I0760553

FANTASY & FAIRYTALES
BOOK THREE

# GOLDEN CROWN

M. LYNN

Edited by Melissa Craven

Proofread by Patrick Hodges

Cover by Covers by Combs

ISBN : 978-1-970052-68-8 (Hardcover)

# Also by M. Lynn

# THE SIX KINGDOMS

# PALACE OF GAULE

# For Owen

*Whose smile can make any day a good day*

# CHAPTER 1

It may as well have been the edge of the world. The white cliffs stretching above the frothing sea, their razor-sharp edge dropping over open sky.

The danger was in getting too close to where the earth dropped off. To where the dark depths gurgled. But there was a thrill in going where no sane person would go, in focusing on nothing but the steady balance that would keep you from tumbling into the deep.

Etta walked that line, between sanity and crazed daring. She flung her arms out to her sides and hung her toes over the edge.

Behind her stood the ruins of the palace of her ancestors. It still bore the memory of what they'd done. The scars were etched deep into the soul of Bela, never to be forgotten.

But they were here. Her people had returned and they worked night and day to make the village everything they needed it to be.

And she wanted to step off the edge.

She didn't want to die. That was the opposite of everything she longed for. It only held nothingness and she didn't want nothingness.

She wanted everything. To feel everything. To rid herself of the chill that entered her soul the day she faced La Dame.

Her legs wobbled beneath her, just enough to throw her off balance. She pitched forward, her feet knocking a shower of rocks over the edge.

Should she be afraid? The question struck her as she failed once again to regain her footing and slipped farther forward.

Her left foot hit open air, suspended for a moment of disbelief before the right foot joined it and she tumbled over. The water neared and her stomach dropped, but she didn't scream.

A rush of wind pushed underneath her, lifting her in an arc, and a sigh escaped her lips. As her back slammed onto the grassy cliff, stealing the air from her lungs, she lifted her eyes.

"Edmund." Brushing her pants, she got to her feet.

His brow scrunched in worry. "That's the third time I've kept you from falling. You shouldn't be coming up here anymore."

She brushed past him. "Then it's a good thing you don't make my decisions for me."

He fell into step beside her. "You could've stopped yourself if you'd used your magic."

She grunted.

"Have you used it since Matteo put that crown on your head?"

"Drop it, Edmund."

He stopped walking. "I'm worried about you."

"And I'm worried our people won't have adequate supplies when winter comes." Against her better judgment, she turned to face him. He'd been nagging her all week.

He rubbed his knuckles against the stubble on his jaw. "We've had quite a few new arrivals and they're all bringing carts of supplies from the villages in Gaule. That along with their magic and the ship that arrived from Cana should speed things along."

As soon as word got out that Bela once again belonged to the Belaens, some of the old allies from across the sea came knocking. Cana arrived first. A kingless land ruled by clans, the histories called them Bela's number one trading partner. Back when the Belaen docks bustled with activity. The Madrans followed them, the king of Madra wanted to cement an alliance, fearing they'd turn their magic on him.

Edmund wouldn't quit with the frown so she grabbed his arm. "Edmund, I'm–"

"Fine," he finished for her. "I've heard it before."

"I was going to say I'm not the one who matters."

His lips curved up just the slightest bit and he shook his head. "You sound like a queen I guess. I shouldn't be surprised. I've spent so much of my life around a prince."

He gripped both her shoulders and ducked his head to look into her eyes. "But you're wrong. You matter. You always have."

Her shoulders sagged and he pulled her against his solid chest, dropping a kiss on the top of her head.

"I'm glad you stayed." After they saved Alexandre Durand and battled La Dame, she'd been sure Edmund's loyalty to the prince of Gaule would override any love for his ancestral home. Tyson's had. Her own brother. But Alex's brother too.

She tried to keep Alex from her thoughts, but it wasn't easy when everything in their lives seemed forever entwined.

When Edmund made his choice to stay with her, she'd never been more grateful for anything.

A laugh rumbled through his chest. "Why, Persinette Basile, that might be the first compliment you've ever given me."

She pulled away. "It wasn't a compliment, merely a statement of fact."

He grinned. "Of course, my queen."

"Don't call me that."

"Why not? It's what you are."

"Only because of the magic that flows through my veins and the name I bear. The crown is an illusion. I can't lead these people." She gestured to the people walking to and from the village.

He dropped his arm across her shoulders as Matteo spotted them and hurried over.

"You guys hungry?" Matteo asked.

"Sure."

As Etta followed her cousin to the cook fires, people bowed. Some uttered 'Your Majesty.' Trust shone in their eyes. They'd seen her fight their greatest enemy and drive her away. They'd watched as she came into the power of the Basiles.

Those who'd arrived since the fight were told the stories every night, making her into the hero of their dreams.

Etta didn't feel like a hero.

She was crushed. Broken. Empty.

The curse she'd lived her entire life vowing to break turned out to be the only thing holding her together. It was the cruelest sort of irony.

And she was scared of herself. The power she'd unleashed. It sat under her skin, like a thousand tiny ants, begging to be released. She held it back, afraid that if she went down that road, if she experienced the immensity of it as she had before, she wouldn't be able to come back. But in holding its fiery hatred in, she lost all other emotions.

She didn't want to let the magic control her.

Her people had been sharing supplies, using a few cook fires at the edge of the village to prepare their meals. After accepting a bowl of grain mush and salted fish, she made her way into the woods.

Little feet ran after her and as soon as she heard him, she turned. "Henry, you shouldn't wander off from your mom."

Henry and Analise had been among the magic folk being held in town by La Dame. She'd created an illusion of a grand palace. The only thing that hadn't been an illusion was the small village and Etta now knew it was because her people had been forced to build it. They'd been prisoners, unable to leave, instead, being forced to arrive at the palace for a ball each night.

When La Dame left, her magic had faded from the land, leaving behind a broken landscape.

"Where are you going?" Henry asked. His magic cloaked them in silence. It was as easy for him as breathing.

Envy choked her words and she turned away. "Head on back. I'll return before you go to sleep."

He hesitated for a moment but then obeyed her as he always did. Relief bloomed within her when the edges of his power no longer tried to draw hers forth.

But she couldn't, wouldn't use it. Not since... she rubbed a hand across her face and sat on the soft pine pillow of the forest floor, leaning her back against a tree.

Grass struggled to poke up through the pine needles, begging for her help. Wanting her to make them grow. Life was the first power she knew. Flowers. Grasses. Trees.

It was the only power that felt like hers, but it had been tainted. The ancient Basile power now coursed through her veins, mixing and confusing what was there before.

She heard him before he spoke, but kept her eyes focused on the bowl of mush in her lap as if willing it to become a feast. But even that would've been tasteless to her.

"People are beginning to wonder about you," Edmund said. "You come out here every night to eat alone."

Music drifted through the air from the way he'd come. She hadn't known many Belaens throughout her life, but she'd learned they loved their music. Dancing. Laughter. Joy.

Edmund followed her gaze to the path behind him.

She shook her head. "They celebrate, even after everything they'd been through. They've been persecuted for generations. Now they have nothing."

"They have Bela. We all do. A country to call our own. One where we need not hide." He sat down beside her and nudged her shoulder. "And they have a queen."

"Right," she scoffed. "Queen."

"I seem to recall a coronation."

"Edmund, the crown is no more real than La Dame's illusions."

"They chose you."

"No, they didn't. They chose my blood. Edmund, I'm not a leader. None of them even know me. They shouldn't follow me."

"I know you." He bumped her shoulder again, leaning close. "And I will follow you right up to the gates of Dracon if it comes to it."

She pushed a breath past her lips. "I hate you."

"No, you don't."

"I try so hard not to feel sorry for myself and you come along and make me feel like an idiot."

"You are an idiot."

"Gee, thanks." She stuffed her spoon into her mouth to hide her smile.

Edmund sighed and leaned forward against his knees. "Can I say something without you punching me?"

"That sounds ominous."

"I think you miss him."

"Tyson? Yeah, of course I miss him."

Edmund made an annoyed sound in the back of his throat. "You know very well that's not who I mean."

"I thought it must be, because anyone else would just be absurd."

"What's so absurd about it?"

She bit off a bite of fish and chewed to avoid his question. When the curse had first been broken, all her magic felt for Alexandre Durand was a hatred so intense it could've burned the sun. But that hadn't been her. Her magic was born to be at odds with him. What if she'd been born for something else? Could hatred and love for the same person exist inside her together?

Each day, memories of their time together ran on repeat through her mind.

"He's my enemy," she finally said.

"Only because of your ancestors and his. The enmity need not be yours."

"Edmund, do you forget everything he did to me? To you?"

"He had no choice."

"There is always a choice."

Edmund's back shuddered as he released a shaky breath and Etta kicked herself for her words. She might be conflicted about Alex, but Edmund wasn't and it was killing him to be so far from him.

She rubbed his arm. "Hey, I'm sorry."

He turned his head to look at her, the side of it resting on his knees. "He went home to war. I've always been at his side. For everything. I should be with him."

"Do you regret staying?" She held her breath, not knowing if she could handle the answer.

"No." He grabbed her hand. "Not at all. I'm just worried. If something happens to him..."

He didn't need to finish because she understood. It may have been because of the curse, but she still remembered what it felt like to love a king. To love Alex. Edmund had been in love with him since he was just a teenager and he would probably love him for the rest of his life.

"I'm supposed to protect him," Edmund breathed.

A familiar urge rose up in Etta. To protect. The need to bathe her sword in blood for no other reason than to guard the life of a royal. She'd been raised to be the protector, her father never imagining she'd get to live any other life. Was that why he named her Persinette? As the only rebellion he'd ever get against La Dame? The Draconian translation for Rapunzel was a sad excuse for a fight but maybe it was all he'd had.

Maybe she wouldn't know another life. Even now as her old charge fought for the soul of his kingdom, she had to guard her own land.

Maybe wearing the crown was no different from bearing a sword.

Before, she'd been charged with keeping safe the life of one man. Now she had an entire people behind her blade.

And Edmund was right, although she'd never tell him that. She missed Alex. When she'd acted as his protector, she hadn't also been asked to lead. Could she do both?

"He's going to be okay," she finally said.

"You think?" His sad eyes brightened.

Etta got to her feet and held her free hand down to him. "We need to believe it because Gaule is no longer our worry. The time has come for Bela to rise and soon, we'll have to go to battle ourselves."

A grin stretched across his face. "That sounded very queenly."

She narrowed her eyes. "Don't make me retrieve my sword."

"Oh, please do. I'd love to show you a thing or two about dueling."

"Ha, you teach me? Right."

They dropped their dishes back at the cook fire and Etta headed off to find Henry, a smile still firmly in place.

# CHAPTER 2

"You're telling me I can't get into my own palace?" Alex scanned the face of each officer crowded into the tent.

Anders stepped forward. "Essentially, your Majesty, yes."

"My mother is behind those walls." His mother and those loyal to her had been betrayed by many of the realms nobles. They now sat trapped within the inner palace with an enemy army at their gates.

They'd made no progress on the walls despite sitting there for days just miles from the palace. Duke Leroy's forces sat in the valley just outside the gates, allowing the soldiers Alex had drawn together to get no closer without a confrontation.

He scratched his tired face. There'd been little rest since they'd left Bela behind. Beside him stood a man he didn't recognize instead of the one who should be there. But Edmund hadn't come.

He'd stayed... with her. No, he refused to dwell on her when his country teetered on the brink of civil war.

As soon as he reached Gaule, Alex had pulled Duchess Moreau's force from the border. Village militia men and women who were more accustomed to protecting their communities from bandits and breaking up the occasional drunken brawl than marching into battle. And now the Belaen border sat unguarded. But Etta gave her word. They wouldn't attack.

The Draconian border was unguarded as well, but only because after seeing La Dame's power first hand, he knew none of them stood a chance if she attacked.

Camped near the palace, they'd found Anders with the royal guard he'd brought to fight the traitors. So, his force consisted of one hundred guardsmen and a band of partially trained civilians. They'd be no match for Leroy's much larger force. A force that was supposed to be sworn to the crown.

Leroy was the worst kind of counselor. He'd advised Alex's father on many things prior to the old king's death. He would rather throw the kingdom into civil war than allow magic folk any freedoms.

Alex tried everything to quiet him. He'd banished him from court. Stripped him of his land's revenues. Even taken the care of Amalie, his youngest daughter, from his hands.

The steady drum of a horse's hooves filled the air, stopping just outside the tent. Anders left, returning only moments later with an unkempt man. His eyes darted around the tent wildly before he forced himself into a bow.

"Your Majesty," Anders started. "Conners has been inside the walls for the past couple of weeks. He has much to tell you."

"Begin." Alex narrowed his eyes.

The man straightened and pulled at the ends of his dark hair. "I... I lived in the outer palace. Just one of the guardsman who took shifts at the gate. I didn't hear any traitorous talk until moments before the attack. I swear."

"Go on." Alex nodded, leaning forward.

"Half the guard turned on the queen mother and stormed the dungeons to release the nobles being kept there."

"All of them?"

"Yes, sire. Lord Leroy took control from there and the other nobles fell in line. They gained the support of the people who lived in the outer palace by decreeing that all those with magic be brought forth and put on trial."

Alex turned away and paced the length of the tent, his generals scrambling to get out of his way. How had he been so wrong about his people? They hadn't been ready for the new world he'd thrust upon them.

This was his fault.

"There was cheering, sire." The man's voice broke. "The people... they cheered as a man was found guilty of being one of the magic folk and put to death right there in the center of town."

Alex stopped moving and pinned the young man with a stare, resisting the urge to ask him the question burning in his brain with this many witnesses. If he'd been so wrong about his people, none of them were trustworthy.

"How did you get away?" he asked instead. "How did you get out?"

"Persinette Basile." His lips curved up. "She created quite the distraction when she left. It allowed a lot of us who didn't agree with the nobles and their followers to escape to the inner palace where the queen mother is protecting all those who ask for it."

"How did you get out from the inner palace?"

The man scratched his chin. "I'm not really sure. I volunteered to be the one to go and Amalie Leroy showed me through some tunnel that came out into a cove at the ocean. I walked for a while before I found a horse grazing."

Alex should have known. Hope knocked into him for the first time since his abduction that seemed so long ago. There were only two tunnels into the palace. One came out along the outer wall facing the forest. He'd used it with Etta to get back into the palace. The other, he'd only heard about. He pushed past Anders and left the tent in search of his brother.

Tyson leaned against a boulder on the edge of camp with a cap pulled down over his eyes and his arms folded across his chest. Alex didn't want to wake him.

"I can sense you watching me," he said with a muffled voice. He pushed the cap off his face, revealing eyes that he'd barely been able to look into since leaving Bela. They weren't his mother's. They weren't Durand eyes. They were hers. Peering into the face of his brother was like seeing Etta. How had he never seen it before? It hurt too much, so he looked away.

Tyson watched him with the cold stare he'd perfected since leaving Bela. He may have chosen Alex, but the ill feelings between Alex and Etta tore him apart. If they weren't resolved, part of Alex worried his brother would never forgive him.

"I need to talk to you." Alex moved to lean against the boulder. "A man arrived today after escaping the palace and evading Leroy's forces."

"You sure he's not a spy?" Tyson's distrust stung Alex. There'd been a time when his brother had been open and kind. But that was before he'd had to leave his home to run for his life.

"He says Amalie showed him out through a tunnel."

That brought the light back to his eyes. "Amalie? Is she okay?"

Alex nodded slowly. "Yes. But I need to know about these tunnels."

"I tried to tell you about them a long time ago. Back when dad–"

"I know," Alex cut him off. "And I'm sorry I never listened to you, but right now I need you to tell me if they can get me into the palace."

Tyson's shoulders dropped, and he sagged back, his head swinging in a slow arc. "You can get into the tunnels, but the passageway into the palace can only be opened from the inside."

Everything inside of Alex deflated.

"I'm sorry."

Alex patted the back of his head. "It's okay."

"No, it's not."

Alex spun around and slapped his palm against the stone. "Dammit, it's not. Nothing is okay. Our *mother* is in there. She's surrounded by people who want their king's head and it's all my blasted fault."

"Are you whining, brother?" Tyson raised an eyebrow. "That's supposed to be my job."

Alex couldn't tell if he was joking or not. He couldn't tell anything at the moment. All he knew was that the people he loved were trapped, and he had to get them out. He gave in to his brother who was obviously waiting for him to speak. "Then what is my job, oh knowledgeable one?"

"To be king." Tyson stood. When had he gotten so tall? He'd grown enough to meet Alex's eyes without tilting his head back. "You have to do what no one else can do. Figure out how to take back your throne and save our mother and Amalie, all while not taking back any of the progress Gaule has made toward accepting Belaens."

"Easy, right?"

"Noble actions are never easy."

"Did you learn that one from Edmund?" Alex fell into step beside Tyson.

Tyson ducked his head to hide his sheepish grin. "We spent a lot of time together after we escaped the palace."

"I wish you hadn't had to do that."

"Me too." He raised his hand in front of Alex's face and snapped it open.

Alex sputtered as water rose from the ground in a flash and slapped him in the face.

"That was for being a dick to my people for so long."

Alex wiped his face on his sleeve. "You didn't even know they were your people."

"You were still a dick."

"Yeah." Alex sighed and pushed damp hair off his forehead. "I guess I was."

"Still kinda are." Tyson shot him a final grin but didn't stick around for Alex's retort.

Alex shook his head and reentered the tent where his officers continued to confer. They glanced up hopefully. "Sorry, we have to find another way."

The room deflated and no one spoke until a guard ran in, jostling Alex. His eyes widened.

"My… My king." He bowed clumsily.

"What is it?" Anders snapped.

The guard turned to him, shrinking back from the general's large presence. "The scouts spotted riders, sir. A lot of them."

Alex cursed as Anders took charge, issuing orders to prepare the soldiers for battle.

"Sire," he said to Alex. "You should stay with the archers."

His first instinct was to argue, but then common sense kicked in. He was a much better archer than swordsman. His hand shot out, grabbing onto the tunic of a guard nearby. "Prince Tyson was just here. Bring him to me." The man nodded and hurried away.

There was no way he was letting Tyson near the fight.

A horn sounded from the far side of the valley and riders crested the hill, stretching across the horizon.

"Reinforcements for the duke." Alex rubbed his jaw. It had to be. Holding his bow aloft, he hurried to the other side of camp where the archers gathered.

"Archers, to me!" he yelled. "Ready your bows."

Nearby, Anders forced the soldiers into battle lines. Most of them had never been in so much as a fistfight. The royal guardsmen and women stood straight with steely eyes and calm demeanors. The Moreau fighters circled in chaos. Alex pulled his eyes away as a guard shoved Tyson forward.

"Seriously, Alex? I'm a better fighter than three-quarters of those soldiers."

Alex shoved a bow into his hands. "Today, you're an archer."

"I'm a shit archer."

Alex cuffed him on the back of the head as his eyes scanned the oncoming force. "You're almost as good as me, Ty, so no more."

Tyson cursed and rubbed his head but otherwise remained silent as he readied his bow.

Alex had never been in an all-out battle. He didn't know exactly what to expect. But he was pretty sure they didn't begin with a single rider galloping forward, a white flag billowing in the breeze.

Alex pressed his bow into Tyson's free hand. He stepped up next to Anders.

The rider stopped midway between the forces.

"You think it's a trap?" Alex asked.

"I don't know, your Majesty."

The rider slid gracefully from the dappled mare and approached the envoy for Alex's army. Long silver hair spilled from her helmet as she removed it. A woman. Alex sucked in a breath as her gaze pierced them even at that distance.

"Hello." The voice was quiet, no more than a whisper.

Alex and Anders both twisted around looking for the source.

"I'm not your enemy." A musical quality lilted the words.

"It's her," Alex said, his eyes widening.

Revulsion flashed across Anders' face, reminding Alex how his general felt about Belaens. Her magic allowed her to speak across the distance.

"I need to speak with her." Alex couldn't explain it. The draw of her magic. Other than Tyson, he hadn't been around any magic folk since leaving Bela and it had left a hole in his life.

"Come," her sweet voice said.

"Stand down," Alex called to his force.

"You can't go alone," Anders argued.

"Then send your best soldiers, but you are not coming." He didn't need Anders angering the woman with his disdain for her kind.

Tyson ran up beside him and he opened his mouth to tell him to stay put, but then shut it without uttering a word. Tyson had as much right to meet the magic woman as he did. The eagerness on his face spoke volumes. Tyson hadn't shown much interest in anything since leaving Bela.

Anders handpicked three guards and horses were brought forward. They cantered across the field they'd intended to be a battlefield.

When they reached the armored woman, her eyes caught on Tyson and widened as a smile spread across her face. "You have magic," she said softly.

"Who are you?" Alex demanded, looking down on her from atop his horse.

Tyson slid down before Alex had a chance to stop him. "You sensed me?"

She shook her head with a laugh. "We've all heard the rumors. I was only looking for confirmation."

Alex scowled at his brother as he jumped down from his horse. "I will not ask you again. Who are you and do you intend to attack?" He scanned her force at the other end of the valley.

She finally turned her piercing gray eyes on him. "It is a pleasure to meet you, your Majesty. Like I said before, I am not your enemy. In fact, we can be of service to you. A messenger reached me saying that my father was trapped inside the royal palace, surrounded by traitors. I thought this must be a lie, but he was supposed to have returned with his wife. The risk was too great not to come."

"Your father," he said dumbly.

"Yes, Duke Caron. Recently wed to the princess Camille."

It suddenly clicked and Alex glanced back at his guards. "Stand down. These are the Caron forces. Thank God."

"I'm Ara. It truly is a pleasure to meet you, Alexandre Durand. My father always spoke most highly of you."

"You have no idea how relieved I am to see you." Did her father know of her magic? He had to. There was no time for Alex to express his surprise as she spoke again.

"So, it's true then? Gaule is at war?" she asked.

"Call your units to camp next to mine," Alex said, gesturing to where pointed tents rose up across the valley.

She nodded and spoke softly. Alex couldn't hear her words, but her lips were moving. Her soldiers started across the valley and she gave him a shrug and vaulted onto her horse. Had they heard her words as he had from afar?

He'd seen a lot of things in his short stint as king. A lot of magic. But he'd never get used to it.

He climbed into his saddle and dug his heels into his horse's flanks, anxious to tell his men and women that the greatest threat still lay within the palace walls. There'd be no battle this day.

But a battle was coming. No one doubted that.

# CHAPTER 3

As she sat among the trees, Etta dug her knife into the wood once again, carving out as much as she could. She'd seen her father make their sparring poles many times before. They'd been smooth and light. Hers had jagged edges and oddly shaped ends. She was useless for anything that didn't involve wielding a sword.

Frustration rose within her and she flung her knife at the nearest tree. Even her aim was off and it landed in a pile of dead leaves.

"You know," Matteo said as his shadow fell over her. "You could use your fancy new Basile magic to do that."

Edmund appeared next to her and she pushed to her feet. "What would you know about it?"

It was cruel and she shouldn't have said it. Matteo was the only Basile in generations with no power of his own. He'd grown up thinking he'd one day inherit the Basile curse, but then he'd found out about a cousin born weeks before him. Etta. And that the curse had fallen to her instead.

Etta would gladly give Matteo every ounce of magic she possessed. She didn't want it.

His expression shifted in sympathy and that worsened her guilt. Matteo struck her as a jerk when they first met, but he soon proved to be more ally than anything else. He'd lived his entire life as a prisoner to an evil woman.

Now that he was free, he'd changed right before her eyes.

Edmund wasn't as forgiving as a scowl marred his handsome features. "Do you insist on making everyone else around you just as miserable as you are?" He directed the words to Etta.

"Edmund." Matteo placed a hand on Edmund's arm and to Etta's surprise, her friend backed off. "Another ship arrived this morning. We'll start unloading it after lunch."

She nodded. "I'll be there." Some hard work would be good for her.

Matteo and Edmund locked eyes, seemingly having some silent conversation and then Matteo trudged back the way he'd come.

Edmund continued to stare at her. "You can't keep doing this, Etta."

"Doing what?"

"Hiding out. Snapping at people who care about you. One of these days, you're going to need to step up. If not for me or Matteo, then for your people."

Not wanting to hear it, she gripped one of the rough staffs she'd made.

Edmund picked up the second one. "Spar with me." He raised a brow. "I may even let you hit me a time or two."

"As if you'd have a choice," she grumbled. "Fine." She led him to the clearing a short walk away.

"I'm going to cut my hands on this thing you're calling a staff."

"I've never carved them myself before, give me a break."

He faced her and winked. Edmund loved throwing people off guard. Winks. Smiles. The grace at which he moved. It didn't matter if they were men or women.

But Etta had always been immune to his charm. She was determined to beat him. Maybe it was an effect of the way they met, their first battle. They were meant to fight to the death. Those kinds of stakes instilled a singular focus. And each time she fought him, she slipped back into tournament mode. Cold. Calculating. The only objective: winning.

She made the first move and her pole cracked against his as he blocked and stepped back. She attacked again, a series of swift moves. He matched her thrust for thrust. Always her equal. That's how it was between them. Neither was superior.

Edmund grinned as he advanced forward and all sound faded. His magic. She shook her head. It wouldn't be a true battle with Edmund if sound entered their arena. He'd used his magic every time he'd face her. Inside their bubble, the only sounds came from the meeting of their poles and the shuffling of their feet.

Etta spun with her leg raised to catch him in the side. He grabbed her foot and pulled, forcing her to twist away.

"You'd actually beat me if you used your magic," Edmund said, sucking in air.

"Stop." She jabbed, hoping to catch him off guard.

Edmund was never off guard.

"Are you scared?"

When she didn't respond, he swung his staff in a wide arc, meeting hers above their heads.

"Persinette Basile doesn't fear anything," he said, staring into her eyes.

She twisted away, trying to ignore his words and the expectation in them. They all expected so much from her. Their faith was suffocating.

"What do you have to be scared of? That La Dame will win?"

He blocked another one of her attacks. "That's it. You don't think you can beat her. At least not without a little darkness. You think you'll have to give in to the power, let it control you."

Etta surged forward, her movements stilted with anger. She swung too wildly, moved her feet too quickly.

"What if you do? Isn't it worth saving Bela?"

She stood panting as he narrowed his eyes.

"No, you're afraid you'll destroy us."

She charged, jumping into the air and spinning. He knocked her away easily and she went tumbling to the ground. Picking herself up, she threw her pole to one side and charged him again.

"Are you La Dame?" He tackled her to the ground, and she tried to kick him away. "You aren't her, Etta. But one day, if you don't stop the hate growing inside you, you might be. Use your powers." He released her and backed up. "Use them," he screamed. "Don't be a coward." He gripped her arm and hauled her to her feet. "Coward. Traitor. You're no queen."

The anger overwhelmed her and she couldn't stop the burst of magic as is exploded from her hands. Edmund flew backward, turning over in the air until his body collided with the branch of a tree and he slammed into the ground.

Shock kept her frozen for a long moment until reality crashed in and she ran toward him. Edmund's body bent at a weird angle and blood dribbled from his mouth. A sob pushed out of her.

"No. No. No." She bent over him. "I'm sorry. I'm so sorry."

As she pressed her face into his chest, it rose slowly and she jerked her head up.

People ran toward them, led by Matteo.

He stopped when he saw Edmund, his eyes welling up. "Is he—"

"No," Etta said quickly. "We need Esme."

Matteo yelled to the people behind him. "Someone find Esme!" He knelt on the other side of Edmund and pressed his fingers to his neck. He sagged in relief and touched Edmund's face gently. "He wanted to draw out your magic, but this..."

"I..." Tears clogged her throat. She wiped her face and tried again. "No one should have this much power, Matteo. Do you see what I did? It's nothing but evil."

"This wasn't your fault."

His forgiveness only made it worse. "Of course it was. I almost killed him."

"But you didn't." He reached across Edmund to take her hand.

Esme arrived quickly and knelt beside them, immediately putting her hands on Edmund's chest. She closed her eyes and Etta had never been more glad they let the Draconian healer stay after she'd escaped La Dame's employ. Since that night, Esme kept her distance from the Belaens, most of whom still didn't trust her. But now she was here.

Edmund's breathing evened out and before long, his eyes fluttered open.

Etta refrained from throwing herself across him and begging his forgiveness. She frantically shifted through his blood-stained blonde hair but there was no cut there. The healing worked.

Unable to look into his eyes, she jumped to her feet and started running with no destination in mind. After a while, she found herself atop the cliffs once again looking into the abyss. The swirling waters resembled her powers. Dark. Overwhelming. Uncontrollable. With each passing day, they threatened to pull her into their dangerous current.

A warm presence stood beside her, bringing her away from the edge, and she let the tears flow as she turned to bury her face in Vérité's mane.

His nose nudged her cheek and she pulled back to lose herself in his wide understanding eyes. She couldn't explain it, but Vérité got it, got her. Their souls were entwined. He'd saved her more times than she could count. From her enemies. From herself. She could no longer differentiate between the two. She was her own enemy.

Power surged down the length of her arms and she pulled back. What if she hurt Verite? She'd never forgive herself.

Her breath wheezed in and out of her throat rapidly. No, she told herself. Edmund was going to be okay. He was fine.

Her hands shook as her fingers sank into her long hair, wanting to pull it free. Vérité's eyes pleaded with her. He wanted to go for a ride. To feel a part of her once again. As her heart hammered in her chest, she turned and walked away. His eyes followed her, but she didn't turn back.

Before long, she was back in the place she'd sparred with Edmund. It was where she always went to think, to lose herself in the forest. She'd always felt her best when surrounded by trees that protected her from the harsher realities of the world.

In Gaule, the Black Forest hadn't only been her home. It'd been her sanctuary. She'd lived with her father, hidden by his wards. It was the only time she'd been safe. The people who killed her mother couldn't find them there. The king who'd once been her father's friend couldn't hunt them down if they were nowhere to be found.

Her father had kept many secrets. Some of which had been revealed slowly since his death. She hadn't known the full history of their line or that he'd secretly fathered a child with someone who wasn't her mother. Not just any child. A prince.

She'd been taught to hate Gaule and the family that ran the kingdom, but also that hate wasn't enough. It wasn't freedom. If anything, it was another prison. Especially when forced to stand by the side of the one you hate... to... She shook her head. Harder than hate was the end of hatred when that barrier fell. Because then, you risked losing everything you were.

She'd fought it. Fought her feelings for him, but the curse tying them together amplified everything inside of her. Fighting it was useless.

Now she saw her feelings for what they really were. Another curse. She wouldn't let herself give in to them. Not when a crown sat on her head.

Because that's what she was. A queen. She hadn't earned it. She hadn't defeated La Dame, only chased her away for a time. But Basile blood coursed through her and to her people that was enough. They would follow a descendant of Aurora and Phillip to the ends of the earth.

Whether she used her magic or not.

As she wiped the tears from her face, she looked up into the afternoon sun, knowing the time for indecision was past. She'd wallowed. She'd grieved. She'd let her fear overcome her.

Not anymore.

Heading off toward the beach, she pulled her magic back, holding it in, refusing to let it out. When it was inside of her, she could control it.

And she would.

Because she was Persinette Basile.

She arrived at the beach as a wooden rowboat pulled ashore laden with supplies. Their ancient allies across the sea were determined to see Bela regain everything it once had. The Madrans had no magic, and it was plain they feared it. The sailors refused to leave the ship or speak to the Belaens, but their king knew La Dame was the greater threat.

Matteo spotted her, and she jogged over.

"Thought you'd be with Edmund," she said.

He pressed his foot down on the bow of the boat and hopped off, splashing through the water to walk toward her. "He'll be fine. I was needed here."

The unspoken words were plain. He was needed because she hadn't been around. Matteo and Edmund had been fulfilling her duties.

A woman stood farther down the beach holding out a hand in front of her. The water receded from around the boat, allowing others to descend and begin carrying off the supplies. They worked in sync with one another and Etta realized they must have done this very same thing many times before as each ship came in.

She couldn't take her eyes from the woman who was grinning as she made the water splash up to hit one of the men.

The trick with the water reminded her of Tyson.

Matteo snapped her out of her depressing thoughts. "Glad you finally joined us."

An apology stuck in her throat but she couldn't push the words out. There was so much she was sorry for. That she hadn't been strong enough. That she'd let their enemy leave to fight another day, leaving the threat hanging over them. That she didn't know how to be a part of a community. She never had.

Her people thrived on finally having a community to call their own. They no longer had to live in secret, alone.

But that was all she'd ever known.

So, as she looked at Matteo, one of only two living souls who shared her lineage, she thought of so many things to say, settling on only two words that couldn't possibly encompass any of it. "Me too."

She worked all afternoon unloading supplies and lugging them to the village.

As the sun sank on the horizon, her people settled in around the cook fires for mealtime. Some pulled out odd stringed instruments, sending notes into the night.

Etta walked past them through the village where homes bustled with activity. She accepted greetings as she ducked inside one of the homes being used for healing. Edmund rested on his bed. Matteo sat next to him, leaning forward to hear him speak as he offered him a bowl of rice and beans.

When Matteo's eye caught hers, he jumped away. "I'll give you a moment."

Etta took the spot Matteo vacated on the end of the bed, her eyes focusing on her hands.

"Etta," Edmund said quietly. "Look at me."

She shook her head.

"Persinette Basile, if you don't look me in the eye right now, next time we spar, I won't let you win."

Her eyes blazed as they snapped to his. "Let me win?"

He chuckled. "Knew that would get you."

She frowned. "Edmund–"

"I'm sorry I pushed you so hard," he interrupted.

"Wait, you think this is your fault? I almost killed you."

He flinched at her words but tried to hide it. "I'm tougher than I look."

"If Esme hadn't come..."

"I know. But Etta, you can't let this stop you from using your powers again."

He read her too well. "I can't control them, Edmund. You saw that. They're too much."

"Nothing is too much for you."

"How do you have so much faith in me?"

"You're my best friend."

Warm pride spread through her but an awkwardness settled in her mind. So, of course, she had to ruin the moment. "I thought Alexandre was your best friend."

"First." He held up one finger weakly. "His name is Alex. You're only calling him Alexandre to pretend you really do hate him like you think you should. But I know better. Second, my feelings for Alex will always be complicated. You know the feeling." He shot her a smirk, and she opened her mouth to protest, but he went on before she could. "But you, little queen, you are my family."

Her eyes glassed over, but she was able to keep herself from crying. She nodded, soaking in the strength he always gave her. He made her believe in herself and belief had power. Almost as much power as magic. "I need your help, Edmund."

"Anything."

She sucked in a breath. Once the words were out, Edmund wouldn't let her take them back. "I need to learn how to control my new magic."

His lips curved into a smile and she put a hand over his mouth to keep him from responding before she got it all out.

"If people are going to insist on making me the queen, I need to be able to protect them. I can feel the power crawling underneath my skin and it's only a matter of time before I explode. We can't let that happen. When it first came to me, I could grasp it, mold it, and use it against La Dame. Since then, it's grown and amplified."

When he finally spoke, his words were muffled underneath her hand. "I'm in."

"You might get hurt."

He shrugged.

"I don't know what it'll do to you."

"Are you trying to talk me out of helping? Because it won't work. I'm going to be there for you no matter what happens."

She nodded and withdrew her hand. "I was afraid you'd say that."

"Esme will demand I take another day to rest." He grinned, something evil sparking in his eyes. "But I told Matteo that you'd be more than happy to hold court tomorrow because you'd feel guilty about what happened to me."

"No way."

"Etta, you're the queen."

"So, you're using what happened for personal gain?"

"Not personal." His grin didn't waver. "It's for Bela. Your people need to see you acting like their queen."

"You're evil."

He nodded. "That is an accurate assessment."

"Fine, but now I'm leaving before I try to knock you unconscious again just for the sake of shutting you up."

Glee danced across his face. "So, we're at the joking stage of me almost dying?"

She matched his grin and turned to walk away. "Oh, don't be so dramatic."

# CHAPTER 4

Fires lit up the night sky outside the gates of the palace as Alex looked on. That army wasn't going anywhere. Other forces had joined them in the night, no doubt summoned by the nobles who were splitting Gaule in two.

Alex scooted forward on his belly to the top of the hill to get a better vantage point. He hadn't come to gather their numbers. That would need to be done in the light of day. No, on this night, he'd crept out of his tent and away from the guards who were his constant shadow because he needed to see it for it to be real.

They were trying to take his throne. It wasn't a throne he wanted. He was raised to be king but had never embraced it. Before his father was crowned, a council ruled Gaule. The king headed the council, but he had very little authority on his own. He was a figurehead.

But his father took his power. He stripped it from the council with the support of some of the most powerful people in the kingdom. He'd said it was the only way to keep them safe from

La Dame as Gaule's young men and women fell on battlefields, surrounded by a dying hope.

Life ran in circles and now Alex was forced to fight for his crown as his father had. Then La Dame would come.

Maybe Etta could defeat her, but that filled him with another kind of dread. If something happened to her... No. La Dame wasn't only Bela's problem. She'd destroy them all.

If they didn't destroy themselves first.

"How many fighters do they have?" Ara whispered, crouching down beside him.

"More than us," he grunted, shooting her a questioning look.

"I saw you sneaking away from camp. You really shouldn't do that, your Majesty."

He rubbed his knuckles against his jaw and shifted his eyes back to the walls of his home. "Outside the palace, I'm just Alex. Please."

She nodded seriously. "Alex."

They stayed there, side by side watching in silence for a while longer before Alex pushed himself up. Ara matched his stride to walk through the darkness until they saw the waning fires of their friendlier camp.

"I came looking for you for a reason," Ara said as she followed him into his tent without an invitation.

He glanced back over his shoulder. "Yeah?"

She sat on the end of the bed as if she owned the place. "Can you tell me about her?"

"About who?"

She raised an eyebrow as if the answer was obvious. "Persinette Basile."

His first instinct was to deny her. Nothing good would come from discussing Etta with a near stranger.

Breaking the curse shifted his feelings. Instead of the intense joy he'd once had, all he could summon was regret.

"I..." he started, swallowing hard. "Why?"

"She was in your household. You must have known her well." She paused. "You obviously know I have magic. My mother hailed from Bela. She raised me on stories of the Basiles."

Alex drew his brows together and busied himself by splashing water from a washbasin onto his face. He'd known Duke Caron's first wife. She hadn't been Belaen.

As if sensing the direction of his thoughts, Ara sighed. "You're thinking of the lady Emily. She wasn't my mother. My father is a good man... but he also has many weaknesses. Women are one of them."

Alex turned to her once again, this time thinking of his sister. Would he have matched her to such a man if he knew?

The answer was yes, of course. He'd had no choice. He needed Caron. And the man was kind, much more so than any other eligible nobles who'd vied for her hand.

Ara sensed she'd said something she shouldn't have. "Be assured, he will make Camille happy. They're all happy. My father has so much to give that none of them are lacking in anything. After my mother died, he took me into his household to be raised with his three legitimate sons and two illegitimate ones."

"You have five brothers?"

She grimaced. "And I'm the youngest. Imagine their protests when my father put me at the head of the army."

Alex laughed, feeling something break loose in his chest as he imagined five large men being passed over for the sprightly Ara.

She smiled, her lips tight. "Not to mention two of them are soldiers who now have to take orders from me. They thought the messenger was a fake meant to lead us into a trap. But I had the final say and here we are."

As if on cue, someone called Ara's name. She scooted from the bed. "That would be Hendry."

Alex followed her out and an impossibly tall man crossed his arms, his eyes flicking from Ara to Alex and then back again. "What is going on here?"

"Show some respect to your king, Hendry." Ara stomped her foot.

"I will when he isn't luring my little sister into his tent unchaperoned."

Ara rolled her eyes but didn't get a chance to respond as a loud crash sounded behind them and Tyson barreled through camp, colliding with a large cook pot. His curses reached them, but he didn't stop his forward progression. By the time he reached them, he was panting. Once he caught his breath, he scanned Hendry from head to toe. "Dude, you're tall."

"Ty," Alex said. "Why are you running through camp like your hair is on fire?"

He ran a hand through his hair as if making sure it was indeed intact and Alex held in a laugh.

"I remembered something," he finally said. "Something important."

Alex scanned their surroundings for people listening and then pulled his brother into his tent with Ara and Hendry behind them. The space was cramped with the four of them, but Alex barely noticed as he focused on Tyson's intense face.

"There's a messenger's hole."

"What?" Alex snapped. "What are you talking about?"

"The tunnels used to be used for messengers to come and go without alerting the rest of the palace to their presence. Most kings used them for their contacts with agents of La Dame when she was our ally."

"La Dame was never Gaule's ally," Hendry said harshly.

Alex started to refute his statement, but Ara beat him to it. "Don't be stupid, brother. Of course, she was. Why else would Gaule still be standing when Bela was destroyed generations ago? We may not like it. We may be ashamed. But we cannot pretend our history doesn't exist."

Tyson waved a hand at them. "None of that matters right now. What I'm trying to tell you is we have a way to get a message into the palace."

They all stopped moving, stopped talking. Alex would have sworn they even stopped breathing.

Ara regained her wits first. "Explain."

"The tunnels only open from the inside, but messengers had to have a way to inform their contacts of their presence. Of the need to open the tunnels. I didn't remember it because I've only ever seen it once and then completely forgot about it." His pleading eyes fixed on Alex. "This is how we save them."

Alex knew Anders didn't agree with the plan, but he obeyed his king. They must pretend as if Alex and Tyson were still in camp. Not to mention Ara and Hendry. Their brother Renner would keep their absence under wraps.

The next obstacle was getting to the other side of the palace without being seen by Leroy's forces. They were camped right in the valley between the village and the castle.

They passed the village, quiet in the night. Some villagers hid behind the inner palace walls, protected by the dowager queen. Still, others chose the side of the traitors. They were angry to find friends and neighbors were Belaens, the very people they were supposed to fight against.

Alex rode at the head of their procession. A few extra guards accompanied them as Tyson explain exactly how to get to the cove at the end of the tunnels.

The Black Forrest.

Memories assaulted Alex as the tree cover enveloped them. Everything was the same. A peaceful quiet that only seemed to exist among these trees settled over them. It smelled of damp earth and blooming flowers, of a time when his heart had beat inside his chest.

He didn't want to remember. It would be easier to wash it all away, to focus on saving his mother, on taking back his throne.

Easy didn't seem possible. Not when every second he'd spent with Etta in the woods was burned into his brain. Why couldn't he just despise her? His enemy. The girl with the most beautiful smile in the world. As amazing as it was rare.

The woods weren't where he'd first kissed her, but they were the place he'd first seen something deeper than the fierce face she put on for the world. It was the place he'd had all of her. No confusion. No anger. No crowns to worry about.

He shook his head and met his brother's sympathetic gaze. He was thinking about her too. About how their father's desire to erase magic had forced her to live in the woods for years. How she'd fought for everything she had.

And how she'd looked at them when they left Bela. As if she'd never see them again, and yet, she'd been cold.

Not the Etta either of them knew.

She'd been Persinette Basile. Nothing more.

"This place is freaking me out," Ara grumbled. "Aren't these woods haunted?"

The corner of Alex's lips curled up. Viktor Basile's wards had hidden the magic folk among the trees for years, but they were occasionally heard. Alex scanned the woods for any sign of them, but he suspected they'd bolted for Bela at the first chance.

"Yeah," he said, his smiled falling. "It's haunted." Because, for him, it was.

It took two days, but they followed the path all the way to the far end of the forest where it met the sea. Large trunks stuck up through the swirling waters.

"We aren't going in there," Tyson assured them, turning his horse.

A few hours later, he led them out into a cove. The palace walls rose before them, more imposing from the outside.

Every time Alex saw the high structure, he doubted he'd be able to get inside.

Tyson was different. His mind constantly ran over every possibility, finding optimism in each. Alex envied that.

Tyson scrambled off his horse, his tired legs almost collapsing beneath him. He stumbled and righted himself before heading for the wall and spreading his arms against it. "Oh, sweet palace. It sure is good to see you."

Ara laughed as she slid down, landing in a puddle. Sand stretched out to each side of them, hard from the constant pounding of the waves. The tide was out, but the waterline almost reached the walls.

The cove was a tiny inlet, too small to notice along the coastline. Dark water stretched along the horizon. Alex turned toward the castle and followed his brother down the sharp decline that led into the narrow tunnels underneath the walls.

They came to a dead end at a wall of slate. Tyson ran his hands along every rock, losing showers of dirt.

"A little help," Tyson called.

Hendry and the other guards stayed back, but Alex and Ara ran forward to follow Tyson's motions.

After a while, defeat slowed Alex's movements, and he stepped back, his head hanging low. It wasn't there. He released a long breath and almost didn't hear Ara's gasp.

Tyson grabbed his arm and pulled him over as Ara wiggled a loose rock free. "It's here," she said.

The messenger's hole was small, not large enough to stick an entire hand in.

Alex pulled out the letter he'd written and slipped it through. "Where will that end up?"

"There's an unused chapel on the other side." Tyson shoved the rock back in the hole.

"You mean to tell me that we just did all of this to get a letter into a room where no one will ever find it?" He huffed and hurried back through the tunnels.

Once outside, he sucked in the fresh air and put his hands on his head.

"Alex, listen to me."

Alex turned to his brother. "We're on the edge of war and I am a king who just left his army to ride for days to deliver a message to no one. Forgive me if I lose my shit right now."

"It isn't no one. It's Amalie."

"What?"

Tyson pushed out a long breath. "Amalie and I spent a lot of time in that chapel. It's... ugh, it's going to sound stupid and childish to you, but that was our place. I'm kind of hoping she's still going there. No, not hoping, I know she is."

Alex's anger deflated. "She told me you guys were close, but I..."

"Hadn't noticed?" Tyson shook his head. "Of course you wouldn't. You were lost in your own world with your art and Edmund and then Etta. But I had Amalie. Even though I knew one day you'd take her from me. That she was always meant to marry you. For a little while, I had her. She's my best friend." He smirked. "She's my Edmund."

Alex draped an arm around Tyson's shoulders, knowing Amalie was much more than just a friend to Tyson. She'd told him so herself after Tyson escaped Gaule with Edmund.

"I guess we should settle in for a wait." Ara started giving orders to the guards as if it was what she was born to do. Alex saw a bit of what her father must have seen when he named her general. Hendry watched his sister with amusement on his face.

Before long, they'd set up camp past the water line, hoping that by morning, they'd know if it was all for nothing.

Alex leaned back against his bedroll next to Tyson. "Is it weird to be back?"

Tyson refused to look at him. "When I left, my entire life was falling apart. So much has happened since then. I don't feel like the same boy who ran in the middle of the night."

"Did you really think I'd let anything happen to you if your magic was found out?"

A beat of silence passed between them and Tyson lifted one shoulder in a shrug. "I didn't know what to think. You'd imprisoned Edmund. And you did come after us when we escaped."

"I charged Etta with breaking Edmund free. I wanted him safe. When I learned Etta had been lying to me the entire time about her true identity, something inside me broke. I couldn't think of anything but getting answers from her. Finding out if any of it was..."

"Real? How's that working for you?" When Alex didn't respond, Tyson spoke again. "What about now? Do you think it was real?"

"I don't know, Ty. I really don't. I hope so." Alex slouched down and closed his eyes, ending the conversation before his brother could ask more questions he wasn't ready to answer. More questions he didn't have time for. He had to do what was best for Gaule.

It no longer mattered if any of it was real.

Shadows moved among the trees, dancing against the darkness, and Alex's eyes snapped open. He didn't move as footsteps surrounded them.

It felt as if the leaves themselves were muffling all sounds. Magic. It had to be.

Beside him, Tyson stirred. He gripped his brother's arm to keep him still. Had Leroy's men found them?

Before he got any answers, a blaze of light spread through the woods, shooting up toward the sky, blinding any who looked too closely. Alex shielded his eyes, the movement catching the attention of the man holding the light in the palm of his hand. It dimmed, and he directed it right toward their prone forms.

No one spoke as Alex's face was bathed in light and he held his breath as his hand slid under his bedroll to grip the knife he kept there. His sword was out of reach.

Silence stretched as they waited for someone to make the first move. Uncertainty hung in the air. Ara bristled, looking ready to pounce. Hendry had somehow retrieved his sword. Their guards were on full alert.

Until a man pushed past the beam of light and Alex recognized him immediately.

Simon dropped to one knee and bowed his head. "Your Majesty," he breathed. "Thank the heavens."

Alex relaxed and dropped the knife. "It's damn good to see you, Si."

He hadn't known Simon for long. The man had been in his guard but Alex never took notice of him until Si took it upon himself to try to fix Alex's dreadful sword technique. After that, Simon had been his man, with him every step of the way. When Etta could no longer be protector, he'd stepped in.

And Alex had never been more grateful for anything.

Except for maybe the fact they found them instead of the traitor noble's forces.

Simon stood and extended a hand down to Alex. The king grasped it and allowed himself to be pulled to his feet. Simon's eyes found Tyson. "Your mother is going to be so happy at your presence, young prince, she may even forget about the enemy at our door." One side of his mouth lifted. "For a minute at least." He turned back to the man playing with the light in his hands. "Put that out, man. Do you want everyone to know we're out of the palace?" He shook his head and crossed his arms over his chest. "Please, sire, tell me you're here because you have a way to beat those bastards back."

"Let's get into the palace and we'll discuss it."

Simon gave a silent command to the people who surrounded them still. They weren't guards. Alex had been told his mother was protecting some of the villagers in the inner palace. Were they magic folk?

They trudged from the woods and into the long tunnel. It was the middle of the night and exhaustion tugged at all of them, but Alex shook it from his mind and pushed on. The musty air rattled in his chest and he rubbed a hand across his eyes. The man with the ability to create light guided them. The tunnels seemed longer in the dark of night.

"Did you get the letter we sent through the messenger's hole?" Alex asked Simon.

"Amalie found it." The large man scratched his chin. "We send a man out on patrol every night to make sure this way out of the palace stays clear and when we found the note, we moved up the patrol schedule."

"If you knew it was clear, why haven't you abandoned the palace?"

Simon scratched his strong jaw. "We have a lot of people to protect. We wouldn't have been able to get them to safety without notice."

They reached the end of the tunnel where a door stood slightly open. Alex hadn't even noticed it before. When it was closed, it looked like the stone wall surrounding it. They pushed it wider and stepped through into a room that had seen better days.

Alex ran his fingers along the wall. They may be in a run-down chapel, one he'd never given much thought, but he was home. He'd made it.

The halls were packed with servants and soldiers but none of them recognized him. His clothes were travel-stained, his hair long and unruly, and days' worth of growth coated his cheeks. People jumped out of Simon's way and when they reached the royal family's wing, all sound faded away. The hall was empty, lonely. He passed by the door to his room, running the tips of his fingers along the wood. Etta's room was next, but he turned his head away, unable to look.

Finally, they reached his mother's door. The guard gazed at them skeptically. "The dowager is sleeping. It's late." His eyes rested on Alex's face as if trying to place him. After a moment, they widened and he bowed clumsily. "Forgive me, your Majesty. I didn't know it was you."

Alex patted him on the arm as he knocked on his mother's door. Tyson bounced on his toes beside him, but the rest of the party was still.

The door opened and his mother's voice drifted out before she saw them. "Simon, is that you? It's late, so the report is going to..."

She stopped, her mouth dropping open, frozen in shock. Her eyes glassed over and Tyson was the first to move. He ran toward her and wrapped his arms around her. A sob escaped her lips as he buried his face in her shoulder.

Tyson had never been ashamed of his emotions. He wore his heart like a badge of honor.

"My boys," she finally said, reaching out toward Alex.

As he let her pull him into a crushing hug, the events of the past months crashed over him and he held on tighter, afraid his legs would give out if she let go. He'd been taken from his home. Beaten. Held in a tower. Seen so much death. Forced to bring himself low. Then had everything he thought he'd known ripped away with the curse.

Having his mother with him again was the first thing that felt right in so long.

"Mother," Tyson whispered, fighting his own demons.

"Shhhh." She patted the back of his head. "I know."

When they pulled back, tears streaked down her face. She cupped each of her son's cheeks. "I didn't know if I'd see you boys again. There's been no word while we're locked up here."

Alex glanced from her to Simon. "We think we can do something about that." He gestured for Ara to step forward. "Meet Ara Caron. She's brought us troops."

Simon looked to the ceiling as if thanking something above. "We must wake your father. Seems we aren't as hopeless here as we thought."

It didn't take long for Duchess Moreau, Duke Caron, and Camille to appear. The Duke radiated pride when he saw his son and daughter.

The door to Tyson's old room that connected to his mother's opened and a hesitant young lady appeared. "I heard a commotion."

At the sound of her voice, Tyson lifted his head slowly, taking a deep breath before turning around.

Amalie's face lit up. "Ty? Is that really you?"

Tyson rushed toward her but stopped short of wrapping her in a hug. They faced each other for a long moment, neither speaking.

Finally, Tyson smiled. "I used the messenger hole. I was sure you'd find the letter and open the doorway. But you didn't."

She shook her head. "I only go there when I have to. It's been too–"

She didn't need to finish.

"Yeah." He dropped his eyes to his hands. "It's been..."

She reached out tentatively to take his hand. "I just needed to make sure you were really here."

Alex turned away from their reunion feeling a burning in his chest.

"Are you okay, brother?" Camille stepped up beside him.

Alex narrowed his eyes. He'd never seen eye to eye with his sister. In his mind, he could still see her and Leroy trying to hang magic folk.

The Durands might have been as screwed up as they came, but crisis brought them together. No matter what happened in the past, they'd fight together to preserve their legacy, their kingdom. He understood that about Camille. She might still have an issue with magic folk, but when her family was being threatened, that didn't matter.

She leaned heavily on her cane and waited for him to answer. He shook himself. "Of course I am. I'm finally home."

She looked as if she didn't believe him, but she didn't press him further because their mother leaned forward, ready to begin.

"Alexandre," she started. "Take a seat and tell us everything."

For just a moment, he thought she was talking about his abduction, about Etta. But that would be for another time. Right now, there were more pressing matters.

"Anders has our forces camped on the other side of the village. He has the unit of royal guardsmen under his command, the Moreau soldiers, and now the Caron units as well."

"Is it enough?" his mother asked.

"We are still outnumbered."

She sighed and closed her eyes for a moment.

Duchess Moreau scratched her chin. "If you pulled my forces into the fight, who is guarding the border?"

Tyson jumped in to answer. "We've seen La Dame." A gasp ran around the room. "If she comes for Gaule, no amount of soldiers at the border will stop her."

"What about Bela? Magic folk are flocking there. Should we not worry they'll come for some kind of retribution?" Camille asked.

Tyson shook his head. "No. The queen made us a promise."

"Queen?" Their mother said at the same time as Camille said, "Bela has no queen."

Tyson rose to his full height as if that would keep anyone from disputing his next words. "My sister is the queen."

A tiny whimper sounded from Catrine's throat as the realization struck her. Her pleading eyes met Alex's with a question in them. Alex nodded. His brother knew his true parentage. He was more Basile than Durand.

Duchess Moreau didn't look surprised, but the rest of them waited for answers.

Alex rubbed a hand across his face. Where did he start? "Persinette Basile has been crowned queen of Bela."

His mother rested a hand on his shoulder. "How?" Alex knew what she was really asking. Where was Etta, and how were they separated while the curse tied them together?

Alex rose to his feet. "It's gone." He didn't look at her as he strode to the door. "All of it."

Behind him, his mother dismissed everyone back to their beds, saying they'd pick up the strategy meeting the next morning when they were all more rested.

They filtered out past Alex. Even Tyson disappeared with Amalie leaving Alex alone with his mother.

Alex shook his head as her hand landed on his back. "What did they do to you, son?"

He swallowed back the words he wanted to say. They destroyed him. Opened him up and scooped out everything that mattered. Emptied him. Broke him. He stilled his shaking jaw and gripped the handle of the door, pulling it open.

"She..." He shook his head. "I'm fine, mother, just tired."

He closed the door behind him and didn't glance at the guard as he made his way to his old room, sinking into his bed before his mind pulled him into the dark void of his own emptiness.

When Alex woke the next morning, it took him a few moments to realize where he was. His heart beat frantically as he dug his hands into the soft bed and his head jerked from left to right.

His surroundings finally struck him as familiar and he sucked in a calming breath. Not the tower. He'd never be in that tower again. He was home. His palace. Where his rule meant something.

Except it didn't. Not to the people outside the palace walls. He ran a hand down his face and pulled his aching body from the bed as he scanned the room. Someone had been in there and he hadn't woken.

A platter sat on the table in his sitting room but it wasn't loaded down with fresh fruits as he'd come to expect growing up. A bowl of mashed grain and half a loaf of bread stared at him. There was fresh butter at least.

The entire palace must be on rations. It didn't bother him for his own sake. Despite the pains of hunger in his stomach, he didn't think he could eat a thing, but how long had it been since the others inside the palace had full stomachs?

In the washroom, the tub had been filled. He assumed the water had been warm at some point, but that may have been hours ago. What time was it? Sunlight danced in ribbons across the stone floor. He couldn't remember the last time the sun had woken before him.

He scrunched his nose as he sniffed his tunic. Living in a camp full of soldiers didn't exactly provide much opportunity for good hygiene.

He stripped off his worn tunic and peeled the dirt crusted trousers from his legs, shaking his head at how he must have appeared to his mother yesterday. He'd fallen asleep without even changing.

He bathed quickly, scrubbing rigorously and taking great pains to remove all signs of hardship from his skin and hair. The water was a hideous shade of brown by the time he finished, but he smelled like the roses the maid had put in the water.

His wardrobe was the same—untouched in his absence. His fingers reached for the soft wool of a simple tunic before he released a sigh and shook his head. Not today. Today he had to show them the king was back.

He slipped a padded tunic over his head before donning his chain mail and pulling a surcoat over it. If the traitors were going to force the kingdom into war, this was the king they'd get. Not one who would sit back and let them take control of Gaule.

When he strapped his sword to his waist, his lips curled up into a smile. It'd seemed like years since he'd had the weight of his own sword at his side. He'd used others, but it wasn't the same.

He turned toward the door, but at the last moment, reached for his crown and nestled it into his dark hair. The weight settled around him and any hint of a smile fell from his lips.

Simon was waiting for him in the hall. So, it began. It should have shocked him to find out Simon had magic as well, but Alex had grown numb to secrets. To magic. It had been around him his entire life. He just hadn't realized it.

Simon nodded in approval when he took in Alex's appearance.

"Morning," Alex grunted.

"They're waiting for you in the council chambers."

Simon was a man of few words so the walk through the crowded palace halls was quiet. When people saw them, eyes widened, mouths dropped open. Those with their wits dropped into bows. Others murmured. He only made out a few words. *The king has returned.*

Before turning into the council chambers, Tyson's voice drifted toward them. Alex stopped. Simon glanced at him and did the same.

"I'm so sorry, son," their mother said.

"You said that last night." Tyson sounded like the sullen teenager he was, not the powerful magic man he'd become.

"Viktor was..."

"I don't need to hear about you and that man. My *sister* told me plenty about him."

"Oh dear." Her breath hissed and Alex imagined her cheeks puffing out like they did when she was nervous. "Persinette... is she...?"

"I could have stayed with her, mother." His voice shook. "I wanted to. There's nothing I wanted more than to stay with Etta and Edmund and everyone else who is just like me. Do you know I even have a cousin?"

"But you came back?"

"I had to," he burst out. "I'd never abandon you and Amalie and Camille. I have to be at Alex's side when he takes back his kingdom."

"And then?"

"And then, Mother, I'm not sure I can stay in Gaule."

"You're just a boy."

Tyson huffed out a laugh. "I haven't been a kid since the day I discovered my magic."

Their words drifted away and Alex closed his eyes. His brother had wanted to stay. Simon patted Alex on the back awkwardly and gestured to the room. Alex took the hint and entered; ready to tell them everything that had happened since he was taken from the palace.

And everything that would happen from here on out.

He had a plan.

# CHAPTER 5

Etta tried out a smile. One that didn't look fake. It stretched her face unnaturally, but the family didn't seem to notice as they waved to her excitedly. A little girl with angelic rosy cheeks ran toward her. "You're the queen," she said.

Etta smiled again but this time it wasn't so forced as she nodded.

"You have hair like mine." The girl grinned, pulling on her own blonde locks. The sun caught in the strands making them glow golden.

Etta touched the end of her braid. Not so long ago, she'd had to cut it off, and it hadn't seemed important.

"Sasha!" A petite woman ran up. "Come here." She curtsied quickly. "I'm sorry, your Majesty."

She scurried away, pulling the girl alongside her. Etta watched after them, wishing she'd said something. The people who'd returned to Bela respected her. Edmund said they revered her, loved her even. The ones who hadn't been present when she fought La Dame had heard the story. But they rarely talked to her.

Even after she'd fulfilled her promise to Edmund. She'd held court and nothing had felt more silly, at first. She'd sat on a raised chair and people bowed in front of her while offering platitudes.

That part had been a waste of time. She wasn't the queen they needed. But then they began discussing what still needed to be done. They were expecting more ships soon. The village was to be expanded to accommodate more of their people seeking refuge. Old alliances were to be rekindled.

Winter was upon them and their food stores might not get them through it.

She shook her head. She'd known none of it would be easy.

Matteo had been there, always by her side, ready to help with any decisions, and she was beginning to wonder if she needed other advisors. She couldn't do it on her own.

Pulling her cloak tighter about her, she hurried down the path to the beach. Edmund promised he'd meet her there.

A single flake of snow landed on her cheek, melting instantly. She looked up to see a few others fall as her breath floated in front of her face.

The birds had long since left Bela for warmer kingdoms and for the first time since leaving, she missed Gaule. It didn't snow in the winter and the temperatures weren't anywhere near as harsh. They didn't have to huddle around fires at night in their ramshackle huts to keep from freezing to death.

Edmund was already at the beach, facing the rolling waves. The white cliffs rose up at their backs. Before Etta could alert Edmund to her presence, another person came into view. Esme.

Etta sucked in a breath. Esme had saved Edmund twice now and countless others, but it was hard to look at her without seeing her daughter. Maiya's betrayal still clung to Etta like a fist around her heart.

Esme's dark lips stretched to reveal impossibly white teeth. "My queen."

It was on the tip of Etta's tongue. The fact that technically La Dame was Esme's queen since she was Draconian. But she bit back the words as Edmund turned.

His shoulders lifted in apology as he glanced between Etta and Esme. "If I'm going to be around while you're testing out your powers, I'm going to have the healer nearby."

"Okay." Etta swung her arms in front of her, loosening her muscles.

"Okay?" Edmund quirked an eyebrow.

She nodded. He was right. No matter how much Etta distrusted the woman who'd spent her life working for La Dame, she trusted herself even less. She wouldn't put Edmund at risk.

Tilting her head to the side, she cracked her neck and stretched her arms over her head. "So, how do we start?"

"You think I know?" he asked. "I've spent my life hiding my magic just like you."

"You're the one who pushed me so hard to use it."

He shrugged. "And look how well that turned out."

Esme started laughing, her shoulders shaking as she folded her arms across her stomach.

"Care to share what's so hilarious?" Etta narrowed her eyes.

Esme swallowed down another laugh. "You're supposed to be Bela's hope for survival?"

"And?"

"And you two are going to get yourselves killed." She shook her head.

Etta stepped toward her. "What would you know? You're just a healer?"

"You have no idea what you're talking about. I am a healer, yes, but healing isn't my only magic."

She closed her eyes and Etta suddenly felt every bit of defiance draining away as if it had never been a part of her.

A dumb grin lit Edmund's face.

"Edmund," Esme said softly. "Tell me your greatest fear."

He wouldn't just obey her, would he? Etta watched her friend struggle with his words. His forehead scrunched as he fought her command, but then smoothed out as another wave of peace pulsed out.

"That..." He tried to keep them in. "That they're right about us."

"Who, Edmund?" Esme asked. "Who is right?"

"Gaule. Everyone. That we're dangerous. That our magic isn't to be trusted."

Etta stared at him as the peace snapped away like a rubber band stretched too far. Red crept up into his cheeks as he realized what he'd just said.

"Etta," he said softly.

She turned away from him to fix Esme with a glare. "If I find you using that on any of my people, I'll send you back to Dracon and whatever fate awaits you there."

Esme didn't flinch under the harsh stare as she nodded once.

Etta faced Edmund once again. "You're right, Edmund. We are dangerous. We shouldn't be trusted. Because the time of Bela has come. They should fear us, but we should not fear each other. Let's begin."

It was too strong. Etta felt it vibrating through her. This magic. This power. It didn't feel like hers. She'd always been comforted by her ability to create life. Even now, her mind's first instinct was to latch on to the weeds poking through the rocks where sand met grassy hill. She closed her eyes and tugged on the tight string, imagining the weeds stretching up toward the sky.

The tight string loosened quickly and Etta's eyes popped open as it unraveled within her. Her head jerked back as she tried to hold it inside but her control was gone. Her mind reached out, grasping, straining, for something to hold on to.

Wind rushed in her ears, a deafening roar drowning out the screaming of those around her.

"No," she cried as she felt it slipping. "Agh!"

She fell forward and her knees hit the sand as the power exploded out of her, draining every bit of energy inside.

The sand rose up around her as she pitched forward onto the now scorched ground. She turned her head in time to see Edmund flying into the air.

Her cheek was still pressed to the warm ground as the sand settled in a haze of dust, mixing with the still falling snow. Edmund's head popped up among the waves and he made it to the shore with a few strong strokes.

Etta sucked in a breath as if air was in short supply, her heart drumming rapidly against her ribs. Edmund crawled out of the water and collapsed shivering.

Esme ran forward and dropped to the ground beside him.

"How," Etta wheezed. "How did you avoid it?"

Esme didn't look up from checking over Edmund. "The range of my magic is much farther in front of me. I took a chance standing down there, hoping your range was similar."

She pointed toward the far end of the beach. "Edmund here thought you'd have more of a chance if you could see him."

"Obviously not." She crawled toward them and looked down into her friend's face. "You okay?"

"Just c-cold." His teeth chattered.

She shrugged out of her cloak and laid it over him, but it was soaking wet in seconds. "You need dry clothes."

"Are you hurt?" Esme asked.

"I d-don't t-think so."

"That is why we're doing this at the beach." She helped him to his feet. "If we were in the woods, he could've been seriously injured."

"I don't think you guys should be helping me anymore." Etta kicked at the sand as a gust of wind blew it into the air. The chill felt good on her burning skin. The snow sizzled when it touched her.

"T-Too bad." Edmund trudged up the path in search of dry clothes, but Esme stayed behind.

"He's right, you know," she said.

Etta strode across the beach to the rocks and sat down. "About what?"

"You can't do this alone and if you don't learn to control your magic, it not only takes the one weapon against La Dame we have, but it'll kill you." Esme was quiet for a moment before trying a different tactic. "Can I tell you a secret?"

"Aren't you usually pulling secrets from other people?"

She nodded. "I deserve that. I have spent my entire life in service to La Dame. I admit it. I joined her ranks of my own free will when I was a teenager. I worshipped the ground she walked on."

"What changed?"

"I had a daughter."

"Maiya."

Esme nodded. "Her father was one of La Dame's dragons. That's her network of spies. Pierre is the only dragon who managed to get close to Viktor Basile. He is a hero in Dracon. And my greatest nightmare. La Dame gave our daughter to him to use for his cover in Gaule. Before that night at La Dame's final ball in Bela, I hadn't seen her since she was a baby."

"I'm sorry."

Esme lifted her eyes. "You're a queen. Don't be sorry. Tell me I'll have my revenge. For years, she's used my daughter's life as a way to keep me in her control."

"But you still left her to join us."

Her shoulders dropped. "I know."

Etta leaned in, dropping her voice. "You'll have your revenge."

"And you'll have my loyalty." She cocked her head. "But can I ask you a question?"

Etta nodded.

"Why would your father name you Persinette? In Draconian, that means—"

"I know. He named me Rapunzel." She scrunched her brow and blew out a breath. "I don't understand anything my father ever did. Was he taunting her? Did he want her to come for us? I'm never going to know because he died with so many secrets."

Etta slid from the rocks as she watched Edmund approach in dry clothes. He'd tied his wet hair away from his face.

"Persinette," Esme said.

Etta turned. "Yeah."

She took a breath as if weighing her words. "La Dame believes she will own you one day. That's why..."

"Why what?"

"Deep in the recesses of the Draconian palace lays a crown. Your crown. The Basile crown was not lost as the legends say. She has kept it for the day the Belaen ruler stands at her side."

"That doesn't make any sense." Etta's eyes drifted out over the water but she didn't take in the sight. "Why then did she want me dead?"

"Think about it. She's never actively tried to kill you." She shook her head. "She's kept your family cursed for many generations looking for the one she deems worthy."

Etta jumped to her feet and spun. "Why am I worthy? Why not my father? I am nothing. I can't even control my own magic." Etta's chest heaved as her voice rose.

Edmund reached them and draped a dry cloak over her shoulders. "You're wrong."

"It's just another thing she's stolen that I have to get back." Etta rested her hands on top of her head. "I will never stand at her side, but I will have my crown."

Edmund grunted. "Glad someone is finally realizing she can't escape destiny."

"Not destiny, Edmund. Revenge. Blood. Magic."

"There's something else," Esme said hesitantly.

After a long pause, Edmund gestured for her to continue. "Don't leave us in suspense."

Esme breathed deeply. "Your power is the opposite of La Dame's."

"What does that mean?" Etta met her gaze.

"Many centuries ago when the Basile magic and La Dame's were first revealed, they balanced each other. One held immense darkness and the other light. Since then, they've both grown darker, but the same rules apply. They will battle each other any chance they get, but at the same time, they attract each other. Your power will try to draw hers in, stealing it from her."

"Is that even possible?"

"It had never been done... but yes. And, Etta, you must resist the urge to take what is hers."

"Why?" Etta asked. "Shouldn't I try to strip her of power?"

"If your power and hers meet within your body..." Esme shook her head. "I'm sorry, Etta, but it will destroy you."

"Come on Etta," Esme called. "Focus. Do it again. Try to only release it in bits. In battle, when the adrenaline courses through you, you must fight the urge to expel too much at once. If you do that, the power will leave you forever."

Edmund got to his feet once more and stumbled backward. Esme reached for his arm to keep him upright.

At Esme's healing touch, Edmund stood straighter, his eyes regaining clarity.

Etta shook her head. "It's been too much."

"I'm fine," Edmund said, his voice strained.

He was anything but fine. They'd been training for days and Etta lost count of the number of times Edmund had been knocked unconscious or thrown into the icy water. She was improving, learning to control when the power was unleashed, but pulling it back was another story. The impact reached far enough that they'd cleared the beach of all people except the three of them.

If she was ever going to have a chance against La Dame, she needed complete control over her powers. The more she used it, the greater her stamina became.

But would it be able to match that of the most powerful sorcerer in the world?

She'd been able to focus enough to expel bits of the power without releasing it all at once. If she strained, she could draw on her ability of growth—the very same thing she'd tried that first day. They stood at the base of the cliffs and the vines crept up the sheer rock wall, slithering like snakes.

She closed her eyes, seeing her old home in her mind. The Black Forest with the meadow of flowers she'd created was her safe place, despite its location inside Gaule. It calmed her and allowed her to contain the magic trying to break free.

A hum sounded low in her throat as a hand landed on her shoulder. She startled out of her trance and instinctively sent a blast of power behind her, striking Edmund in the chest.

She turned in time to see him land halfway down the beach, his body bent at an odd angle.

Esme reached him before Etta and laid her hands on his chest. He was back with them in moments.

"Do you enjoy almost dying?" Etta spat, pushing to her feet.

"Not particularly," Edmund wheezed, staring up at the sky. "No."

"Why did you touch me?"

"You were doing it. Focusing your magic." He rolled over onto his belly and pushed his hands under him. "Forgive me for being proud."

The corner of her mouth lifted. "I was doing it, wasn't I?" She turned back toward the cliffs where a series of vines now crisscrossed the surface. She clenched her fist, feeling the magic pool in her fingertips. It wanted the same thing she'd spent her life seeking. Freedom.

The curse had been her master and now she was the magic's master. She could do this. The power inside of her was a living thing, but it attached itself to everything she was with promises of everything she could be.

"Edmund needs to be done for the day," Esme said, ever the voice of reason.

Etta nodded. "You two go up to the cook fires and rest. I'm going to keep practicing."

"Not alone," Edmund argued.

"Edmund, I am the queen. I will do as I please." She softened her eyes. "Just go. Please. I'm okay."

They hesitated a moment longer before disappearing up the path. Etta held her palms over the ground and started by releasing magic in small amounts, working up to a continuous stream, blasting sand into the water. She walked forward, a cloud of dust surrounding her.

The air turned frigid as the sun disappeared from view, but Etta's skin was blazing. She unhooked her cloak and tossed it behind her, raising her arms. Her golden hair flew back away from her face as she enjoyed the feeling of strength, of power.

It was a dizzying mix of fear and a desire for more.

"Etta," someone's voice broke through her trance. "Etta!"

The power fizzled out as she lowered her arms. She'd done it. She'd pulled it back. She hadn't hurt anyone. A breath rattled in her chest as she turned her head to meet her cousin's gaping stare.

"You..." Matteo couldn't get any other words out so he just pointed. "Your..."

"What?" Exhaustion struck her suddenly and forcefully. Taking a step toward him took every ounce of energy she possessed.

"Hair," he croaked.

Etta raised a heavy arm to the hair that had come loose from her braid and pulled it forward, dropping it immediately. It was glowing as it had the day it grew from where she'd cut it off. She squeezed her eyes shut, thinking when she opened them, none of it would be real.

But it was. Her hair had an ethereal golden shine. It began to fade as they stood there gawking at it until it returned to its normal blonde shade. It wasn't the first time it had happened, but part of her thought she'd imagined it before.

"What was that?" she asked.

"I don't know."

She managed to get herself to the rocks before her legs collapsed beneath her.

They didn't speak for a few moments until Matteo broke the silence. "I've lived most of my life in La Dame's household and I've never seen anything like that before."

Etta buried her face in her hands. "There's so much I don't know. Has the curse kept this power from every generation of Basiles since Phillip and Aurora, or am I the only one? What am I supposed to do with it? Is my magic strong enough to beat her?"

When he didn't respond, Etta spoke again, but this time it was more to herself. "Why do I miss the feeling of the curse filling me?"

"The last one is easy." Matteo took her hands and pried them away from her face. "The curse gave you a single purpose. There was no question as to what you were supposed to do. Protect the Duran king. That left no room for interpretation and there was nothing you could do to change it." He paused. "Now you are a queen and none of us know what being queen of a kingdom that was destroyed generations ago even means."

"You make it sound so simple."

"How's this for simple—you miss serving someone instead of having people serve you."

"That's just stupid."

"Is it?" he asked. "Okay, then let's try this. You don't miss serving. You miss serving Alexandre Durand."

She forced out a laugh. "There's only one Durand I want with me and that's Tyson."

He bumped her shoulder. "For the record, I think Alexandre Durand is a spoiled king who had never tasted hardship before La Dame took him."

"I don't disagree with that assessment."

"And now he's gone back to his palace. He'll have won it back by now and Gaule will return to its glory days of persecution and torment. We should take advantage of their internal struggles and make our move."

Etta slid from the rock, Alex's face appearing in her mind. Was he okay? Were Tyson and Catrine? "No," she sighed. "I made a promise. Their borders will remain untouched." She gave Matteo a reassuring smile. "But at the first sign of Belaens being persecuted in Gaule, we ride."

# CHAPTER 6

Disgust churned in the pit of Alex's stomach as he stood atop the inner walls looking out on the traitors residing in the outer palace. They'd taken his home, but that wasn't the worst of it. They'd found magic folk who hadn't been able to flee to Bela or seek refuge in the inner palace. Lines of them were chained along the wall, a shield of prisoners. At any hint of their magic, one of the guards would kill them.

Persinette once told him that most magic folk possessed a magic that was quite weak, only allowing them to do simple tasks. Then he'd seen the kind of power she possessed and he didn't know what to believe anymore.

But they didn't try to break free. They appeared truly broken.

"You shouldn't be atop the walls, your Majesty," Simon said, stepping up beside him. "Your guard says you refused them when they tried to accompany you."

"I am the king, Simon." Alex patted him on the shoulder. "There are few benefits, but being able to command my guard to let me be, just for a moment, is one of them. I didn't have that as the prince."

Simon nodded, not looking at him. "I remember. You got quite good at evading us."

"Not as good as Tyson."

A rueful smile appeared on his lips. "That boy would disappear for days. I never envied the men he slipped when they had to face the king." His smile fell and hawk-like eyes scanned the small town in the outer castle. "But I'm serious, sire. One well-placed arrow and we are suddenly lost."

Alex ran a hand through his hair. "The fight would go on without me."

Simon didn't respond right away, but Alex felt him tense as if prepared to block an attack if necessary. "There wouldn't even be a fight without you."

Alex scoffed but Simon went on. "You stood up for something, sire. You broke away from your father's cruel rule. The purge is still remembered by some of us. I was a young man when they came for us. Gaule was the only home I'd ever known. Bela was a place of distant stories. It was the dream, an unattainable one. Gaule was real and our kingdom turned on us. My wife was killed in the first round of the purge."

Alex sucked in a breath and turned to stare at the profile of the guard beside him. A man he'd known so little about.

"But you came to serve my father, anyway? You must have hated him."

"I did." He rubbed the back of his neck. "When I first came to the palace, I was angry. I was going to kill the king."

Alex stopped breathing as the traitorous words settled around him. "But you didn't," he croaked.

"No." His lips tugged down. "I didn't. I was assigned to his son. I knew if I raised my hand against you, it would hurt the kingdom far more than the kingdom hurt me. It would have been easy. But the purge was ending by then and to take your life would have caused a resurgence of the hatred. So, I waited, hoping that one day I could help my people."

Alex pushed out a breath. "And instead, they're either imprisoned in this palace or down there with chains around their ankles." He pointed to the prisoners below.

Simon faced him. "Or in Bela rebuilding what should be ours with our queen. Your Majesty, my people finally have a future. Even the ones here. I didn't think I'd ever see a day when they trusted another Gaulean king. You say you don't matter to this fight, but you are the fight. You showed an entire people you will go to war for them. They will follow you." He gripped Alex's shoulder. "Now, let's get off this wall before your mother has both our heads."

Ara was waiting for them at the base of the stairs. He could see it now, the resemblance to Duke Caron. Her brother was with her. "I've spoken to Renner."

It took Alex a moment to understand what she was saying. She hadn't had a two-sided conversation with her other brother, she'd used her magic to reach her voice out toward him.

Alex motioned for them to walk with him. "Tell me."

"He knows the plan. He's sending some men our way and the rest will be in position at sunrise three days from now."

"Good. What we really need are horses."

Hendry jumped in. "The tunnels should be just big enough to bring them through. Renner will get us what we need."

The siblings had faith in each other. That was good because there were so few people Alex could say the same about.

"I don't want my mother near the fight. She needs to be kept under guard along with the children and anyone else who does not know how to wield sword or bow. Ara, I'm going to want you with the archers atop the wall."

She opened her mouth to protest, but Alex stopped her. "Your skill with a sword is well-known, but you are of more importance to us directing everyone."

She clamped her mouth shut, acknowledging the truth in his words.

"You should lead the archers," Simon said to Alex.

He shook his head. "No."

"Sire—"

"I've gotten better with a blade, Si. I need to lead the soldiers who will be riding into the worst of it. They need to see me among them, not high atop the wall as my father would have done. The royal guardsmen who fight at Lord Leroy's side must be forced to take arms against the king they betrayed. I will not be swayed in this."

"Oh look," Ara said quietly, nudging her brother. "It's our new mother."

There was no mistaking the sneer in her words as Camille stepped into their path. Alex had known Duke Caron had many children, some older than his new bride, but it hadn't hit him until then the position he was putting his sister in with the marriage. At the time, he'd only been focused on tying her to someone whose loyalty would never be in question and who would never be outwardly cruel. As much as he sometimes disliked his sister, she was still family.

Camille's eyes flashed with something a shade darker than annoyance when she saw Ara. She was trying to accept magic folk as her husband did, but it didn't come naturally to her. Their father had twisted her deeply.

"Sister." Alex took her arm and pulled her away from Ara and Hendry, leaving them behind. "Is everything okay?"

Simon followed them closely but didn't say a word.

Camille sighed dramatically. "You see the way they look at me."

"Maybe if you tried to hide your disdain for Ara, even a little."

She huffed. "Of course you're on their side. Ever since your precious Etta showed up at the palace, magic folk mean more to you than your own blood."

His steps faltered at the mention of Etta. "Now you know that isn't true, Camille."

She stopped walking and slammed the end of her cane into the stone floor. "Do I?"

"Camille..."

"Where is she, Alexandre? I used to think you were doing this because you loved her. Even if she was insufferable, I could understand that. You always were a fool." A small smile played on her lips but then she shook her head and it dropped. "Now she's not even here and you're still allowing our kingdom to be torn in half. Is all of this still for her?"

How did he answer that question? He'd started his mission to end magic's persecution in Gaule as a way to protect her, to prove he wasn't his father. Now...

"Sometimes there doesn't have to be a reason," he said softly. "Maybe I just want to do what's right."

"And then what? Say we win this battle, preventing an all-out civil war. Are you going to send the magic folk fleeing into Bela? That's what they should do. It's safest for all of us. From what you've said about Etta's new powers, she could probably rebuild her father's wards. We could be protected again. Magic folk were never meant to live among us."

Alex had to tell his lungs to expand to allow air to flow into them. Was his sister right? Separating Gaule from Bela once more would protect them from La Dame, but then what would happen to Bela?

What would happen to its queen? To his brother and Edmund?

Everything that mattered in his life was wrapped up in magic. How could he abandon them?

"I don't know, but Camille, I am the king. I need you to trust that I will do what is right for Gaule." He didn't give his sister a chance to respond before leaving her outside the council chambers. Those were questions he'd have to answer later. For now, he had to prepare for a more imminent fight.

Alex sat atop his steed. Waiting. He hated waiting. But every part of this plan had to be executed to perfection. His horse snorted in agitation and he realized it felt the same tension in the air.

A hundred and some odd horsemen crowded the courtyard with foot soldiers waiting just inside the palace to follow.

Most of the soldiers had been in the palace already, choosing to stay loyal to the crown when Lord Leroy showed his true colors. Others had come in with the horses, using the Black Forest to evade detection.

And still, some were just magic folk. Until this point, they'd lived ordinary lives and kept their magic hidden as if it was something to be ashamed of.

Alex had come to see that none of them were ashamed. They hid their power for fear of what would happen, but they were a proud people. They knew the history of Bela. It was passed down from generation to generation through stories and legends.

Just as Alex knew Gaule's colorful past. If it hadn't been for his father, would Gaule be fighting so hard against magic? Would they be so divided?

Before his father became king, there was much less power in that title. Did Alex want to allow a council to rule Gaule instead of only a king?

When his father consolidated his power, taking it from the council piece by piece, it allowed the purge to come about. No one was there to stop him when he ran magic folk from their home.

Alex shifted in his saddle, pushing those thoughts from his mind. He didn't want to think about where his power came from or if he even deserved to have it.

Lifting his face to the rising sun, he caught sight of the archers lining the top of the wall. They were crouched down, hidden by low barriers. Ara was among them. Her gaze connected with Alex's. He was too far away to see her lips move, but her voice rang softly in his ears. "Be ready, my king. The forces are in position. The gates will open soon."

He nodded and turned to Tyson. "Are you prepared for this?"

Tyson grinned, sliding his sword from his scabbard. "Will you let me have Leroy?"

"You know I can't do that, brother."

Tyson's shoulders dropped. "I'm not sure I could kill Amalie's father, anyway."

"Is she with mother?"

"She better be," he said darkly. "She wanted to join us. Can you believe that?"

Alex shrugged. If there was one thing Etta taught him, it was never to underestimate a woman with a mission.

Simon formed up on Alex's other side. Duke Caron and Hendry were nearby. Alex shot the Duke an approving nod. He respected a man who didn't rely on others fighting for him.

The traitors in the outer palace still slept, unaware of what was about to be unleashed upon them.

A groan reverberated off every stone in the courtyard as the gates began to move. There were shouts of warning on the other side, but they were cut off by arrows striking the guards in their throats. Chains rattled as the prisoners began to wake.

As one, the archers revealed themselves atop the wall and released a volley of arrows at the soldiers who were now running from their beds.

"To the gates!" Alex yelled, kicking his heels into his horse and charging forward.

The enemy soldiers scrambled toward their horses, but they weren't fast enough as the force behind Alex cut a path through the mob. Cheers from the prisoners rang in his ears until it was the only thing he could hear, a siren's song calling to him. He'd free them.

"Caron," he yelled. "To the prisoners." He swung his sword down to cut at a man near his feet and snapped his reins. "Tyson, Simon with me!"

The outer palace was steeped in chaos. Soldiers scrambling to protect their position. Townsfolk whose only misdeed was choosing the wrong side and getting caught in the crosshairs. An arrow whizzed past him and he spared a single glance at the archers.

Ara's voice drifted toward him. "Renner is engaged with Leroy's forces. Get to the gates now."

They'd left just enough soldiers in the outer palace to hold it, but not enough to withstand the oncoming stampede. Leroy had counted on their lack of horses and fighting men.

Heart beating in his throat, Alex mowed down someone in full armor who tried to stand in his way. Tyson hacked through someone behind him.

"Sire," Simon called. "Archers!"

Alex whipped his head around, seeing the men climbing onto the surrounding rooftops, bows in hand.

"Come on." He rode forward, dodging one arrow as another flew straight toward him. He didn't have time to get out of the way.

"Alex," Tyson screamed.

Alex waited for the pain but it never came as the arrow stopped midair as if hitting some invisible barrier and clattering to the ground.

Alex's eyes darted around until landing on a young girl with golden hair pulled back in a braid. He sucked in a breath.

"We have to get to the gate," Simon interrupted his thoughts.

Alex barely heard him. The girl had saved his life. She reminded him of... Before Etta invaded his mind, a guard yanked the girl back.

She screamed when he put a hand over her mouth. Without thinking, Alex jumped down from his horse and ran after them. The guard was too preoccupied to see him until the king's blade was sinking into his chest. He released the girl and fell back.

The girl chewed on the end of her braid looking so much like Etta had when they were children.

"Alex," Simon called again.

A man ran toward them and took the girl in his arms.

"Thank you," he said as he pulled her through a doorway to hide her from the fight.

Alex shook himself and swung back onto the horse as another arrow narrowly missed him. With Tyson and Simon on either side of him, he rode through the very heart of the battle, not stopping until the gate loomed over them.

Three men ran out of the gatehouse and Alex readied for a fight. Tyson raised one palm and a burst of water rushed forth, knocking them to the ground and pushing them toward the streets that now ran with blood.

Alex stared at his brother in wonder. "When did you learn to do that?"

"One day," he said, "If you ever see Etta and Edmund again, you should ask them how they found me in Bela."

"After we win this." Alex shoved past Tyson. "Today we need to win this."

Two more guards came from the guardhouse but stopped when they took in the sight of their king.

Alex held his sword aloft. "You two have two options. You can either try to prevent us from getting this gate open and receive a sword in the belly for your troubles. Or you can decide not to be a traitor this day. Decide not to take up arms against your king. You have three seconds to make up your minds."

The two men looked at each other and then back at Alex. "We'll get it open, your Majesty."

Alex nodded. "Now would be good."

They retreated into the guardhouse while Alex, Tyson, and Simon fended off anyone who tried to stop them.

Hendry came charging toward them and leaped from his horse. "We have taken control of the outer palace, your Majesty."

"The prisoners?" Alex asked.

"Freed and preparing to help us."

"Have you taken any of the nobles?"

"No. They would have stayed with the larger force for protection."

Alex's hope crumbled. He was right. This day was far from over. Taking the inner palace was the easy part. Only a minimal guard had been left along with the villagers.

Ara's voice drifted over all of them. "To the gate," she said. "Be ready to charge."

At her command, their men and women who were still standing approached the gate, some on horseback, most not.

"The wounded have been sent into the palace to be tended to," Duke Caron said as he joined them. "There's one other thing." He nodded to one of his men who brought a struggling soldier to the front. As soon as her helmet was removed, grumbling sounded around them.

Amalie stood in full armor with blood streaking down her face. Her sword gleamed red to match the fire in her eyes.

"Amalie?" Tyson stammered. "What the hell?"

She stuck out her chin. "This is as much my fight as yours."

"But..." No more words came as his mouth hung open.

Alex looked to Caron. "Can you spare a man to escort her back to the palace?"

"Of course, sire."

Amalie's eyes flashed. "I won't go."

"This is not the time to be stubborn, girl," Simon growled.

Amalie's eyes met Alex's. "My father is a traitor, Alex. I deserve a chance to right some of his wrongs."

Alex studied her face. "You're right."

She went on as if she hadn't heard him. "You don't get to tell me what I'm allowed to fight for. If I want to risk my life for you, then..." Her eyes narrowed. "Wait, what?"

"Bring her a horse," Alex called to one of his men. "I don't want her on foot."

"Alex," Tyson pleaded. "Don't send her out there."

He turned to his brother. Before Etta, he might have sent Amalie away. But she'd changed him. Made him see his power differently. Why should he get to decide what someone deems worthy of their life?

Amalie climbed onto a horse.

"Let her do this, Ty." He said, turning back toward the opening gates. "She has a mind of her own. Allow her to use it."

The sound of battle reached him before the gates were fully open. Caron and Moreau forces were engaged with Leroy's soldiers. They were outnumbered and losing.

As soon as the gates stopped moving, Alex charged, hoping his soldiers followed him. They cut a path through the center of Leroy's forces as the traitors tried to scramble out of the way.

Their distraction allowed Renner to order his men to move forward, closing the circle they had around Leroy's men. That had been the plan. Encircle them and force them to stand down.

A burly man charged toward Alex, sinking his ax in his horse's chest. It reared, throwing Alex to the ground.

He rolled to his feet as his horse collapsed beside him with a trembling sigh. Sparing one final glance at the beast, he ducked out of the way of his attacker and turned to meet him blow for blow.

The large man yanked his ax free and brought with it a spray of blood that struck Alex in the chest. He blocked the swing of the ax with his sword but the other man was stronger, forcing the king's weapon to the ground. Alex stumbled back, his eyes shifting to the side for any spare weapon.

The traitor soldier advanced. His mouth was set in a grim line and there was no pleasure in his eyes. The people of Gaule didn't want to be rising up against their king. They'd thought they had no choice. It was rebel or accept magic into their lives.

Alex's wild eyes caught sight of Simon nearby tearing through the ranks using the strength his magic gave him. It was frightening. Those who had magic would always have an advantage over those who didn't. If they were allowed to use it openly, the power shift would be swift.

Alex hadn't understood.

But there, in the middle of that battlefield, he knew why these people had come to fight and he couldn't fault them for their fears.

"You don't have to do this," Alex said, trying to calm his rapid breath. "None of you do."

The man stopped, surprised his opponent spoke in the middle of their battle. He grunted and took another step forward. "Magic folk killed my little girl." When he swung again, there was less energy in it and Alex jumped back easily.

He saw the moment the fight left the man's eyes. Maybe it was the mention of his daughter or the fact that the battle was turning. Caron's forces closed in, pinning Leroy's soldiers in closer to the palace walls. Alex's men still guarded the gate, preventing them from seeking refuge behind the walls.

Alex bent and retrieved a fallen sword from the ground, but before he raised it, a blade pierced his attacker through the back, the tip of the sword slicing clean through.

A scream stuck in Alex's throat but never made it out as the man who'd just wanted to avenge his daughter crumpled to the blood-stained grass, all life fading from his eyes.

Alex didn't see who struck the killing blow because his eyes were on something else. A small soldier faced off against Lord Leroy. The portly man was no match for the quick steps of the girl Alex would recognize anywhere. Amalie's helmet obscured her face from view as she blocked her father's jabs. She spun with a quickness Alex hadn't known she possessed and jammed a steel-clad foot into her father's knee. He cried out as he fell. Amalie knelt behind him and held a knife to his throat.

She pulled off her helmet and her father's eyes widened.

"Amalie," Tyson yelled, running to her side.

She didn't spare Tyson a glance. Instead, she screamed at the top of her lungs. "I'll do it! Put your swords down now or the leader of your rebellion will not see his next sunrise."

Those close enough to hear obeyed, and the command made its way through what was left of Leroy's troops.

Alex scanned the faces looking for any of his other traitorous nobles, but they'd disappeared from view. He stepped forward, taking advantage of the temporary cease in fighting. "Lower your weapons."

Running a hand through his sweaty hair, he glanced from Leroy to the tired eyes of the men he'd roped into his rebellion.

The loyalist forces weren't doing much better as they leaned against their swords, breathing heavily. None of them had been untouched by this. Gaule would forever be changed. But maybe this could be the end of all the strife.

He pulled on the ends of his hair as the words ran through his mind. None of them seemed right.

Caron's troops remained in a tight circle, controlling the circumstances. Alex shook his head. "We are all Gauleans."

"Not all of us," Leroy spit, shooting daggers toward Tyson and Simon.

Amalie pulled his hair back. "Say that again."

"Amalie," Alex said, surprised at the venom in the normally sweet girl. "Release him."

"What?" she snapped.

"Alex..." Tyson warned low enough for only Alex to hear.

"Do it," he commanded.

Amalie removed her knife and kicked her father in the back so he fell forward. It didn't escape Alex's notice that she kept her knife in her hand and stood over him, preventing him from standing.

Alex raised his voice. "Every person here has called Gaule their home. It is not my kingdom. It's not your kingdom. It's *our* kingdom. Together we have created greatness." He swallowed past the lump in his throat. "I am your king. My word is law." He scratched his jaw. "But maybe it shouldn't be." What was he saying?

He sighed heavily. "What has happened this day is a tragedy. Good men and women have lost their lives. Our children are no safer. La Dame is still on our doorstep. But she isn't only our enemy. She is the enemy of all who are free and that includes the magic folk within our borders. It includes the Belaens. If we are busy trying to destroy each other, we are giving her exactly what she wants, and she will crush us." He crashed his fist against his armor for emphasis.

Raising his eyes to the palace at their backs, he shook his head. "Return to your villages. Live your lives until I call on you to protect Gaule. All who are here today are pardoned. Except for one man." He hung his head and pushed through the crowd. "Simon, bring Leroy to the throne room."

Refusing the offered horse, Alex walked the long road through the outer castle to the palace where his mother awaited him. She gasped when he appeared. He released his hold on his sword and it hit the stone floor with a jarring crash as she wrapped her arms around him.

"Is it over?" she asked, her words barely audible.

He shook his head against her shoulder. "Not yet." Without another word, he walked up the steps, leaving muddy boot prints in his wake. He sat heavily.

Those who'd stayed hidden in the palace watched their king make his way wordlessly up to the throne room. He hadn't been in there since the night he'd ended the war on magic—or thought he had. The same night he'd finally had Etta. The true, honest Persinette. The same night he'd been abducted.

His own words rang in his ears. Had he really said them? That maybe his word alone shouldn't be law? There'd be time enough to consider those implications later.

The sound of heavy steel-toed boots fell behind him and brought him back to the current predicament. He closed his eyes and leaned forward against his throne. If the nobles had risen up against his father, they'd all have been executed. But Alexandre Durand was not his father. And killing a man who held so much power, so much loyalty in Gaule was not something he was prepared to do.

Taking another deep breath, he turned and motioned for Simon to force Leroy to his knees. Duke Caron hurried in with Camille and Queen Catrine. Amalie and Tyson weren't far behind.

Alex walked forward until he was standing over Leroy, Alex's muddied, blood-spattered boots right under his face.

"I should kill you," he said, his voice dropping. "For ripping my kingdom in half."

"You did that all on your own," Leroy spat.

Alex raised a brow toward Simon and the big man jerked the lord forward.

"Get your filthy magic tainted hands off me," Leroy growled.

Alex leaned down. "You aren't in a position to be making demands." He narrowed his eyes. "If I kill you, there will be another uprising on your lands. We can't have that." He shook his head. "But I will also not allow you to return home only to stir up more rebellion."

Every face in the room turned to Alex in surprise, but he wasn't done.

"I tried to be a merciful king, but your chances have run out. You will now spend your days as a prisoner of Gaule. Your home will be a cell in this palace. My guards will watch you constantly. You have forfeited your freedom. I won't kill you, but I can make sure others don't die for your folly. Everything you now have will be because I allow you to have it. Everything you do will be what I allow you to do. Your life is under my control. Your lands and everything on them will pass to your eldest daughter Liza. You have no more claim to them."

Alex straightened and motioned to a guard to take the disgraced lord away. He walked toward the ornate wooden door meant only for the king, leaving behind a bewildered crowd. They'd wanted blood, but Alex was so tired of blood.

He left his guards outside his room and when he shut the door, he sagged against it before dragging himself to the washroom.

The water ran red as he washed the day away from his face and shaking hands. His armor was dented, but he'd managed to return uninjured. For now, he'd consider that a victory.

After scrubbing every trace of the battle from his skin, he didn't bother to put clothes on before he sank into his bed, his tired muscles crying out in ecstasy.

Alexandre Durand had never been a fighter. He'd had Etta for that. Beautiful, fierce, enemy Etta. But he'd spent the last part of the battle trying to convince his people that Belaens were not the enemy.

Adrift in a sea of confusion, her face swam across his mind and he wished more than anything to feel the curse even for a moment. To feel connected, tethered. To know something still bound them together.

As he reached for the bonds, his heart came away empty because he knew he may never get to lay eyes on her again.

A shadow moved in the corner of his room and he wiped his eyes, thinking he must have imagined it. Shaking his head, he tried to relax into sleep.

There was a scuffing noise against the floor and he sprang up knowing he hadn't imagined it that time. Getting to his feet, he looked around, his eyes latching on to the shadow as it moved once more and came into the light.

A man in dirty, blood-spattered clothing lunged forward, his eyes still crazed from battle. Alex didn't get the chance to scream before the blade of a knife sank into his naked chest.

He shoved the man back with every ounce of strength he had left. The attacker stumbled, knocking over a table with a loud crash, before jumping forward once again.

"For Gaule," he cried.

Stars swam before Alex's eyes as the man yanked the knife free. Alex got his arm up to block the next thrust and the sharp steel sliced into his arm like it was nothing.

A cry left Alex's throat, strangled with pain, as the attacker brought forth a second knife and lunged.

Alex didn't feel it this time as his knees buckled beneath him before slamming into the stone. Blood streamed down his chest, hitting the ground in a pool of liquid life. He was vaguely aware of the door to his room crashing open.

"Your Majesty!"

Simon. His lips formed the name, but no sound escaped. A fight surrounded him, but they were a blur before his glassy eyes.

He tilted forward and the floor rushed to meet him before everything turned black.

# CHAPTER 7

The energy was sucked out of Etta until she couldn't even stand. She fell forward, her hands digging into the sand in front of her. After practicing her new magic for weeks, Etta was now testing its every edge, every limit she had, pushing her boundaries as much as she could. Each day stretched her stamina but by the time the sun disappeared from view, she could barely move.

"Etta." Edmund knelt at her side.

She didn't know why he insisted on being there for her every time the power built. They'd all lost count of how many times he'd been rendered unconscious or flung into the icy waves. It would be funny if each time didn't prove just how little control she still had.

She'd had magic her entire life. Her earliest memories were of making things grow and come to life. Creating beauty in her forest. But the Basile power that had been unleashed when the curse ended was not that. Darkness lurked underneath it. It wanted to take over her whole body, controlling her. She had to be the one to control it.

If anyone had told her that her duties as queen would be the easiest part of her life, she'd have laughed in their faces. Compared to the days she spent molding and targeting her magic, dealing with her people was nothing. They were building something they could finally call their own. For so long, the Belaens only had what they'd been allowed to have in Gaule.

"I think we're done for today." Esme wiped a hand across her tired face.

Etta flicked her eyes back over her shoulder to give the woman a grateful nod before watching her head back toward camp. A trust had been growing between the two. Each day, Esme and Edmund trudged down the path to the beach to help her. They never complained. They never even called her queen. To them, she was Etta. Not Persinette Basile. There'd been little talk of the danger looming overland behind the high mountain walls.

Everything seemed quiet, but they knew it was not. La Dame was only biding her time. She would come for them.

Etta pushed up to sit back on her heels.

Edmund dropped down beside her, twirling a lock of her glowing hair around his finger. "I'll never get used to this."

"You won't?" She rolled her eyes. "I can feel it."

"What do you mean you can feel it?"

She shrugged one shoulder. "I don't know." Pulling the golden strands over her shoulder, she fingered the ends. "It's hard to explain. It's like... a living thing. That sounds stupid."

"What do you think it means?"

She shrugged again and lifted her eyes to the dark waters. "When I was a child, my mother would spend hours brushing it. She'd tell me that one day my beauty would give me power. Do you think this is what she meant?"

"Like it's the source of your power?"

"I don't know. I've always had magic. You have too... but now... I'm not used to the amount of power I have. I guess I'm just looking for a reason."

"This is really odd. You know that, right?"

She laughed. "Yes, Edmund. My life is just about as odd as you can get. I'm well aware of that fact."

He bumped her shoulder. "But also exciting. You have more power than I've ever seen." He shook his head as if unable to believe his own words.

A small smile played on her lips and she rested her chin on her knees.

Edmund stood up slowly and dropped into a bow, extending a hand to her. "Your Majesty, may I have the pleasure of escorting you to a meal?"

She took his hand and let him pull her up. "You may." She grinned.

He tucked her hand into the crook of his arm and started up the path. Matteo greeted them at the door to their small ramshackle residence. He dipped his head in respect as he insisted upon doing. Etta was getting used to being treated like royalty. She didn't like it, but she accepted it.

"The final hunting party of the season returned this afternoon," he said.

She snapped her eyes to his in anticipation. Food stores were their biggest worry for riding out the winter.

Matteo smiled. "They brought back quite the haul."

She exhaled the breath she'd been holding.

"With the salt we've acquired from Madra, a team has been working to prepare the meat."

She nodded. The last ships that arrived on their shores not only brought trade goods but more Belaens returning to their kingdom from countries across the sea. Word was spreading about the imminent battle and they were a proud people. Magic folk who'd never set foot in Bela would give their lives for the kingdom that should be their home.

Etta sat down as Matteo set a wooden bowl of stew in front of her. She tasted the fresh rabbit with the first bite and let out a low moan.

Edmund chuckled from his place beside Matteo and her cousin looked at the big blond affectionately.

They were speaking in low voices when Etta finished and decided to walk out among her people. Many of them were sitting out around fires instead of in their homes. She nodded as she passed by and curious eyes followed her.

"Henry." She smiled, leaning down to hug the young boy from behind. He jumped and spun, a smile splitting his face.

"Etta!"

Someone coughed behind him and he looked down at his feet. "I'm sorry. Your Majesty, it's good to see you." He attempted a bow and Etta stifled a laugh as she leaned in to whisper in his ear.

"Just between you and me, I prefer Etta."

When she leaned away, he was grinning. She looked past him to the circle of people. A few more children sat nearby, their eyes wide with fear at her presence.

"Would you like to have a seat, your Majesty?" Analise asked in her sweet voice.

Etta shook her head ruefully. "I must be getting back. I only wanted to say hello and make sure you all were doing well."

"We've never been better," Analise said honestly. "Living so openly among magic folk is more than we could have ever dreamed of."

Etta couldn't help but glance at their surroundings. People had been using their magic and hard work to build a new Bela they could be proud of, but it still only consisted of the small village where her people had to share homes.

But Analise was happy and Etta felt something stir within the emptiness inside her. It had been a long time since she felt anything. No fear or hope or love. She thought everything she had was tied up in the curse, but maybe it didn't have to be.

She was the queen of Bela. Maybe everything she had could be tied up in her people.

When she fell asleep that night, the loneliness she'd known since La Dame lifted the curse, felt like less of a burden after all.

As the sound of the first cook fires of the morning began outside, Etta sat on her bed with her knife between her teeth. It was time for a test.

When she'd disguised herself to save Alex, she had cut off her hair, but it grew back the moment the Basile powers woke within her.

Pulling her hair to the front, Etta studied the golden locks and held a section in her hand. Grabbing her knife with the other, she held it against the strands and sucked in a breath as she began to saw.

It sliced through her hair easily as she jerked it back and forth. Hair fell around her on the bed but she didn't stop until she was all the way through.

For a moment, she stared at the jagged edges of the hair that was left, waiting. The door banged open, and she jerked upright, accidentally dragging the blade of her knife against her arm. Cursing, she dropped it and pressed her hand over the cut.

Matteo rushed forward. "Etta, what on earth are you doing?"

She held back the tears that sprang forth. Her arm stung and now her hair was a wreck. Her assumptions about her hair were wrong.

Her cousin grabbed a towel and pressed it to her arm. "You're needed in the throne room."

She almost laughed at that. The throne room was basically a tiny room that had a single chair and no other adornments.

She stood silently, letting the cut hair flutter to the floor.

Matteo shook his head. "I don't think I'll ever understand you, cousin."

"What's so urgent that I can't wash first?" she asked. "Or at least fix this." She gestured to her lopsided hair.

"I think you should hear it from the messenger that has arrived."

"Fine." She swung her cloak around her shoulders.

Edmund met them outside. "What happened to you?" He eyed her lopsided hair

She grunted and picked up her pace. People were crowded into the throne room. They parted for her as she walked toward the chair.

Arguing commenced among those present.

"She can't go," someone yelled.

"There's no choice," another retorted.

"She promised to protect all her people, not just those who came to her."

Etta sat, smoothing her cloak around her. A few of the quieter attendees seemed confused by her haphazard appearance, but none spoke of it.

"Quiet," she snapped.

The fight continued.

"Hey," she yelled.

Still no use.

She'd never used her magic around so many people, but as her frustration grew, she saw no other option.

Putting a hand to her throat, she poured magic into her voice, making it reverberat around the room. "Quiet."

The room stilled.

Edmund grinned proudly. That was the most control she'd shown yet.

As soon as the power shot through her, her head began to tingle as the golden strands of her hair lit up and began to lengthen where she had cut them, until it was as if her test had never happened.

Wide eyes stared at her from every corner of the small space. Her power sizzled around them, but she kept the reins tight, not letting it break free. It strained within her. *This is wrong,* she thought. *It shouldn't be leashed.* But those weren't Etta's own thoughts. The magic invaded her mind. She used every bit of energy to push it away.

"Now," she said, trying to infuse calm into her voice. "Someone tell me what has happened."

A man in travel-stained clothing lurched forward as someone pushed him. He fell to his knees before her, raising his face to her in awe. "It's true. We've heard the stories in Gaule... but you really do have the ancient Basile power."

Etta was losing patience. "I do and I will release every bit of it on you if you don't tell me why I'm here."

He gulped as if he believed every word.

"I come from Gaule."

She leaned forward. They hadn't had news from Gaule since learning of Alex's victory against his traitorous nobles the month before.

"Tell me," she growled.

"T-they... M-my father sent me. He's a farmer on land owned by one of the nobles who went against the king."

"Go on."

"People have been disappearing. Not all magic folk could just pick up their entire lives and go to an unknown kingdom. Now they're being taken prisoner."

Etta clenched her jaw. "What has the king of Gaule done about this?"

"No one can get to him. After the battle, he shut the palace. The outer castle is abandoned by all but the royal guard and no one is allowed inside the inner castle. He isn't holding court or meeting with his people."

"Duchess Moreau... Duke Caron, what about them?"

"They have yet to return to their estates, your Majesty."

Etta leaned back and closed her eyes briefly. "So, the king is not running his own country."

"He is, your Majesty. He's sending out his guard to keep order. The problems occur once the guards leave a territory. He isn't a bad king, just a trusting one, and in Gaule, no one can be trusted. The king is allowing his council and his generals to have control over keeping order. They are the ones appearing to the people, trying to restore faith in the king. But the citizens of Gaule need to see their king. I'm sorry, I don't have any more information for you."

"Thank you," she said. "You can go."

Matteo and Edmund cleared out the throne room and then stayed behind.

Edmund was fuming. "How could Alex just stay behind his walls and turn his back on magic folk? After everything he's done... he basically went to war with his own nobles to protect our people!"

"Edmund," Etta warned. "Calm down."

Matteo put a hand on his arm to hold him back and his breathing relaxed.

"Alex isn't stupid," she said almost to herself. "What is he doing?"

Matteo released Edmund and leaned against the wall with his arms crossed over his chest. "I don't want to defend that Gaulean bastard... ever... but I think he's just trying to avoid a civil war."

"They already had one." Edmund sat on the arm of Etta's chair.

"No." Matteo shook his head. "They had one battle, not a war. Alexandre is walking a thin line. He can't round up the troublemaking nobles without an even bigger uprising on his hands. The only tool he has in his pocket is the army – which is much depleted without men from the nobles he's policing."

"He's waiting," Edmund jumped in.

"For what?" Etta leaned her head back to glance up at him.

"For La Dame to make her next move."

"Not only that," Matteo mused. "Alexandre isn't acting like a king with absolute power. He's going to roll back the decrees his father pushed through."

Understanding lit in Edmund's eyes. "Because he thinks the rebellion was against a king, not the kingdom. I know Alex better than anyone. I should've seen this coming. He's never believed one person should have control over Gaule."

Matteo nodded. "Makes sense. That would be why Duchess Moreau and Duke Caron are still at the palace. They're his biggest allies. They'd help with the transition."

Etta sighed. "This doesn't address the bigger issue. It isn't our concern whether the people of Gaule rise up. Our job is to ensure the safety of the Belaens who still reside in Gaule."

"What do you want to do?" Matteo asked.

"I have to go to Gaule."

Matteo shook his head vigorously. "Absolutely not. Not when the people here need you and La Dame is our biggest danger."

"Cousin." She pursed her lips. He wasn't wrong, but something didn't sit right with her. If La Dame was coming for them, she would have done so by now. She sucked in a breath, recalling Esme's words. "She won't attack."

"How do you possibly know that?"

"Because she's waiting for us to come to her. For me." *She wants you to stand at her side.*

Matteo crossed his arms. "Going into Gaule is too dangerous. We can send someone else."

She stood and fixed him with a stare. "No. I refuse to abandon my own people."

Matteo met Edmund's eye as if pleading him to talk sense into her, but Edmund only nodded. "She's right."

Matteo sighed. "Then you have to take our best fighters."

"No. We don't have the horses to spare and you need every man and woman here."

"You can't go alone. You're the queen."

She got to her feet and walked toward him. "Matteo, there is only one person on this earth who could do me harm and if she comes for me, no amount of Belaen fighters will help. I need to do this. Our people need me. Plus, I won't be alone. Edmund is coming with me."

"Damn right I am." Edmund draped an arm over her shoulders.

Matteo's lips turned down. "And what am I supposed to tell everyone here? That their queen has just wandered off?"

"No." Her hair slapped against her back as she shook her head. "No lies. Be honest with them. Always. When I return, our people will be safer. Until then, it is up to you to take charge of things here. Can I count on you?"

"Always."

She squeezed his arm on her way out the door. "Tomorrow, we return to Gaule."

# CHAPTER 8

Gaule stretched out before them like a flower, ready to be picked. It was no secret that the kingdom had thrived over the years due to the wards Etta's father had protected them with—even after they'd betrayed him.

He could have brought the wards down and left Gaule open to La Dame's desires, but he'd never blamed the people for their king's misdeeds, and there had still been a need to keep the king alive, if only so Viktor himself lived.

Etta was not her father.

She stood next to Edmund atop a hill that looked down into one of the prosperous villages on the Leroy lands, cursing every person below who allowed her people to suffer. They were complicit. They were hateful. She had experienced enough scorn from the Gaulean people to rid herself of her father's noble ideas of equality.

These people were not equal to her. She could destroy that village with one wave of her hand. The power boiled in her blood and it took every ounce of strength she possessed to hold it back. Was this what she'd been afraid of? She hadn't wanted to accept the power and everything that came with it.

The magic made her angry, calling for the blood of all who went against her.

Vérité snorted, resting his soft nose on her shoulder, and the anger began slipping away. Closing her eyes, she slammed up the rest of her walls around her magic to keep it from breaking through. She was getting better at holding it back, but that didn't mean she liked it. Keeping the power under control felt wrong. It wanted to be free.

Edmund stiffened beside her as he craned his neck to see something in the distance. A small gasp escaped his throat. "Are you seeing what I'm seeing?"

Etta swallowed back the rising bile and nodded. Outside the village, bodies dangled from trees.

With a grunt of disgust, Etta mounted Vérité and snapped the reins. Edmund followed her down into the village. As they neared the trees, faces came into view. Men. Women. Children. Etta didn't allow herself to divert her eyes. They deserved to be seen. Something had happened here, and it sent a chill straight to her heart. A stillness sat heavy in the surroundings and Etta lowered her head, hoping they were at peace.

Once inside the village, they were able to get lost in the crowds of the market. It was much busier than any village she'd ever seen, but a heaviness choked the air. These were the people who had been called to rise up against Alex. Despite her complicated feelings for the king of Gaule, she hated those who would defy him and try to take his throne.

They dismounted and walked the rest of the way to their meeting point. One of her people still living in Gaule was taking an enormous risk in helping them.

A hooded figure appeared next to her. "Your Majesty."

Etta pulled Vérité to a stop. "Tanner?"

"Keep moving." The voice was obviously that of a woman, which surprised Etta. She glanced once at Edmund before allowing herself to be led into an alleyway.

"My husband will tend the horses." They stopped at a slightly broken door and an older man appeared, wordlessly taking the reins of their horses.

Tanner ushered them inside and shut the door. Etta pushed back the hood of her cloak and took a turn around the room. Sparse furnishings sat haphazardly in the corner near a cook stove. A small bed rested against the opposite wall. Was this how all her people lived in Gaule?

"Did anyone stop you in the streets?" Tanner asked.

"No." Edmund shook his head, his short blond hair catching the glow of the candlelight.

"Good. The village hasn't been patrolled in a few days since the last batch of prisoner executions."

"The bodies outside the village?"

She nodded.

"Some of them were children," Edmund growled. "What could they have possibly done to warrant losing their lives?"

Tanner looked quizzically at Edmund. "Do? They don't have to do anything. They have magic. That's enough."

Etta paced. "I should have had people watching Lord Leroy. These are his lands and we should've seen something like this coming."

Tanner shook her head. "Lord Leroy hasn't returned from the battle. He's now a prisoner in the dungeons."

"Then who..."

"His daughter."

Etta sucked in a breath. "But Amalie wouldn't—"

"Not Lady Amalie. Her sister, Lady Liza returned after their father was captured. Her husband is said to have died, leaving her in charge of both his forces and her father's. She's increased the hangings since her father was taken."

"What about the king?" Etta asked. The Alex she knew would never stand for this.

"The king hasn't been seen since the night of the battle. His soldiers patrol the roads but many of them are of similar views as Leroy and his eldest daughter so they don't take their guardianship of all Gauleans seriously. The king posted guards at the Leroy estate after the battle but they haven't been seen. My man inside says they were killed."

"Why are you still here if it's so dangerous?" Edmund asked.

"We can't abandon those with no other way to get out. We've been smuggling people to the Caron and Moreau lands but the last group we sent was captured and now dangle from trees."

Etta pressed the heel of her hand against her eyes. "If the king of Gaule won't protect the people within his borders, I will. But I can't start a war. Can you get me into the estate?"

A smile spread across her weathered face and she dipped her head. "Of course, my queen. It would be my honor."

Preparations only took a day and before she knew it, Etta was standing in the shadowy hall surrounded by the more well-to-do villagers and nearby nobles. Tanner was at her side, but

Edmund had been forced to stay behind to prepare for their swift departure.

The plan had come to her quickly and now she knew it was the right thing to do. Lucky for her, the people who lived in this part of Gaule had never seen her. Some of the nobles had, so she avoided being too near them as she walked the length of the room.

Liza Leroy sat in a chair that was raised almost as if it were a throne. Did she fashion herself a queen? Etta had met the girl once before when her father brought his daughters before the king at the coronation ball. She'd only just arrived at the palace and become protector, so the night had been a blur. But she remembered the girl now. The giggling young woman with delicate features now had a scowl set firmly in place. What happened to her? Why had she chosen to follow her father so blindly instead of taking her sister's path?

The man standing beside her turned and locked eyes with Etta. Flashes of the ebony council room table entered her mind. This was one of the nobles who'd sat there in the days after Alex was taken.

Etta tried to remember his name and failed. As if sensing Etta's thoughts, the man's eyes widened in recognition, but he didn't move to warn Liza. Etta only had a moment before her presence would be known.

She placed a hand on her throat to amplify her voice.

"Liza Leroy," she said darkly.

Those in attendance turned wildly to find the source of the voice. Etta stepped closer to the front and continued. "You have failed."

The lady's gaze finally found her and she reveled in the fear she found in Liza's eyes.

"You thought you could destroy us as your father did before you, bring us to our knees. You considered us weak, unworthy, but it is you who is weak." She stopped right in front of the woman, feeling every set of eyes on her back.

Throwing one hand out to the side, she let the edges of her magic leak out. The flames lighting the room extinguished and party-goers yelled in fear as they were thrown into darkness.

Their fear kept Etta going. She wanted to be feared. Leaning down, the only light coming from her glowing hair, she met Liza's eyes, hers narrowing.

"Remember me, my lady?" She smiled.

"Sorcerer," she spat.

She nodded. "I can see it. The fear seeping from your every pore. You're right to be scared of me. Tell me, were my people scared before you strung them up?"

"Your people," she scoffed. "They were Gauleans living on my father's land. They belonged to us and I had every right to do with them as I saw fit."

Etta pursed her lips and straightened before turning to the assembled people. "I am Persinette Basile, Queen of Bela. Anyone who harms the magic folk, my people, has harmed me."

"You're just a girl." The growl came from behind her and she turned to face the man beside Liza. Lord Hinton. The name came to her as she studied his face.

"You can't beat us," he went on, "just like that boy king can't."

"Just a girl?" Etta cocked her head. "Okay." She made like she was going to walk away before loosening the tight control on her magic and letting its light curl in her hands before throwing it squarely at the lord's chest.

He was lifted into the air and slammed back against the wall. His arms flew over his head and stuck to the wall. He couldn't move as Etta stepped closer.

"Do I have your attention now?" she asked simply.

Her magic begged her to rip his heart right from his chest. To allow it to drain the life from his eyes.

But the queen of Bela couldn't march into Gaule and kill nobles.

She refused to give in to the whims of the power inside her. She knew it was only a short jump into darkness.

She directed her next words to the people. "I am taking Lady Liza and Lord Hinton to the palace of Gaule. If you try to stop me, I won't hesitate to destroy this entire despicable estate and every village that rose up against Alexandre Durand. If you don't believe I can, then try to stop me. I promise you'll regret it."

The candles roared back to life, and no one stopped her as she ripped Lord Hinton from the wall, using her magic to render him unconscious. She pulled Liza forward, sending her mind into the same darkness.

The crowd gave her a wide berth and Leroy was pulled along behind her with her power. Tanner appeared at her side and jerked her head to a cluster of people who looked more well-dressed than the simple villagers.

"Some of the other nobles who joined Leroy in his rebellion," Tanner explained.

Etta stopped. They cowered as she turned toward them. Two men and one woman who looked different from the rest.

"Have they been arresting magic folk?" Etta asked.

"That one has." She pointed one long finger at a young woman in a dress of purple velvet. Her beauty concealed her rotten core.

"What's her name?"

"Lady Hinton."

"Ah, the lord's wife." Etta considered the woman for a moment. Lady Hinton's eyes were made of ice. "Lady Hinton." The woman began walking toward her against her will. Etta tugged as if she had the lady on a string.

The scowl never left her face as she met Etta's eyes without any of the fear Lord Hinton had possessed.

"You'll be accompanying us as well." With that, Etta turned and marched from the room, her magic pulling her three prisoners after her.

Night had descended outside, but Etta didn't want to spend any more time in this place than she had to. Relief flooded her when she found Edmund with a wagon. His horse and another were pulling it while Vérité waited to the side. He lifted his head when he spotted her and kicked the ground.

Tanner thanked them, but Etta waved her off. "What kind of queen would I be if I didn't protect all of my people?"

One corner of the woman's mouth lifted. "The normal kind."

Etta shrugged and climbed onto Vérité's back. She gave Tanner a small wave and kicked her heels to get off of Leroy's lands as quickly as possible.

Etta had spent her life preparing to be a protector. It was the role she'd been born into. Maybe being queen wasn't so different from that. She must sacrifice her life for theirs. She was made to serve. To fight.

The curse had given her no choice but to fulfill her purpose. The crown wasn't so different.

It was just a different kind of curse. At that thought, the emptiness inside of her began to fill. The curse had always connected her to something, someone. Without it, she'd been alone.

But she wasn't alone. She had Bela and every one of her people. The crown connected her to them.

Curse. Chains. Crown. None of them made her a prisoner. Not anymore.

# CHAPTER 9

The walls hadn't changed. In Etta's mind, she'd expected them to be battered from the battle for control of Gaule. But unlike the Gaulean people, they hadn't broken.

Etta had kept Liza Leroy and Lord and Lady Hinton unconscious for the entire journey. They'd encountered no trouble and now Etta stood looking up at the impregnable fortress, a foreign queen demanding to be heard.

But there was no one there. The outer gate looked all but deserted.

Annoyance sparked the inferno of Etta's magic and the wind blew around her, lifting her hair from the back of her neck as she tried to rein it in.

Suddenly, returning here didn't feel right. She should have stayed in Bela.

Her control slipped, releasing sparks from her fingers as she tried to hold the power back. Memories rushed toward her. The day her father died and she'd been brought behind those walls for the first time. Becoming protector.

Alex. Every moment they spent wrapped up in each other assaulted her.

Her imprisonment.

Then her escape. Twice, she'd been forced to flee from Gaule.

The memories warred against each other, the bad fighting for dominance over the good.

Her magic rose, pushing out through her skin. She jerked her head from side to side. "Edmund," she pushed out. "I can't."

"Etta," he said calmly. "Get control."

An image of Edmund sitting in a dirty cell flashed across her mind. The people inside that palace had done so much to hurt them.

"I can't," she bit out moments before the power blasted out of her.

It struck the wall, surging through the barrier, breaking it apart. They dove behind the wagon as a barrage of stone rained down. Etta covered her head with her hands, unable to call enough magic to form a protective barrier.

The drumming of rocks slowed amid screams from the horses and Etta lifted her head to check for injuries.

"Edmund," she called, coughing as the dust entered her lungs.

"Damn, Etta," he groaned. "You really hate this place, don't you?"

Etta didn't respond. She couldn't explain it, how the emotions fueled her magic. She didn't hate the palace... her magic did. She'd lost control, the very thing she was afraid of. She tried to use the wagon to pull herself up, but her legs gave out beneath her and a sob pushed past her lips.

They'd been working to control her magic and one look at the walls she both hated and couldn't hate, and her strength was gone.

People came running, but they didn't near Etta as her hair was still aglow.

Edmund threw his hands in the air. "We're only here to see the king."

Murmurs of disbelief worked through the guards who now had their swords at the ready.

A harsh voice echoed among the others. "If you're here to see the king, why the hell did you just destroy the only thing keeping him safe?" Camille stepped forward, leaning on her cane. "Wait, don't answer that. I don't care, Etta. You can't see Alex." She turned to the guards. "Arrest them."

# CHAPTER 10

Etta lifted her head off the cool ground of the cell, her energy failing her. It wasn't the same cell she'd been kept in before, but it might as well have been. Stone walls rose on three sides with a wrought-iron gate for the fourth.

No comforts existed within those walls. Nothing that would make her believe she was anything but a prisoner. Again.

No, she couldn't be a prisoner. She was the queen of Bela, not merely Etta anymore. She wanted to scream for someone to let her out, but no sound came out.

"Hey." Edmund kneeled next to her. "You're awake."

"Seems so." She pushed up before falling back.

Edmund put a hand on her back to help her sit. The magic she'd used sucked everything out of her. As soon as the cell door slammed shut, locking them in, she'd fallen asleep.

The fog in her mind began to clear as she shook her head. Golden strands broke free of her braid, falling forward around her face.

"Where are our prisoners?" she asked.

Edmund shrugged. "At least this time we're in here together." He suppressed a grin.

She raised a brow. "Of course you'd make jokes right now."

"Oh, come on, Etta. It's like coming full circle. You and I are prisoners of Gaule again. There has to be some sort of irony in that."

She curled her fingers into fists, trying to build the magic in her arms and push it through the rest of her body to wash away the exhaustion. Her limbs began to strengthen until she no longer had to rely on Edmund's assistance to sit.

Edmund's eyes widened. "When did you learn to do that?"

She lifted one shoulder in a shrug. "Just now, I guess."

His eyes twinkled. "If you can replenish your magical energy..." He didn't need to finish the thought as he blew out a long breath.

"Now we just need to figure out how to get out of here."

"Do you think Alex knows we're his prisoners?"

Etta didn't miss the hope in his voice. He didn't want to imagine Alex betraying him again. "He's the king, Edmund. Why wouldn't he know?"

Edmund shifted his eyes to his hands. "Camille may be doing this all on her own."

Etta wanted to believe his words. Had the Alexandre Durand she'd known changed so much in just a short time apart? He was letting her people suffer. Did he now side against magic folk? What happened to him?

She scooted closer to him and wrapped an arm around his back. "I'm sorry, but when you stayed in Bela, you chose a side. Alex has determined that side is the enemy. He's probably released Leroy and his daughter by now." She closed her eyes and her breath stuttered. "And he has Verite."

"I'm sorry. I know what Vérité means to you."

Etta climbed to her feet. "It's okay. I can get him back. I'll tear this place apart stone by stone if I have to. If Gaule is once again turning on magic folk, we must return to Bela to prepare."

"Prepare for what?"

"Whatever comes." She extended a hand to Edmund. "We are no longer prisoners, Edmund. I am a queen and you are everything Gaule lacks. If they stand against us, they will lose."

He clasped her hand and stood.

"Not prisoners," he said as if to remind himself. "Not this time."

Etta shot him a grim smile before turning to the door. Her control had returned, and she blasted the door off its hinges. It crashed against the wall with a loud clang. Other prisoners roused themselves with yells of surprise. Etta tried to pick out Lord Leroy's voice among them. Tanner had said he was being held here.

Once the ringing in Etta's ears quieted, an eerie stillness crept in. "Come on." She led Edmund through the labyrinth of halls past full cells.

It wasn't until they reached the stairs that they heard it. Footsteps.

"Camille," someone snapped. "You had no right."

"Of course I did. I have every right to lead Gaule when he—"

"He wouldn't want you anywhere near his throne," the man growled. "And he wouldn't let you imprison—" The steps on the stairs stopped as Camille and Tyson came into view.

Tyson's eyes widened when he caught sight of Etta and Edmund before a slow grin spread across his boyish face. He turned to Camille. "I told you they'd probably have escaped by now. You can't hold Persinette Basile."

"Ain't that the truth," Edmund barked out a laugh, his shoulders relaxing. "See, Etta. If Ty didn't know we were down here, what are the chances Alex did?"

The smile slipped from Tyson's face for only a fraction of a second before it came back. Unkempt scruff covered his cheeks and dark circles ringed his eyes, but he was still Tyson.

They stood staring at each other for a long moment before Tyson bounded down the rest of the steps and didn't stop moving until he had Etta wrapped in his arms. A shudder ran through him as he buried his face in Etta's shoulder.

"I'm so glad you're here," he whispered. "Everything is so wrong."

Etta wound her arms around his back. They may not have been raised together, but Tyson was her brother and she'd missed him every day.

"I'm so sorry," he choked out. "Camille had you put here without me or mother knowing."

Etta glared at the princess over Tyson's shoulder.

Camille held her hands in front of her chest. "What was I supposed to do? She blew apart our gates! For all I knew, we were being attacked."

Tyson pulled back and shot Camille a frigid look before regarding Etta with a quizzical frown. "We have so many questions for you. Why did you attack? Why were Liza Leroy and Lord Hinton with you? Why won't they wake up? Why are you even here in Gaule?"

Etta breathed deeply and Edmund put a hand on Tyson's shoulder. "If we can get out of the dungeons, we'll explain. Maybe the king and the queen mother should join us?"

Tyson's face fell, and he shook his head. "They won't. But I'll send for the duchess. Come."

They ascended the stairs and Tyson fell into step beside Etta as they walked across the familiar courtyard. Etta still knew this place better than her own kingdom.

"Where's—" she began but Tyson answered before she could finish.

"Vérité is in his old stall. He'll be taken care of."

Etta nodded gratefully. "And—"

"Liza and the Hintons are being kept under guard near Lord Leroy. They are not trusted in the palace."

She squeezed his arm.

"I missed you," he said in that open way he'd always had.

She smiled in spite of the circumstances and looped her arm through his. Camille let out a disgusted snort behind them.

Tyson leaned in. "I always knew you'd be our queen."

*Our*. She hadn't imagined it. He'd said *our* and that single word infused hope into her. When Tyson had chosen Alex, he'd taken a piece of Etta with him. Our. Tyson considered Bela his kingdom. Etta hid a smile behind her hand.

"I missed you too," she whispered.

His face lit up at her words, the stress lines smoothing out.

"I can't believe you destroyed our gates."

"I'm sorry." How could she tell him she hadn't meant to? That in those moments, the magic controlled her instead of the other way around? Would he fear her too?

It turned out, there was no time to explain before another familiar face greeted her.

"Simon." She nodded with a smile.

He immediately dropped into a bow. "My queen." When he lifted his head, love and admiration resided in his gaze and it warmed her. "Welcome to Gaule."

She gripped his arm and squeezed. "Thank you."

More people waited inside the council chamber and Etta recognized most of them, but they weren't Belaen. To them, she was just a foreign queen, and it was a bit of a relief. Magic folk looked at her as if she were their savior.

Duchess Moreau was the first to greet them, offering familiar hugs. Duke Caron bowed formally. A young woman sat in the back of the room, her wide eyes piercing into Etta. Etta liked her the minute their eyes connected. The woman's gaze flooded with warmth.

"It's nice to meet you, your Majesty," a voice whispered.

Etta whipped her head around trying to find the source. The woman laughed and Etta stared at her once again, the corner of her mouth tilting up.

Duke Caron stepped forward. "Your Majesty, let me introduce my daughter, Ara."

Etta instantly saw the duke in a new light. He had a daughter with magic? Camille must be really happy about that. The thought sent a perverse pleasure through her. Maybe that was why the princess had been forced to be on the side of magic folk.

One quick glance around the room was all Etta needed to register the heaviness in their expressions. Where was Alex? And Catrine?

Edmund voiced her questions. "Where's the king?"

Simultaneously, their faces darkened and a foreboding chill crept over Etta. She turned to Tyson, her brother, the overly honest prince.

"Where is he, Ty?"

Tyson sighed and scrubbed a hand over his face. "They're saying he doesn't have much longer, Etta." His voice choked. "He's..." He shook his head. "I didn't think anything could take him down."

She stepped closer to Tyson, forcing him to meet her eyes. "Ty?"

He pushed out a shaky breath. "He was attacked last month. Our healers thought they'd save him, but then infection… He's dying, Etta."

The ground shifted beneath her. Her legs quaked as she stumbled back, sucking air into her lungs.

She shouldn't care, her magic told her. Forget about him. He meant nothing to her.

Then why did her heart crack right down the middle? She shook her head. "He... he... he can't." Her words shook, and she grabbed for something, anything to keep her upright, latching on to Edmund's arm. He held onto her as if his life depended on it, the news breaking him open just as much as her.

Alexandre Durand, king of Gaule, was the enemy of her magic and all she could think was that if he died, she'd die right along with him.

If they were still tied by the curse, she would. Their lives had been entwined. But this was different. It wasn't her body that would die upon his last breath, it was her soul.

"I need to see him," she forced out.

"Not so fast, your Majesty," Duke Caron said. "You have a lot to answer for. You cannot walk away until we know why our gate lays in ruins and three of our nobles appear to be under the influence of magic."

Etta glanced back at him with a growl. She didn't care how she appeared to these people. Not when the need to see Alex burned through her. "You'll get your answers when I deign to give them to you."

He opened his mouth to protest, and she released a tendril of magic–just enough to push him back into a chair and hold him there.

"Persinette Basile," he snapped.

"Da," Ara slid into the seat next to her father. "No."

Tyson hadn't moved, but Ara's voice sounded in Etta's ear. "He's in his chambers."

Etta nodded gratefully and motioned for Edmund to follow her, preparing to use her magic to stop anyone who came after them. No one did.

The guard outside Alex's chambers stepped into their path to stop them and Etta flung him against the wall, using her power to bind him there before pushing into the room.

Alex's eyelids shifted, but remained closed. His skin had dulled into a sickly gray pallor and his dark hair stuck to his face. On the table beside the bed, a bowl of leeches waited to be used next to small glass vials containing various tinctures.

Catrine sat in a chair with her head resting on the bed, her long dark hair obscuring her features from view.

Etta's eyes focused on Alex's face. Even when she'd wanted to hate him, he'd been so strong, so sure.

Edmund's hand slid down her arm and he laced his fingers with hers, squeezing tightly.

"Alex," he breathed.

Catrine stirred and lifted her head slowly, her heavy-lidded eyes rounding when she saw them. Her shoulders dropped, and a sigh blew past her lips. "Thank God you two are here."

She got to her feet with the slowness of a much older woman. Her lips drew down, deepening the lines on her once flawless face. "He's been asking for you. I didn't have the heart to remind him you were..."

Etta tried to move forward but her feet wouldn't budge. Edmund dropped her hand and walked to the side of the bed with none of the hesitation she felt.

"Why has he been asking for us if he didn't know we'd ever be back?"

Catrine reached Etta's side and put a hand on her back. "He hasn't been in his right mind, honey." She didn't bother with the formalities their ranks insisted upon. Catrine never had. She'd taken Etta under her wing and now the reason screamed with clarity. Catrine Durand had loved Viktor Basile. Tyson's existence proved that.

It should have tainted Etta's opinion of the woman, that Viktor had betrayed Etta's mother. But instead, Etta soaked in the comfort she'd always gotten from Catrine. She sucked in a heavy breath and pushed it back out as her feet finally started moving.

For so long, her magic had been forcing Alex into the role of the enemy in her mind, but now that he was slipping away, nothing made sense anymore. She hadn't been so lost since the moment the curse was broken and their bond disappeared.

Edmund sat on the edge of the bed and took Alex's frail hand in his. The king of Gaule murmured something unintelligible.

"Alex, sweetheart," Catrine cooed.

"You don't need to wake him," Etta protested. Of all the scenarios, this was not how she'd imagined meeting Alex again.

"He's been sleeping all day. It's time for his next tincture." She uncorked a bottle and poured it into a wooden mortar before grinding it together with the pestle. She didn't ask the questions everyone else had for Etta and Edmund. Her only concern was her son. For once, the kingdom's worries faded into the background.

"Alex," she said again, squeezing his upper arm. His eyelids fluttered open slowly, and he stared up at them as if he couldn't place who they were.

Unable to hold back any longer, Etta touched the side of his face, fingering the soft hairs growing on his cheeks. His entire face slackened. "Etta." His voice was no more than a whisper. "I knew you'd come home, eventually."

She frowned. Gaule wasn't her home.

Alex's eyes shifted to Edmund. "She saved you from the dungeons?"

Edmund's pained eyes met Etta's.

"Yeah," he said. "Etta saved me."

"I'm sorry," Alex breathed. "I shouldn't have kept you there." He closed his eyes briefly. "I wish I could have been your savior."

Tears sprang to Edmund's eyes. "You were, Alex. You always were."

"I love you." Barely audible, the words had Edmund collapsing forward and pressing his face to his best friend's chest.

"I love you too. Always."

"Etta." Alex tried to lift his hand to reach for her. "My Etta. Promise you'll stay with me."

Etta jumped back, her eyes shining. "I... I can't do this."

She reached the door in four long strides and didn't relax until it stood between her and the dying king on the other side.

She choked back a sob. With a flick of her wrist, she released the guard she'd left pinned to the wall and turned to find Tyson waiting for her.

She sucked in a breath and did her best to push all thought of Alex aside before going back to the things she could control. The safety of her people.

"I'm ready for those questions, Tyson. I have answers for you, but your council better have answers for me as well. Answers and action. I will accept nothing less.".

# CHAPTER 11

Tyson banged his head on the table in front of him. They had retreated to the suite of rooms belonging to Camille and her husband while they stayed at the palace.

"I don't believe you," Camille said, eying Etta warily. "You're just trying to stir up tensions within Gaule."

The anger snapped within Etta and she held her breath, holding her simmering power in check. What was it about this place that made her control disappear so quickly?

Edmund wasn't there to calm her. Not this time. He'd remained at Alex's side.

If she spoke, she feared her magic would barrel into the indignant princess.

Amalie stepped forward to put a hand on the back of Tyson's neck. She'd arrived soon after Tyson led Etta into the room and kept a protective eye on the prince.

"Didn't Alex have guards stationed in my father's house?" she asked. "They were meant to watch for more unrest among his followers. My sister… she's always been his puppet, but I never saw this coming."

Etta shook her head. "I'm sorry Amalie. Your sister has continued your father's persecutions and murder of my people."

Amalie swallowed hard but didn't divert her steely eyes. That girl was no longer the scared kid who'd had to be rescued from her father's reach.

"Tell us again." Duchess Moreau said over the rim of her teacup.

Etta sighed. "They're killing my people. You all wondered what I was doing in Gaule? It's because I trusted you to keep magic folk safe and you failed." Her harsh gaze cut through each one of them. "While you sit here in your palace, your country falls into darkness. I refuse to let it take Bela with it."

"Is that a threat?" Camille narrowed her eyes.

"Damn right it is. I don't want to have to come against Gaule, but if it comes to it, I won't hesitate."

"Who do you think you are?"

Etta straightened her spine, peering at Camille as if she was nothing. "I am the queen of Bela."

They stared at each other, neither wanting to be the first to look away.

"This isn't helping." The duchess's voice broke their standoff. She set her teacup on the table and buried her face in her hands. Etta had never seen the woman emit anything other than strength, but it seemed there was no strength to be had in the palace.

Tyson. Duchess Moreau. Catrine. Simon. Even Camille. They were broken down, worn out, by war, but mostly because the person they all loved was fading away.

To have such love... Etta couldn't imagine it. Alex's death had the power to destroy them.

She got to her feet. "Now that you all know I didn't come to attack you and have no malicious intent—and some of you even believe me—we have work to do. I'm sorry about... about Alexandre. But a king is not a kingdom and right now the kingdom must come first. Honestly, I don't care what you do with Gaule, but when it affects my people..." She looked to Duke Caron. "You control a large force in Gaule. Why were Liza and Lord Leroy's other allies not kept under closer watch?"

The duke scratched his chin wearily. "The Caron forces have been moved to the border to join with the Moreau ranks to guard against any attack from Dracon."

Tyson nodded in approval.

"We've been using the royal guard to patrol the lands of any noble who took up arms against the crown, but they've been spread quite thin and..." The duke trailed off.

"And?" Etta pressed.

Tyson blew out a breath and his next words burst out of him. "We can't trust them, okay? Half the guard fought against the crown and the other half are probably still of the opinion that the more magic folk hanging from trees, the better." He slapped his hands over his mouth.

Camille sank heavily into the chair beside her husband whose face betrayed nothing.

Duchess Moreau sighed and Amalie closed her eyes.

Finally, Etta understood. The ones who wanted to protect the magic folk represented the minority in Gaule. Even those loyal to Alex didn't all believe in what he was fighting for. Equality. Safety. Peace.

There was too much history in Gaule for them to succeed. Etta thought her task of rebuilding Bela was an impossible one, but her people were of one mind. They came from many places. Some crossed the border from Gaule, others arrived over the open sea. But they were all Belaens. They all wanted to rebuild the kingdom that had belonged to them all along. There was a purpose, a need, a willingness to sacrifice.

What was Gaule fighting for?

"There will never be peace between our people," she whispered as the realization struck her like a bludgeon to the chest. She sat on the edge of the plush velvet couch surrounded by all the opulence she'd grown used to in the palace and all she could think of were her people in Bela living in the overcrowded village, or the magic folk in the villages of Gaule with only thatched roofs protecting them from the world.

Duchess Moreau lifted her head, her expression betraying the truth of Etta's words.

The ever-hopeful Tyson wouldn't hear it. "Don't say that, Etta. We can make it happen. I know we can."

Etta shook her head slowly, hanging it low. Her golden braid hung over one shoulder that was sagged in defeat. The enormity of the problem crashed over her, making it hard to breathe. There were too many magic folk still in Gaule. Those who hadn't chosen to leave for the unknown Bela. She breathed out loudly. "One problem at a time." When she raised her eyes, the desperation in the room nearly choked her. Duchess Moreau and Duke Caron had been protecting magic folk for many years and now knew it wasn't enough. Tyson was coming to the realization that his magic would never be accepted in Gaule, prince or not.

Only Camille looked unaffected and Etta knew it was because the princess had known it all along.

Amalie was the next to speak. "Etta is right. We need to decide what to do with the traitors. My father's followers will continue to fight as long as he sits in the dungeons."

"Who is making decisions in the king's stead?" Etta asked.

Duke Caron released Camille's hand and stood. "The council has been given that power. Alexandre wanted to return Gaule to its former rule. The king used to rule in conjunction with the council. Neither had more power than the other. When his Majesty was attacked, we had no option but to push through the decrees he had set in motion. As of right now, the council is the sole ruler. Duchess Moreau and I hold seats as well as the prince and princess. We will meet and come to a decision."

Etta nodded. "I brought him your nobles as a courtesy to avoid a conflict. I could have killed them outright. Remember that. I expect justice for all those they have harmed."

Etta left them to their discussions and Amalie followed her out.

"Your old rooms should be sufficiently prepared," the girl said, her voice shaking. She didn't speak of her family, but sadness swirled in her eyes. "The rooms haven't been used since you left."

Etta stopped when she was outside her door and turned to Amalie. "How is he?" she asked, knowing what a stupid question that was.

Amalie seemed to sense who Etta was speaking of and her lips turned down. "Tyson is... trying to be strong. For his mother."

Etta put a hand on her arm and squeezed. "I'm glad he has you." With that, she let herself into the room and closed the door, sagging against it as the day's emotions drained every bit of energy from her bones.

The room looked no different from the last time she'd seen it and the familiarity provided a strange sense of comfort. She'd been through so much since calling this place home and it brought her back to the girl she'd been. The one who was cursed and in love.

She kicked off her boots and padded across the room to the canopied bed that called to her. She longed for a brief respite from this strange new world she found herself in. As she sank into the bed, she remembered all those sleepless nights wondering about Alex.

Tears sprang to her eyes, but they didn't fall. Her magic pulsed beneath her skin, urging her to forget, to be unaffected.

In that instant, her magic tried to pull her into the darkness while thoughts of Alex called to her from the light.

She'd almost fallen asleep when someone pounded on the door. Reluctantly dragging herself from the bed, she went to unlatch the door and let in a disheveled Edmund. Red rimmed his eyes and tears ran down his cheeks. He didn't try to hide them.

He didn't say anything as he closed the distance between them and wrapped his arms around her, burying his face in her hair. His back shook and her breathing stuttered as she shut her eyes.

"Etta," he sobbed. "What are we supposed to do?"

She leaned back and brushed the tears from his cheeks with the pads of her thumbs. "I don't know."

After pulling him farther into the room, she moved to stoke the fire that smoldered in the fireplace. When Amalie dropped her off, she hadn't noticed the platters of food on the table by the fireplace. Edmund poured a cup of wine with shaky hands and drank it down in one gulp before pouring another.

"He was talking about you," he said after he'd taken a large sip of his second drink.

Etta continued to crouch in front of the fire, the flames warming her icy skin.

Edmund lowered himself onto the couch. "He's delirious, Etta. The fever has taken any sense he ever possessed. He doesn't seem to remember that you two are supposed to be at odds. He just kept saying he needed you."

"He doesn't need me." She straightened up and turned toward the wine. "He never did."

"Weren't you friends?" He sniffled, trying to get a hold of his emotions. "Before the curse kicked in, you were friends."

She grunted. "That was before I spent part of my life on the run. I grew up, Edmund."

"Well, soon he won't be your problem anymore," Edmund snapped. "Then you can go on living your life as if he was never in it. But me? I don't care what his father did to our people. I'm going to be mourning my best friend for the rest of my life." He bit off the last word, his face flushed with anger, and his chest rising and falling rapidly.

Etta watched him for a long moment before walking with deliberate steps toward the couch and sitting next to him. She wrapped her arms around him. "I'm sorry. I can't..." She rested her chin on his shoulder. "I feel like I'm breaking. Seeing Alex in such a state is tearing me in two. It's not supposed to be like this. I don't want to, but..."

"You can't help it?" he finished. "I know the feeling."

"Yeah, I guess you do." That was why she and Edmund understood each other. They'd both loved Alexandre Durand.

For Edmund, it was illegal—at least in Gaule. For Etta, loving the king of Gaule went against the natural way of things. It ignored history and put the future in jeopardy.

They were quiet for a while before Edmund spoke again. "Before coming here, I'd have sworn I was past my feelings. I still think I am. But whether my love has morphed into the platonic kind between friends or not, I don't want to lose him."

None of them could afford to lose Alexandre Durand. He was the only thing holding Gaule back from the brink. Etta hadn't asked who his successor was. Had he named Camille? The woman who continued to hate magic despite her husband's feelings. Or Tyson? The boy who would never be accepted because of the Belaen blood in his veins.

Edmund slipped toward the bed to get some rest, but Etta's mind continued to rove. As soon as Edmund's breathing evened, she left the room behind and found herself outside Alex's door. Catrine had probably long gone to bed. The guard eyed her, but news of how she'd tied the other one to the wall must have made the rounds because he didn't try to stop her from entering.

"Leave," she ordered, wanting to be truly alone with Alex. "Now."

She raised her hand in threat and he started off down the hall. Alex needed better guards.

A single candle burned low on the table. Soon, no light would grace the room. Alex's pale skin shone in the dim glow. Etta flicked her finger, and the flame grew larger until his every feature was illuminated.

A sheen of sweat highlighted his brow. Etta moved to the bed, the sudden urge to be near Alex taking control of her every move. She found a bowl of water and cloth on the table next to him. Dampening the cloth, she dabbed it across his forehead, wanting, needing to give him any relief she had to offer.

A groan sounded weakly in his throat and his cracked lips moved as if he wanted to speak. Lips that had once been the only thing she thought about. They'd had the power to hold her together when it seemed as though the curse would break her apart.

How hadn't she seen it before? When the curse was broken, the void it left behind was so deep, so destructive, she'd thought it took everything. Alex had been a casualty in the battle with La Dame.

Only he hadn't. He was right there in front of her. For only a little while longer. Setting the cloth down, she lowered herself into the chair Catrine had left and leaned forward, resting her elbows on the bed.

An entire future had once seemed spread out before them, but they'd been kidding themselves. Kings and queens served as sacrifices for their kingdom. They could never think about what they desired, only what their people needed.

At least good ones.

A sigh rattled through Etta's chest and she closed her eyes, resting her forehead against her closed fist. If she hadn't come to take on Liza Leroy, would she have even known Alex was dying? She supposed they'd have heard about it once the news reached Bela. Being beside him, as hard as it was, it felt right. For the first time since her fight with La Dame, she felt whole.

"Why?" she whispered. "Why you? Why us?"

When his hand moved to take hers, she snapped her eyes open. He watched her, his usually bright eyes clouded with fever. She threaded her warm fingers through his chilled ones and held on as if she'd never let go.

"Shhh," he whispered, the sound barely audible. "It's okay."

"Nothing is okay, Alex."

"You're here." He attempted a smile. "That makes it okay."

Edmund had told her he wasn't lucid, but she heard no confusion in his words.

Tears rose in her eyes, but she blinked them away.

"I didn't think I'd ever see you again."

"I didn't want to see you again," she said. "You're a Durand."

He laughed but the sound barely made it past his lips. "Ah, sweetheart, I don't think that matters anymore."

She bit her quivering lip. He was right. It didn't matter. Maybe it never had.

One corner of his mouth quirked up. "I missed the curse after it was broken." His voice cracked. "But now I'm glad it isn't here. I couldn't stand the thought of taking you with me."

She leaned forward, resting her forehead against his. "I missed it too," she whispered. "I just didn't admit it, even to myself."

"Can you stay with me?" he asked. "Just one last time. Don't leave me again."

She nodded against his head and pulled herself down next to him, offering him her warmth. When she rested her head in the crook of his neck, he sighed, and she felt like she was right where she was supposed to be. He was too weak to wrap his arms around her as he used to, but it was enough. It had to be.

Her voice vibrated against the faint pulse in his neck. "This time you're the one leaving me."

"Never," he whispered. "I will love you forever and that means I'll always be with you."

The tears finally broke through, streaming down her cheeks unchecked. How had she denied it for so long? Now it was too late.

"I love you," she whispered. "I love you. It wasn't the curse; I just didn't see it." Tears choked her words, but Alex didn't respond.

"Alex?" She lifted her head to look into his face and felt for a pulse at his neck. It was there, but slowly fading. "Alex." She shook his arm. No response. "No. Please. You can't."

The door opened and Edmund rushed in. "Thought I'd find you here after you disappe-" His face went white as he stepped closer to Alex.

A hole tore open inside Etta. She needed more time. How was she supposed to rule a kingdom without thinking of Alex here in Gaule? How could she live when he no longer did?

Her magic swirled through her chest as she hiccuped back sobs. Edmund tried to wrap her in his arms, but she pushed him away, her control slipping.

"You should go," she said, her tears still flowing. "I can't... I can't stop it."

Controlled by her emotions, the power grew and pulsed, raising the hair on her arms.

"I'm not leaving you or Alex," he said.

Etta looked into Alex's face. Still alive, but only barely. Life faded from him quickly, and she doubted he'd live to see the sun. The power inside her jerked, and threw her forward, forcing her to grab Alex's arms to steady herself. It was coming. Like with the gate, once the flow of magic started, she couldn't stop it.

She was dangerous.

The golden glow started in the tips of her hair and worked up the long strands until it lit the entire room.

"Etta," Edmund yelled, but she barely heard him over the buzzing in her ears.

The magic zipped down her arms so fast she couldn't stop it before it jolted into Alex. "Noooooo," she cried.

His body flew from the bed, taking her along with it. They landed with a thud on the floor as Etta's magic continued to swirl in the air. Alex thrashed wildly, his eyes still closed.

Then all at once, the power snapped back into her and flung her onto her back. She couldn't move as the stillness settled in around them.

It took her a few tries before the words would leave her mouth. "Is he..." She was too scared to see it. Her magic had struck Edmund a few times too, but he'd be okay. Alex was so weak. There was no way he could withstand it.

Edmund breathed heavily and Etta lifted her throbbing head to see him crawl toward Alex and hover over him. She couldn't see Edmund's face, but the stiffness in his posture told her everything she needed to know. Alex was gone.

She laid her head back against the ground wishing he'd taken her with him. Her eyes watered but she didn't have the strength to wipe away the tears. All she wanted to do was curl up and forget her duties.

"Etta." Edmund's voice shook. "He's... you need to come here."

She groaned and rolled onto her side to scoot her tired body toward them, afraid of what she'd see, but knowing she needed to look into his face one last time. She managed to sit up but froze.

Color rose in Alex's pale, clammy skin. His uneven breath that only moments ago had seemed like a struggle for him to get out, now worked smoothly. His eyelids shifted, fluttering his lashes against his cheeks.

Edmund gasped beside her and she hated the hope he was giving her. It wasn't possible.

"No," she said. "Edmund, no."

"You can't deny what we're seeing." He finally tore his eyes away from Alex to stare at her in wonder. "You have Draconian blood."

She hauled herself to her feet, despite her aching legs. "I can't. I'm a Basile. We don't have healing magic."

"The Basile magic hasn't been seen since the days of Aurora and Phillip. No one would know if a Draconian entered the bloodline since then."

A question entered her mind that she was afraid to voice. What if it wasn't her Basile power? She remembered little of her mother... had this been another one of her parent's secrets?

"Edmund," she said, stumbling back. "If we're wrong. If we're imagining things... please, don't make me wish for things. Don't give me this hope."

Someone coughed, and it wasn't either of them. Both sets of eyes snapped to Alex's prone form. His eyes opened with the slowness of a man seeing for the first time. The milky film was gone, allowing the crystal gaze she'd missed so much to reappear.

"Edmund?" he asked softly, furrowing his brow in confusion. "What are you doing here?"

Etta fell to her knees and buried her face in her hands.

"Etta," Alex breathed. "You came back."

She nodded, removing her hands to meet his eyes before crawling toward him. A tear fell from her eye, landing on his cheek, and she wiped it away.

"Don't mind her," Edmund said. "She's only crying because she just found out her bloodline isn't as pure as she thought."

She reached across Alex to shove Edmund and he fell back with a laugh. "Ass," she mumbled, returning her gaze to the man below her. "We thought we'd lost you."

"Why?" he asked. "Where have I been?"

Etta's eyes connected with Edmund's. "You don't remember?"

"I..." he began before a pained look crossed his face. "I was attacked in my own room." He closed his eyes. "I don't remember anything since then." His eyes popped open. "If I was attacked, why don't I feel it?" He pushed himself up until he was sitting and Etta steadied him. His hands patted his chest. "Where are the knife wounds? I know I was stabbed."

"Our little Draconian healed you," Edmund answered. "Apparently a Basile ancestor was very naughty getting it on with a Draconian."

"You..." Alex looked to Etta, and his eyes widened.

She shrugged, uncomfortable under both their curious gazes. There was still so much she didn't know about her own power, but right then, all she could think of was how grateful she was that she couldn't control it. The irony wasn't lost on her. If she'd been able to hold it back, Alex would be lost.

Without warning, she lunged forward and wrapped her arms around him. He hugged her close, his lips finding the side of her face. A jolt of warmth shot through her as he kissed her just below her ear before moving down to her neck. She twisted her fingers into his hair as he brushed his overgrown beard against her smooth skin.

"Thank you for not leaving me," she whispered.

"Thank you for holding me here," he responded.

She got to her feet, drawing on her magic to restore her own strength. Edmund helped Alex up.

"I need to wash," Alex said.

Edmund patted him on the back. "It'll take a few days to recover even with the healing magic. Trust me, Etta likes to beat me up on a daily basis, so I know." Edmund pulled him into a relieved hug.

"I missed you too, Edmund," Alex laughed weakly.

Edmund grunted. "I'll return after you get some rest." He strode from the room and Etta turned to follow him.

"Don't leave," Alex looked to her as if he was a lost boy and she was the map home. "Please."

She turned toward him once again with a single word on the tip of her tongue. She couldn't utter it because it would be a lie. She'd wanted to say 'never' but there were no nevers or always for them. He was still the king of Gaule and she was the queen of Bela. So many unanswered questions lay between them. There was time yet to answer them.

For tonight, she would stay. But soon, she'd have no choice but to put him behind her once again.

She couldn't bring herself to care about that future day. As Alex cleaned up in the washroom, happiness bloomed within her. The boy she thought gone forever was still here. Still him. Always Alex.

He returned with wet hair and a tired smile, his movements slow. "I'm not used to having someone else in here anymore," he admitted nervously.

She breathed out slowly. "I just need you to prove to me that you're real. That I'm not dreaming."

"If this is a dream," he said. "I hope it's the kind that never ends."

He kissed her then. No, not just kissed. He stole her lips and made them his. He burrowed himself into her soul, latching on to every part of her being.

His breath was hers. All the months of hate and secret longing poured into a single moment. And it was brilliant.

"I'm real," he breathed against her lips. "We're real."

His body weak from the healing, she led him to the bed and pushed him down before climbing in next to him and fitting her body up against his. Lacing their fingers together, he kissed the back of her hand.

"Sleep," she whispered. "I'll still be here when you wake."

His eyes drifted shut and a moment of panic had her checking for his pulse. It beat strong, matching her own. She released a sigh and finally let the rest of the world drift away until it was only the two of them and their dreams.

# CHAPTER 12

Etta lied. The moment Alex woke, he knew it. She had promised she wouldn't leave him, but the only sound in the room was his own breathing. At first, he thought he' d imagined her presence. For so long, he' d dreamed of having her near.

But his first glance around the room proved the events of the night before had, indeed taken place. A table along the far wall tilted on its side. His belongings laid around the room as if a cyclone had entered the palace.

He let his head rest against the pillow. No, not a cyclone. Magic. Her magic. She'd healed him. It seemed the secrets of the Basiles never ended.

She wasn't the girl he'd loved before. There was so much more to her now. She wasn't simply Etta. She'd taken up the mantle of Persinette Basile, queen of Bela. Who she was always meant to be.

And that meant her destiny held no place for him.

The door to his room opened and voices drifted in. "Honestly, I don't know what the night guard was thinking leaving his post," his mother said.

"I'll have a chat with him," Tyson replied darkly. "He left Alex unprotected in his final..."

Both sets of feet stopped as Alex shifted to sit up and lean back against the headboard. He was exhausted, just as Edmund said he would be. Each movement was a struggle.

Two pairs of wide eyes stared at him. His mother let out a tiny gasp and covered her mouth. She looked like she'd been through hell. Tyson didn't look much better, but he recovered more quickly and rushed the bed.

"Alex?" he asked, disbelief coloring his tone.

"Hey, Ty." Alex's words broke the dam and his mother ran forward, all but throwing herself across Alex.

"How is this even possible?" Tyson sat on the bed and stared at his brother like he'd disappear at any moment.

"Etta–"

"I told them we should have asked her to come right after your attack, but Camille wouldn't hear of it." Tyson said.

Their mother finally recovered and sat back on the bed, not releasing Alex's hand. "No one thought Etta's presence would do any good. Belaens don't have healing."

"Ones with Draconian blood do." Alex waited for the reaction.

She sucked in a breath.

Tyson's face scrunched up in horror. "Does that mean, as a Basile, I could've saved you all along?"

Catrine put an arm around her son. "Not if the power is wrapped up in the Basile magic. That is Etta's and Etta's alone. She now holds the magic of each Basile who came before her alongside her own growth magic. One such Basile, it seems, had a child with a Draconian." She looked away from them. "Is that why she came?"

Alex coughed weakly. "She seemed as surprised as any of us."

"Then how did she call the magic forth?"

"Probably the same way she blew up our gate," Tyson guessed. "She can't control any of it."

"Wait." Alex tried to push himself up straighter and shook Tyson's words from his mind. They'd go back to the blown-up gate thing. "If you didn't summon her, why is Etta here?"

For one single moment, a spark of hope lit in him. Had she felt him through the now-broken curse? Felt he needed her?

A single match burns brightly only for a moment before the flame travels down to burn your skin.

"She kidnapped Liza Leroy and brought her here."

Alex sputtered. "What?"

"Alex," his mother started. "We just got you back. All I want to do is hold my baby boy as I never thought I'd get to do again. Can we talk politics later?"

Despite how deeply he wanted to understand what motivated a queen to travel into his kingdom when her own sat on the brink of war, he couldn't deny his mother anything. Not when such joy shone in her eyes.

She moved up next to him and wrapped one long arm around his shoulders. He rested against her and before long, the exhaustion took control and he drifted off.

When he woke again, he found Edmund's smiling eyes hovering over him.

"Oh," Alex groaned, trying to sit up. "That's right. You're here too."

Edmund's grin widened. "I couldn't miss the palace seeing their king basically come back from the dead."

"I wasn't dead."

Edmund raised one blonde eyebrow. "If Etta hadn't been here at that very moment, you would be. You should have seen it. I've been training with Etta practically every day and I haven't ever seen anything like that."

"How do you help her when her power is that strong while yours... isn't?"

Edmund laughed. "I guess you can call me her magical punching bag."

"I'd pay good gold to see that."

When Edmund laughed, his entire body gave himself into it. "I've missed you, Alex."

Alex shook his head, a small smile playing on his lips. He'd missed his best friend more than he'd ever admit. "Help me up."

"You really should stay in bed. At least until after the palace healer arrives to check you out."

"Why? I can feel it. I'm healed."

"Alex, healing magic is complicated. It uses your body's own energy to repair the damage. Once it's done, it takes a while to restore those energy reserves again."

"Just help me out of this damn bed."

Edmund held his hands in front of his chest in surrender. "Fine."

"Have you seen Etta?" He asked as soon as he had his feet under him. She hadn't come by and he needed to see her, to feel her, to believe she was real.

"She's been avoiding everyone in the palace but I'll give you one guess as to where she probably is."

"Right." He laughed and then winced as the act hurt. "I should have guessed."

"Come on." Edmund propped his shoulder under Alex's arm to help him walk. "Wouldn't want you to miss out on seeing the love of your life."

"Are you making fun of me?"

Edmund chuckled, shaking his head. "Who, me?"

"You haven't changed."

"Neither have you. I swear, you could be in the middle of the biggest battle of your life and if Etta needed her nose wiped, you'd go."

There was nothing malicious in his words. No jealousy. They were said with a genuine fondness that had always bonded them together. Even when Edmund had feelings for Alex, they'd never gotten in the way of their friendship. But something was different, and he realized what it was. The love between them had changed with Edmund acting more brotherly than anything else. It gave him some strange comfort, not because he minded Edmund's feelings, but only because he wanted his friend to find happiness.

By the time they reached the stables, Alex panted from the effort it took just to remain upright. Most of the horses stood locked away in their stalls, but a familiar dark beast sat in the middle of the exercise ring with his legs folded beneath him.

"Isn't that unnatural for a horse?" Alex asked.

Edmund snorted. "Since when has there ever been anything natural about those two?"

Etta sat in the dirt leaning against Vérité's side, her legs stretched out in front of her. Her mouth moved and as they got closer, her words rang in the air.

"It'll be time for us to return home soon, boy. I know you don't like it here."

Vérité threw his head back and bared his teeth.

Etta sighed. "I know. Gaule isn't our kingdom. I don't like it here either. They don't want us."

Alex wanted to yell that he did. He wanted her there, but all he could do was continue listening. Edmund shifted uneasily, but Alex ignored him. He looked back along the road where his guards were keeping their distance. Soon, Etta would notice them.

"What am I going to do?" Etta continued. "They're killing us, Verite. Our people." She took the blade of grass she'd been playing with and flicked it. "I might be able to do it. I have the power. I can keep us alive and apart."

*Apart.* He sucked in a breath and she lifted her head as if she'd heard him. Their eyes met, and he pushed away from Edmund to open the gate and walk closer. It took every ounce of strength he had to lower himself to the ground in front of her.

Their eyes stayed locked, and he set his jaw. "Tell me what's happening in my kingdom. Why are you here, Etta?"

Lord Christoph Leroy was executed on a hill blanketed in fog. The dawn had come and gone, but hazy colors still stretched across the sky. His youngest daughter hadn't attended as he was hung by the neck. A traitor's death. But the king was there, having regained his strength. He looked directly into the man's eyes in the seconds before the platform he stood upon fell beneath him.

There was no regret in the man's gaze, only acceptance. He'd known it would come to this.

Alex hadn't. He'd been blind to the path that lay before them. He'd tried to spare the man's life. He didn't want to execute his nobles like he'd seen his father do during the purge. He'd wanted Leroy to accept his defeat gracefully, but there was no grace left in the man. As long as breath rattled in his chest, he'd stir up trouble. Liza Leroy was being granted mercy along with Lord and Lady Hinton, but Lord Leroy had exhausted all mercy in Gaule. They'd found a guard who'd been paid to run messages from Lord Leroy to his daughter Liza, instructing her in her actions.

Alex refused to look away as Leroy kicked and twisted and struggled for breath.

The queen of Bela stepped up beside him, her eyes fixated on the man who'd been killing her people. "I'm sorry, Alex."

He only nodded. Leroy's actions weren't her fault. She'd come to Gaule to fight for her people and he respected that.

Her fingers grazed his arm, running over the pulse in his wrist until finally taking his hand. Warmth radiated out from where their skin connected. Was it her magic or just her?

Water hit the top of his head and he looked up into the oncoming rain, the sun still peeking through the clouds. He shook the water out of his eyes and turned back toward the palace. He dropped Etta's hand as he walked away.

Even with Leroy gone, the unrest in his kingdom wouldn't settle. He'd missed a lot from his sick bed. His advisors had been filling him in on the attacks. Both magic folk and the non-magic rebelled.

Many of the magic folk had left Gaule for Bela where they believed they belonged, but he knew it wasn't as easy as just making a journey. There was almost nothing in Bela. Etta and her people had created a kingdom from a land full of ruins and ghosts. It wasn't an easy life, and many Belaens had chosen to stay in the only homes they'd ever known.

Still, something would need to be done. They were dying.

He glanced back over his shoulder at the hill. So were his own people.

He'd reached the broken gates when a horse galloped toward him and reared back. "Your Majesty, there's been an attack in the village."

Alex started running to the stables. His guards chased after him and began shouting orders for the stable hands to saddle their horses.

Simon appeared at his side. "They're saying the people in the village have a family of magic folk trapped in their home."

Was it never going to end? A boy brought Alex his horse, and he launched into the saddle before galloping through the outer castle and away from the high walls. His guards trailed along behind him and another horse took the lead. He glanced to the side, unsurprised to find Etta bending forward in the saddle and gripping Vérité's reins.

Another battle in this same village came to mind. It was the beginning of them, but also the night that started them on the path toward their end. Edmund had been arrested, changing everything Alex thought he knew about magic.

The irony wasn't lost on him as he found himself in the position of magic's protector in Gaule.

A mob crowded into the streets of the village and Alex slowed his horse. Men and women screamed and threw insults.

Rain drizzled down, but it didn't deter them.

Where was Ara when he needed her? These people would never hear him.

"Hey," he yelled. No response. He forced his horse forward. People jumped out of the way to avoid being trampled.

A squat house sat up ahead with a line of people blocking the doors to prevent anyone from leaving.

"Magic has no place in Gaule," someone screamed.

"It's the king," another yelled. Those words worked their way through the throng of people and Alex waited for them to give him their attention, their respect.

That moment didn't come.

"Hey magic lover," a young boy called. Alex's gaze found him seconds before the boy launched a spoiled apple at him. It struck him in the face and there was a stunned moment when it slid down before landing on the front of his jacket.

A roar ripped through the crowd.

"You aren't our king!"

"We will never follow you!"

"Go back to your Belaen whore!"

More food sailed through the air, striking him in the chest. Alex put a hand on the hilt of his sword.

"No, Your Majesty," Simon said.

Alex breathed out. For a moment, he'd forgotten he wasn't alone.

Simon had been right. It would be a mistake to draw his sword in this mess. He tried to push closer to the house, to remember their objective, but his way was blocked.

The eyes of a young girl peeked out the window before disappearing in an instant.

What was he to do?

A flash of light broke through the sky. At first, Alex thought it was lightning, but the crowd had gone silent.

Etta's face twisted in rage as she walked forward. She'd dismounted, and the people shrank away from her. Alex's jaw fell open. Her hair glowed golden with her magic.

She didn't say a word as she continued her forward trek. She reached the line of people blocking the house and pushed her hands apart. They were flung aside, and she entered the house calmly.

"Amazing, isn't she?" Edmund asked in his ear.

Alex wanted to ask Edmund when he'd gotten there, but didn't take his focus from the door. Nervous chatter buzzed around him, only seconds away from turning back into hatred for magic.

Alex gestured to his guards to stay by the door and pushed his way into the house.

A single room living space greeted him.

Etta, hair still bright, stood in front of a couple and three young children.

"Your Majesty," the woman said, curtsying awkwardly. When she rose, her eyes connected with Etta's and in them was a devotion Alex had never experienced before. He'd seen the way the people of Bela followed their queen. They would follow her to the end of the world if so asked. It was the way of the Belaen people. Loyalty. Trust. And they hadn't had a ruler in generations.

Last time he'd seen Etta, she hadn't known what to do with their faith. The Basile powers had been given to her, but her anger clouded everything else in her mind.

This was not that girl.

This was a queen.

Etta touched the head of the youngest child softly.

"Why are you in Gaule, your Majesty?" the man asked.

Etta smiled. "I came to see all Belaens safe."

"Thank you." Tears streamed down the woman's face. "Thank you."

A crack of thunder burst through the air. "You're going to have to leave your home." She glanced at Alex quickly before looking back to them. "His Majesty of Gaule will provide you with horses but you must make your way to the border. Gaule isn't safe for our kind."

The woman sniffled and her husband put a hand on her back before turning to Alex, bowing slightly. "Thank you, your Majesty. Be warned, sympathies in this village are not kind toward you. We are more thankful than you know for everything you have tried to do for magic folk, but it is also what's going to tear your kingdom apart."

Alex pressed his lips together, feeling the truth of the man's words. He nodded shortly.

When they opened the door, the royal guardsmen held back the crowd. Their jeers slid down Alex's back. The children were passed up onto horses and the couple doubled up with him and Etta.

Rain pelted them as they left the mob behind. Their rebellion was not something that would leave Alex anytime soon.

Back at the palace, he had his people deal with their newcomers and marched through the halls, his boots making wet prints as he did.

He barged into his mother's room to find her sitting with Duchess Moreau and Camille before the fire.

"Alex," she chastised. "Honestly. You're dripping all over my carpet."

"How bad is it mother?" he asked.

"How bad is what, exactly?"

"Don't placate me. I am the king. Tell me how close my kingdom is from falling over the edge."

She sighed and set aside her teacup. "Come warm yourself by the fire, son. It is worse than you see."

He lowered himself into a chair, letting the warmth soak through his damp clothing.

"I don't know where to begin," she said.

"I do," Camille jumped in. "They aren't rebelling against the monarchy, Alexandre. They're rising up against you."

"Me."

"Camille," their mother snapped.

Duchess Moreau took a sip of her tea, regarding him over the lip of the cup. "Camille speaks the truth, sire."

Alex sagged against the back of the chair.

The duchess continued. "Inbred hatred is hard to destroy. Never mind the fact that some magic is truly evil. Their hatred means they can't distinguish between the two. Until you, the monarchy stayed either silent on all things magic or spoke out against it. You are the first king in generations to openly support it. You cannot force people to accept something they've been taught to hate. Certainly, not overnight."

"So, they refuse to follow me."

"Not only that," Camille said. "They've spent the past month while you've been ill marching and calling for your demise. They just didn't know how close they came to getting their wish."

"Camille," their mother said. "That is quite enough."

She shrugged but for once, Alex was grateful for her honesty.

"I've failed you," he said after a beat of silence.

"Alex, no." His mother reached out to take his hand, but he pulled it away.

"Father told me I would. When I was a boy. I've been so determined to prove him wrong, to turn this family's legacy around. I thought he destroyed Gaule, but it was me. Everyone told me I acted in haste. I didn't think. I thought changes could be made with a few declarations from the king, but you can't change what's in people's hearts."

"You changed what was in mine," Camille's voice quieted and he wasn't sure if he heard her right.

He lifted his eyes to meet hers.

Her fingers fidgeted in her lap as she bit her lip nervously. "Look, I still don't... like magic. It scares me, okay? It's unnatural and when someone has too much of it, well we've all seen what can happen. Just look at La Dame. We have no chance should she march on us. But, I don't think magic folk should be persecuted. I-I didn't know. I grew up at father's side. I honestly thought he couldn't do any wrong, but he did. Everything he did was so very wrong. I see that now. But Alexandre, you've been trying to fix a country that can't be fixed—not while La Dame is on our doorstep. And definitely not while our king is in love with Persinette Basile."

She crossed her arms over her chest. "You've seen what she did to our gates. Can you honestly say you don't fear the day she turns on us?"

"She won't—"

"Alexandre, we know nothing about her power. I see nothing of the Etta you knew in her."

"She saved my life."

"And son, we will be eternally grateful for that." His mother took his hand again and this time he didn't pull away. "But maybe your sister is right. She's no longer our Etta. She's the queen of a kingdom that was once our greatest enemy."

Alex jerked his hand back and stood. "You didn't see her today. The way she saved her people from the mob in the villages."

"Her people, Alexandre." Camille stared up at him imploringly. "She had to save her people from yours. If that doesn't tell you everything you need to know about the new circumstances, I'm not sure what will."

His eyes shifted from his sister to his mother to the curiously quiet duchess before marching from the room. After closing the door behind him, he released a breath, not sparing a glance for the guards waiting for him. His mind whirled in chaos.

The worst part was he knew they weren't wrong. Gaule would never accept magic. They may never even accept him. And without magic, they couldn't face La Dame.

He had to keep his kingdom safe, no matter the cost.

# CHAPTER 13

Etta led Vérité into the pen outside the stables and removed his saddle. She walked toward the shelter to hang it, enjoying a temporary reprieve from the dampness outside as she walked the length of the dry stables.

Three horses entered the stables at the opposite end. Catrine rode between two of her guards. She slid down gracefully, not needing or wanting the help of her men. After handing the reins of her horse off to a stable lad, she turned as if she'd known Etta was there all along.

"Queen Persinette." Catrine dipped her head formally.

Etta hated the distance between them. Once, she'd been trusted by the queen mother. But that was before the magic took hold of her and Bela rejoined the world.

"Queen mother." Making a quick decision, Etta turned on her heel and walked back to where she'd left Vérité eating from a trough. To her surprise, Catrine followed her into the muddy corral, not even bothering to lift the ends of her thick green skirt.

Etta released a sigh and turned to meet her gaze. "Is there something you'd like to say to me?" She imagined what all Gauleans thought of her and the desire to protect her people within their borders. But as she looked at Catrine, she saw the same burning intensity in her gaze. This was a woman who'd stand for her kingdom until she couldn't any longer.

And Etta suddenly didn't want to be looking at the queen mother anymore. She wanted to see the woman her father must have seen.

"Were you and my mother true friends?" Etta's shoulders tensed, waiting for an answer.

Catrine nodded, sadness etched across her face. "She was the greatest friend I've ever had."

"Then how-"

"How could I love her husband?" Emotions warred in the queen's eyes. "Back then, things were very different for us. My husband was the king, but he was not a good man. He left the palace for months at a time with Viktor at his side. I led Gaule during those years. He made war on the magic folk. It was his one accomplishment. The purge. But the kingdom survived the years of isolation we experienced while the wards were in place because of me and my advisors."

"That tells me nothing of my mother." Etta began to turn away.

"No," Catrine agreed. "But it tells you something of me. I know what you must think of me... of your father."

"Did you love him?"

"Yes," she said with a shrug of her shoulders. "But I wasn't in love with him. I also loved your mother. Our relationship was... complicated. When we conceived Ty, your mother had left the palace."

"Left?"

"She never understood why Viktor insisted on serving a cruel king."

Etta gripped Vérité's mane. "He never told her of the curse…" She lifted her eyes. "But why? Did my healing powers come from her?" She had to know. Was she the daughter of a Draconian?

Catrine's eyes pinched in sadness. "No, dear. The healing powers are yet another gift from your father's line. Your mother was… well, she had no magic."

Etta stumbled back. Her mother… didn't have magic? She wasn't a Belaen?

As if sensing her questions, Catrine continued. "Your mother was from a kingdom across the great sea called Cana."

Cana. She'd never even heard of it. Her father… why hadn't he told her any of this?

"I have to go." She hauled herself onto the horse without bothering to saddle him once again.

"Etta, wait." Catrine stepped forward tentatively. "I never thanked you for saving Alexandre."

Etta nudged Vérité around. "Don't. I don't want this. The Draconian magic. The Basile power. It's going to destroy us all."

She kicked the horse and veered out of the pen, winding her way through the outer palace until she reached the gates she'd blown to pieces. Beyond them, the land opened up.

Her magic burned within her and the control slipped away. If she unleashed it inside the castle, the whole thing would come down.

Today was further proof. Even the villages closest to the king weren't safe for her people. She had to get them out of Gaule once and for all.

She let the anger bubble to the surface and explode from her hands, swinging them in an arc over her head, shredding the grass surrounding her.

Rain pelted her hair, sizzling on her skin where it met the magic.

Her mother left her father because of the curse and Etta hadn't known. But she'd come back. That was what mattered, right? Not the fact that she had no power. She'd loved Etta. At least, Etta wanted to believe she had.

She jumped down and left Vérité at a safe distance. She broke into a run, pumping her legs, the wind whipping water in her face. Adrenaline rushed through her as she jumped and released a bit of magic, pushing her farther than humanly possible. She landed in a roll and popped back up. Light flashed from her hands, illuminating the sky as if lightning cracked it open.

A grin stretched across her face, fueled by a need for more. More power. More life. Another way to forget who she was and where she'd come from.

"Etta!" someone called in a faraway voice.

She bent, ready to release the next wave when suddenly the rain stopped hitting her. Snapping out of her trance, she glanced up to see the water bending around her. She whipped her head around, her soaking braid slapping her in the face.

Tyson waited for her, hands on hips, next to Vérité.

Her control continued to slip.

"Leave," she yelled. He didn't understand the danger. She couldn't hold it back. At least Edmund was aware what he was getting into when he practiced with her.

Then another horse appeared. Tyson said something over his shoulder and when Alex appeared, shaking wet hair out of his face, Etta's control returned with such force she stumbled back.

Confusion warred within her but she shook it off and scanned the land surrounding her. It looked as if a cyclone had come through.

Alex's eyes widened as he regarded her and she wanted more than anything to see inside his mind.

"We need to talk," he said finally. "Ruler to ruler."

She nodded once and crossed the field to where she'd left Vérité.

Once they arrived back in Alex's rooms, there was a moment when all she wanted was to touch him, feel him, to let him wash away every emotion inside her. They hadn't gotten close since the night she healed him. It was as if a barrier stood between them now.

Two barriers actually and they were called crowns.

They entered the room and Alex's guards took up their positions outside. She was thankful no one made her have guards following her back in Bela. She was more powerful than any guard could be so there was no point.

Edmund was waiting for them and Tyson shut the door. It was just the four of them once again. So much had happened to each of them and yet here they were.

Etta slumped down in a chair near the fire, exhaustion tugging at her after the long day. Alex walked behind her, giving her shoulder a firm squeeze before taking a seat. She closed her eyes at his touch.

She opened them as Alex began to speak. "I need to protect my people."

She nodded. "I do too and that means returning to Bela as soon as I can."

He swallowed hard and leaned forward to put his head in his hands. "How do I protect a people who won't let me? How do I keep the most powerful woman in the world from crossing our borders? How do I force them to accept magic when it strikes such fear in them?"

Etta moved off her chair to take the place beside Alex. Her hand hovered over his arm for a moment of hesitation before she touched him. "I don't know."

It wasn't the first time she'd felt completely lost. La Dame was coming for her people as well, but at least they had their magic. And they had her.

Bela was being built up while Gaule crumbled into dust.

Her magic jumped at the thought, yearning for its vengeance. But Gaule was no longer their enemy. She held down the simmering power.

The fire reflected in Tyson's eyes as he regarded them all. "I think I know how to keep Gaule safe."

Alex drew his brows together and Etta held her breath. She didn't like the look on her brother's face.

"Spit it out, Ty," Edmund said.

Tyson moved toward Etta swiftly and knelt down in front of her. "Etta, you have the Basile power."

"I am aware," she replied.

"No, I mean you have all of the Basiles' power. Isn't that how it works? All the magic that has existed in our family line is now in you." His eyes burned into Etta. "O-our… father."

Understanding slammed into her and she shrank back. Yes. It was so simple. If she could do it, Gaule would be protected. They wouldn't be driven to the slaughter. There wasn't anything she could do to keep what was coming from touching her own people, but…

"What am I missing?" Edmund asked.

Alex knew. She saw it in his eyes. The moment when he realized saving his people meant losing her.

She'd come to the conclusion a long time ago that those who loved her would always be taken from her. It had been part of her life since the night her mother died.

Alex, the boy who was used to having what he wanted, had never tasted loss like this.

If she did what Tyson was saying, that was it. The end.

But all she'd ever had were endings.

Alex's entire body shuddered as he looked at each of them in turn. It wasn't only her he'd lose. It was all of them.

He cleared his throat. "The wards. Etta may be able to restore her father's wards."

"No." Edmund shook his head. "That's the worst idea I've ever heard." He met Etta's gaze. "You're really considering this?"

"I don't know what else to do." The words burst out of her and she jumped from the couch to pace the room. "Really, Edmund, what the hell do you want from me?"

"Do you even realize what these wards mean?" he asked.

"Of course I do. My father created the original ones."

"You were a child living in the forest. Alex and I were riding out to border villages with his father's soldiers. We saw what the wards did to magic folk who tried to cross."

She put her hands on her head, spinning around to face him. "I'm out of ideas." Red crept up her neck as she tried to hold back the anger her magic had burning within her.

Edmund crossed the distance between them and grabbed her arms. "Hey, calm down. Breathe." He breathed deeply as if to demonstrate and she closed her eyes. "Etta, control it. Don't let it take over."

She focused on his hands folded around hers. On the sounds of his breath. The magic shrank back, and she opened her eyes to look into Edmund's face. He'd done that for her more times than she could count.

Alex and Tyson watched them silently, their eyes filled with a mixture of curiosity and shock.

"Are you..." Tyson began. "Are you okay?"

Etta collapsed back onto the couch. What was she supposed to tell them? No, she wasn't okay. She walked around constantly on the verge of exploding.

Alex scooted closer and put an arm around her. She sank into his side, the calm beat of his heart calming her frantic one. "Did I scare you?"

Both Alex and Tyson shook their heads emphatically.

Edmund laughed. "Of course you did."

Three sets of eyes shot daggers his way, and he put up his hands in defense.

Ignoring Edmund, Alex asked the question they should have begun with. "How do we know La Dame wouldn't be able to find a way through the wards?"

Etta lifted her head to look up at him. "She never broke my father's wards, and he didn't have the strength of the Basile power. We have to at least try."

He sighed, his breath ruffling her hair. "I know."

Edmund slumped in defeat and Tyson picked himself up off the floor.

Etta pulled herself away from Alex's warmth. "I need some dry clothes and a drink. Have your people make preparations. Send riders to every village with notices that all magic folk planning to leave for Bela must do so within a fortnight." She rubbed a hand over her face. "I can't believe we're doing this."

"I know. I hate it as much as you. We're forcing all magic folk from Gaule. I never wanted it to come to this."

"They're safer in Bela."

He gripped her hand. "That doesn't make it right."

She ran her fingers along his cheek. "But at least they'll be alive. And Gaule will be safe."

She returned to her rooms and changed out of her sopping clothes, setting them to dry by the fire.

A platter of food had been left with an overgenerous pitcher of wine. She poured herself a drink and sighed before sitting in the large wing-backed chair next to her own roaring fire, trying to feel more than she did.

She still loved Alex. That hadn't changed just because of the magic. But the love was clouded in doubt and duty. Nothing was clear to her anymore. It was as if her heart loved him, but her head was incapable.

Would she ever be able to be more than the power inside of her?

It latched on to everything she was, twisting it and hardening it.

She drained her wine and rose to fill the cup again.

After a while, there was a knock on her door. She opened it to find Alex. Before letting the doubts and coldness fill her, she set her cup down and kissed him.

"I don't want to lose you," he whispered.

She didn't have any words for him so she pulled him back to her and walked backward into the room.

"I love you." His voice vibrated against her lips.

She pushed away from him violently without meaning to. Her body betrayed her, giving itself over to the magic brewing inside.

"No more talking," she said roughly. "Not tonight."

He grabbed her wrist to keep her from walking away from him and she rushed forward, slamming him against the closed door, wanting to destroy him the way the magic destroyed her.

He didn't recoil in fear as she expected. That, she could have lived with. He'd have been right to be frightened. But instead, heat blazed in his eyes. His strong hands wrapped around her upper arms and he yanked her against him.

They crashed back against the door once more before he spun and pressed her up against the solid wood.

"Let it out," he said. "I can take it."

He didn't know what he was asking. If she unleashed everything she was feeling… no, he couldn't take that.

"You're not strong enough for that." It wasn't meant as an insult, just a statement of fact.

"Maybe not, but I'd take it, anyway."

He took her lips as if he owned them. She took his as if it was the only thing left to do. Her magic churned unhappily, but she ignored its distaste, using it to fuel her every action.

She wanted to love Alex. More than anything. And she did, she thought. But thinking something was not the same as feeling it.

And that part of her was blocked.

For now, she'd give him what she could.

Soon, there'd be nothing left for either of them to hold on to.

In sleep, Etta looked like the queen she was. Her hair was splayed across the pillow, its brilliant golden strands catching the sun as it streamed through the window.

It was when she woke that she was the girl who'd beaten all of Gaule's best soldiers in the tournament. She'd killed them without a second thought. If Alex hadn't seen for himself what she could do, he wouldn't believe it.

He studied her still features. Nothing about her was fragile, but he couldn't shake the feeling that she was constantly on the verge of breaking. One moment she'd be comforting a Belaen family and the next she was shaking with rage.

None of it made any sense.

He didn't remember that side of her from before.

Her eyelids shifted and a moment later fluttered open. She stared up at him as the cloud of sleep faded from her eyes. Her brow scrunched as her face hardened. He sighed. Some things would never change.

Etta had never truly accepted what lay between them. Before, it was because she worried the curse drew her to him and none of it was real. When the curse was replaced by her family's magic, it became something else, something he couldn't even begin to understand.

He reached out to tuck a tuft of hair behind her ear but then thought better of it and let his hand drop as he moved to the edge of the bed, swinging his legs over.

Clearing his throat, he slipped into king mode. "Riders were sent out last night. All Belaens in Gaule will soon know of the coming wards. I expect you'll have many new arrivals in Bela."

"Alex." She hesitated. "Thank you."

He grunted and got to his feet. Of course, she was only thanking him for aiding her people. It was always about them. For just one moment, he wished she'd ask something for herself.

Etta asked if he feared her and the answer was yes, but not for the reasons she thought. He never believed she'd hurt him—physically at least. But the thing that scared him most was the knowledge that Etta would sacrifice herself for her people without a second thought.

It was what a ruler should do, but she was reckless about it.

If Etta died, everything inside him would die as well.

He slipped into his own room to wash and change before stepping back out into the hall. His guards followed at a close distance as he left to find Edmund. His friend was with Tyson in the main hall breaking their fast.

Climbing onto the wooden bench, Alex leaned forward and rested his forehead against the rough grain of the oak table.

"How much did you drink last night?" Edmund asked with a laugh.

"Nothing."

"Ah." He shared a glance with Tyson. "You're just queen drunk then."

He lifted his head to glare at his friend.

Tyson eyed him. "Okay, I don't want to know about my brother and sister's… ugh… relationship."

Alex groaned. "Stop saying it like that, asshole."

"How else am I supposed to talk when my brother is in love with my sister?"

Alex swatted him upside the head.

Tyson laughed and rubbed the spot Alex hit.

"Just don't say that to Etta." Edmund chuckled lowly. "Although, I'd pay to see her beat your ass."

Tyson shrugged. "I did say it. After I found out Viktor was my father."

"Yeah, but that was before." Edmund shook his head.

"Before what?" Alex asked.

Tyson leaned in curiously.

Edmund's face pinched as if he'd said something he shouldn't. "Just… Etta is different."

"Obviously." Tyson puffed out his chest. "She missed her brother."

Edmund threw a hunk of bread at his head and he ducked out of the way. Alex laughed at them, but something pinched in his gut. Tyson was joking about the reason for Etta's moods but that didn't change the fact that he would miss his brother. He assumed Tyson was going back with them. Gaule was no longer his home.

Plus, Ty could never miss a battle. He'd returned to Gaule to fight the rebellion and now he was going to be a part of a fight much larger than that.

Alex would be able to cross the wards since he had no magic in his blood. He could see his brother. But only if there was something left after they faced La Dame.

It killed him that Gaule would be closed off, safe but unable to help.

A shadow loomed over the table and Alex lifted his eyes to Simon's large frame.

"Your Majesty," Simon said stoically. "May I have a word?"

Alex pushed up from the table. "Of course. I have to meet the duchess in the council chamber, walk with me."

The first part of their walk was silent, but then the words tumbled out of Simon.

"I would like to ask your permission to remain in Gaule."

Alex raised an eyebrow. "I have to admit, this surprises me. You understand what's going to happen? Etta will erect the wards and you will not be able to cross."

"I understand, sire."

"Can I ask you why, Simon? I've seen you with your queen. You're as fervently loyal as any Belaen and yet you do not wish to follow her?"

Simon's steps faltered, and he didn't speak for a long moment. "I have come to realize, your Majesty, that a man can have more than one queen. I am loyal to Persinette Basile and to my people, but my honor would not let me leave my charge here in Gaule."

"My mother." Alex nodded. "So, your loyalty is split?"

"I do not see it as so, sire. Loyalty, just like love, is not something we have in finite amounts. My loyalty is not cut in half to account for both queens. It is expanded to encompass the faith I have with each."

"Then how do you choose?" His mind went to Etta. He loved her more than anything with one exception. Gaule. He'd always love his kingdom and the people in it.

"Your mother depends on my loyalty," he answered. "Yes, Persinette could use me in the battle to come, but she does not truly need me."

Alex sighed. Persinette Basile never needed anyone.

They reached the council chambers and Simon left to return to his post at the dowager queen's side. Alex stepped inside to prepare for their journey to the border and the events that would come after.

# CHAPTER 14

"Are you sure this is the only way, your Majesty?" The intensity of Ara's gaze was blinding.

Over the past few days, Etta had come to appreciate the quiet company of the General. She'd grown up as the bastard daughter of a duke–his only child with magic. Even with an accepting man like Duke Caron, that wouldn't have been an easy life in Gaule.

Discrimination based on magic was not allowed on Caron's lands, but that didn't mean it didn't exist.

Which was why they were in that place on that day, hovering near the line where two ancient kingdoms met. They stood in the shadow of the mountains where La Dame lay waiting behind her walls.

Alex sent his best riders into every corner of the kingdom. Their message? Leave. Get your families to safety. It was time to erect the wards that once stood along the border. The difference being this time there'd be people other than Draconians on the other side.

The only way to protect both magic folk and non-magic folk alike was to keep them apart.

Etta studied the contrasting features of Ara's face. A firm set jaw and high, harshly cut cheekbones, but a soft brow and round doe eyes with sadness echoed in each of them.

She didn't get a chance to answer her before the duke strode toward them. He touched her back and led her away for a private conversation.

Etta let her eyes roam across into Bela and over the lush rolling hills stretching into the distance. After a moment, she turned on her heel and headed back to the row of tents.

They'd been there for days as the flow of magic folk across the border was never-ending.

Tomorrow, the deadline would pass. They'd set a date for the wards to be put in place. It was plastered across the kingdom. One day and then she'd use her magic to cut the land in half. In truth, it would be an invisible line. One who didn't have magic would never sense it. But if magic ran in your blood, you'd be prevented from crossing by unbearable pain leeching the magic from your veins. For miles in each direction, a buzzing in the air told magic folk a ward was near, alerting them to the danger.

She didn't want to do it. God, she wished it could be different.

But wishes were for people who didn't have crowns on their heads.

She didn't get the luxury of pretty fantasies.

Alex stood near the opening of his tent watching her. He looked kingly in his navy-blue doublet and embroidered jacket.

She shivered as a blast of cold air worked through camp. Winter had hit them in full force. In the mountains, the paths would be blocked, but that wouldn't stop La Dame. Still, Etta was under no illusions that she'd come. She wouldn't leave her walls behind. No, all La Dame had to do was wait. Etta had no choice but to go against her. The only question was when.

"Are you cold?" Alex asked.

How did one answer that? Yes, she was cold, but not only on the surface. Once she crafted the wards, she'd never again be able to return to Gaule. That fact alone turned her entire body to ice.

Alex reached for her and rubbed his hands down her arms. She leaned into his touch and met his eye as if he could give her the answers; pleading with him to tell her this wasn't going to happen.

As she closed her eyes, she wrapped her arms around his waist and breathed him in. For once, she was able to keep the magic from tainting her emotions. They'd spent every night together in the past few weeks and some of the ire left her with each moment by his side.

Alex rested his chin on her hair.

"Why are we always leaving each other?" Her words were muffled by his shirt.

He hummed low in his throat and held her tighter. "You don't have to do this."

"Please don't say that. If you... just don't. I'm not strong enough to resist if you ask me to forget about this."

He kissed the side of her head. "You're the strongest person I know."

She pushed away from him. "Don't say that either." She shoved her way into the tent and sat down on the bedroll in the corner.

Alex followed her and crossed his arms over his chest. "Why not?"

Her magic pulsed, trying to rise and expand. She managed to hold it back, but the anger it brought didn't go away.

Alex's voice softened as he repeated "Why not?"

The anger wasn't hers. She knew that now. It was the power inside her. But it felt like she owned every inch of it.

"Because I don't want to be strong," she yelled. "I want to say 'screw it' and forget about every person that's waiting for me back in Bela. I don't want to dredge up my dead father's magic and every memory that'll come with it." She covered her face as the anger slithered away. "I don't want to leave you." Tears slid between her fingers as her back shook.

He knelt down in front of her and pried her hands away from her face before leaning in to press his lips against hers. She'd never get used to kissing him. To running her hands across his firm chest and up under the edges of his shirt.

"Tonight," he breathed, leaning his forehead against hers. "I'm not the king of Gaule and you're not the queen of Bela. Just for tonight can we pretend we have the entire future spread out before us?"

She wound her arms up around his neck, her fingers sinking into the back of his thick hair. "Kiss me please."

He smirked. "Since you asked so nicely."

She forced away the dark emotions swirling in the depths of her magic. It would not control her. Not tonight.

The power didn't make her who she was. Etta was crafted by memories of her father, her love for Alex, and the determination of a warrior.

Alex's hands worked to untwist her braid as he laid her back. "I would touch your hair for the rest of my life."

Tears stung her eyes, and she blinked them back as she pulled Alex down on top of her and got lost in everything she'd never have again.

Alex laughed as Etta played with the tiny hairs on his chest. "That tickles."

She raised her head to look at him and her heart stopped. He'd always been beautiful, but never so much as when he was... unmade. His dark hair stuck up in every direction and his lips were swollen with the memory of every kiss.

"What would you do if you weren't the king?" she asked, a wistful note in her voice.

He ran the tips of his fingers along the curve of her waist. A shiver raced through her, her every nerve on edge.

"I've never really considered it. I was raised to be king. There was never another option for me."

She tucked her head into the crook of his neck.

"What about you?" he asked.

She shrugged. "I'm still getting used to the idea of being the queen. Remember, I grew up thinking I'd spend my life serving you."

"As my shield."

She laughed. "The person who would step in front of arrows—as you once said to me."

"I did not!"

"Oh, you definitely did. You told me it was a ceremonial position, and you didn't think I'd actually be protecting you." She laughed. "I remember protecting you quite a few times."

"Once."

"If that's what you want to believe."

He was quiet for a moment. "I'd like to see something other than Gaule–if I didn't have to be king, I mean. The Kings of Gaule used to travel abroad, but that was before we closed our country off. It's not even safe for me to visit some more distant parts of my own kingdom. Most days, I only see the inside of the castle walls. As awful as my time with La Dame's people was, it made me see that there is so much more than a throne and the life that demands."

"Alex–" She sighed, not knowing what she wanted to say.

"I reinstated the council's powers my father took away." The words were so sudden she startled.

She leaned away from him and met his stare. "That's—"

"I know. But it was the right thing to do. My father's purge showed us what happens when one person has too much power. I don't know who will wear the crown after me but I must safeguard the people the best way I know how. Everything I do is for them."

He didn't say it, but she knew what lay between his words. He'd agreed to her plans to put the wards back into place only because the Gaulean people were no match for the magic that was coming for them. They couldn't face La Dame without being erased completely. Not without magic.

Etta was operating under a lot of assumptions. After her father created the original wards, La Dame stayed away from Gaule. She hoped it was the wards that deterred her. She'd never questioned the strength of her father's magic, but if La Dame couldn't break it, it was unbreakable.

"Just because you won't be able to cross the wards doesn't mean I can't." Light entered his gaze and for a moment, Etta wanted to give into the tiniest bit of hope in his voice. "I can still come to you."

The hope fizzled out as his words sank in and she tucked her head back against his chest. "You know we can't..."

"Etta, there is no way I'm ever going to agree to never seeing my best friend, my brother, and the woman I love ever again. You can just forget about it."

She breathed in the scent of him, committing it to memory. *If there are any of us left.* It wasn't the first time she'd considered the possibility of La Dame beating them. If it were up to her, Tyson would stay in Gaule. Even as she herded the Belaens across the border to bolster their numbers in the fight to come, she wanted her brother safe.

But he wouldn' t hear of it.

"Are you scared?" Alex asked as if sensing the direction of her thoughts.

Etta sat up and turned away from him, her magic coming alive beneath her skin. "No." It was the truth. She didn't fear La Dame. Not anymore. Not when the power of the Basiles coursed through her blood.

She reached for her trousers and pulled them on without bothering with her underclothes.

"Where are you going?" Alex reached for her.

"We can't stay in bed all evening."

"Why not?"

She slipped her tunic over her head and belted it at her waist before shrugging on a cloak. "Come on. Get dressed. I'm not the only person leaving for Bela tomorrow. There are a lot of goodbyes to be had."

She left him to dress. Nearby, a fire roared to life. Their party sat huddled on blankets basking in its warmth.

Tyson held Amalie in his lap. They too would be torn apart. Amalie wanted to join them, but Tyson begged her not to. She was safer in Gaule. At least until after they faced La Dame.

Too many people had faith in Etta.

She joined Edmund and Ara who were having an intense conversation.

"Your father is probably right," Edmund said. "You may very well die."

Ara scoffed. "So could every single person across that border. Why the hell would I sit here and wait for you all to fight a war I have every right to be a part of?"

"Am I interrupting something?" Etta lowered herself down beside Edmund.

"Edmund doesn't want any competition for the general of your army." Ara shot him a scathing look.

"My army?" Etta raised a brow.

"All of these people crossing into Bela will have to fight for you."

"I will not force anyone into this battle."

Ara fixed her with a harsh glare. "Are you trying to lose?"

Edmund scowled. "Don't speak to the queen that way." He crossed his arms. "Only I'm allowed to."

"Children," Etta said, looking to each of them in turn. "Calm down. Ara, you're joining us across the border?"

"Of course."

"You do realize you won't be able to cross back into Gaule once the wards are in place?"

Ara nodded.

"May I ask why you're willing to leave your family behind when you live in the one part of Gaule where magic people are generally safe?"

Ara leaned forward, resting her elbows on her bent legs. "I'm a bastard. That's not new information."

Etta nodded. She'd heard the story.

"My mother was killed by men who hated magic—on my father's land. There is nowhere in Gaule that is safe for us. At least in Bela, I'll get the chance to fight for people who don't want to stab me in the back like I'm sure most of my soldiers do."

Ara's brutal honesty was something Etta respected. "Then we'll be glad to have you."

Edmund grunted out a "sure."

They fell quiet as the crackling of the fire overtook all other night sounds.

When Etta spoke again, her voice was hushed. "Hateful Gauleans killed my mother too."

"Who would have thought a bastard soldier would have something in common with a queen."

Etta smiled at that. "I'm still just the girl whose only skills are magic and weapons."

"With an ancient royal bloodline and the intense loyalty of even the Belaens who have yet to lay eyes on their queen."

She snorted. "Yeah, and that."

"Well, now you have my loyalty. My sword will be the truest in your army."

Etta's eyes flicked to Edmund for his reaction and he didn't disappoint. A smirk appeared and challenge danced in his eyes. "We'll see about that."

Alex joined them, taking the seat next to his mother. Around that fire were the royal families of both Gaule and Bela. Etta wished her father could see them now. Would he be proud of her? He'd prepared her for sacrifice and here she was, making the greatest sacrifice of them all. It wasn't her life—losing that might have been easier. This sacrifice was one of the heart.

But she wasn't alone. They were all being separated from the people they loved because of something as fundamental to life as magic. Tyson was leaving his mother and Amalie. Ara would miss her father. Edmund had already left everything he'd ever known, just as had each and every one of the magic folk who were crossing the border.

This life had never been easy, but it had been theirs. What future waited for them in Bela? Etta was anxious to return to her people, but it was as if they were all walking into darkness.

The cloud blocking out the sun was La Dame and the power that lurked within her.

"You okay?" Edmund whispered, bumping her shoulder with his.

Her eyes didn't leave Alex as she nodded. Did she have any choice but to be okay? Alex said something to his brother and then got up to approach them, his long legs reaching them in a few slow strides. He lowered himself to his knees, facing both Etta and Edmund.

"Promise me you'll take care of each other," he said.

"Alex–" Edmund started.

"Promise," he growled.

"I won't leave her side."

"Like I could get rid of Edmund even if I tried."

Alex nodded. "Anders is nearby. As soon as the wards are in place, he'll disperse his men throughout the kingdom to restore some sort of order. I'm sending Duke Caron and Duchess Moreau to their respective estates."

A harsh laugh burst from Edmund's throat. "Does my father know I won't be returning? The great Anders wouldn't show up to wish his only spawn well?"

Alex sighed and scratched the back of his neck. "I'm sorry."

"I should have known better than to expect anything more."

Etta took his hand between both of hers. The flames lit the sadness on his face. His lips drew down, and he pressed them together.

Alex watched him for a moment, words of comfort failing him. He turned to Etta. "I understand magic folk can't cross the wards, but does magic work across them?"

Etta's brow scrunched in thought. "I don't know."

"Well run a test to see if Ara's magic can be of use to us. If you need me."

"Alex, I'm not dragging Gauleans into the fight with La Dame."

"If you need us," he repeated, clenching his teeth. "We will come."

"Don't be stupid."

"Don't be stubborn."

He was impossible. Etta had no intention of calling on them and he wouldn't listen. Her magic enhanced the anger already brewing. "You don't have magic," she yelled as it boiled over. "What do you think the few Gaulean soldiers who are actually loyal to their king can do against an army of magically armed Draconians? Gaule is useless to us." When her words stopped and her chest heaved, the magic shrank back and she realized what she'd said.

Alex stood slowly. "Good to know what you really think."

With those final words, he strode back toward his tent and disappeared inside.

"That wasn't okay, Etta," Edmund said gruffly.

"I know." She pulled her knees in and rested her chin on them. Maybe it was better to make him hate her before she left. His life would be easier if he never thought of her again.

As quickly as the thought came, it dissipated, replaced by the shattering knowledge of what tomorrow would bring.

Alex wasn't sure how long he'd been asleep when a warm body pressed into his side as Etta crawled into bed with him.

Her words had been a stinging indictment. When she'd said Gaule was useless to her, he imagined she spoke of him. He didn't have magic and would be no use at her side. He had very little skill with a sword even. What need would she have of him in a war?

None.

Could he really be angry at her for the truth?

That's what it all was. He didn't know which parts of the Gaulean army was loyal and which turned a blind eye to the persecution he outlawed. Many of them had even taken up swords against him. His own people.

He longed for the unwavering loyalty of the Belaen people. Etta hadn't been raised to be queen and yet they left everything behind to follow her blindly in a direction that could lead to ruin. Again. Bela had been destroyed once before. Would it be again?

"I'm sorry," Etta whispered, pressing a kiss to his neck as she burrowed farther under the blanket.

Alex kept his eyes closed, enjoying the feel of her. He didn't want to be angry on their final night and he couldn't remember Etta ever apologizing for anything before.

When he finally opened his eyes, he turned to face her. "It was only the truth."

"No, it wasn't." She propped her head up on her hand and bit her lip. "Sometimes I say things and can't stop myself."

"That's always been your problem." He smiled but the intensity of her gaze didn't waver.

"It's different now. This magic..." She sucked in a breath. "It has a darkness to it. Ever since the curse was broken, and this power flooded me, it's like I can't control anything. The power... I think it's angry. It has a mind of its own and intensifies everything I feel. If I'm the slightest bit irritated, it turns into anger and hatred so deep that sometimes it's all I have."

Was it true? The ancient Basile power was dark? But the girl before him was the light of his world.

He tucked an errant strand of silky golden hair behind her ear. "You can beat it."

She shook her head. "I can't. There are two people living inside me. Etta—the girl who will leave her kingdom to protect her people. And Persinette Basile, the queen who was always meant to have the Basile magic. One is just trying to survive each day and keep her kingdom alive. The other yearns for more. More power, more magic. Persinette Basile wants to raze Dracon to the ground no matter what she has to give up in the process. Etta doesn't want to leave this bed and the one man who can make her forget she's anything but that girl who won a tournament once upon a time."

He kissed her, his lips searing his own faith into her. "Have you ever thought Bela needs both Etta and Persinette?"

She nodded. "I think I need both too if I'm going to beat La Dame. She has all the power of Persinette, but what she lacks is an Etta. She wants revenge on my family, but vengeance will never win."

He pulled her head down to his chest. The silence of the night hid the fears of the morning as time slowed and they drifted into the land of dreams where the time for separation would never come.

# CHAPTER 15

Etta left Alex once before. After Alex imprisoned Edmund for his magic, he'd asked her to break his friend out of the dungeons and get him somewhere he'd be protected. It was amazing how far the king of Gaule had come since then.

When she'd gotten free of the castle with Edmund and Tyson, Alex hadn't known her true identity, and she hadn't known the true implications of the curse. She hadn't known that every moment she spent at a distance from her charge would be shrouded in agony.

She hadn't planned to return, but instead to seek out La Dame and break the curse.

She'd been naive.

When Alex learned who she was and of the magic in her blood, he'd sent his men after her and the small string of hope she'd had for him had been broken.

She never imagined it would be restored, but it had.

Now, she stood on the border between Bela and Gaule next to Alex, unsure of any words with the power to make this anything other than the end.

Because it was.

After everything they'd been through, the imprisonments, the battles, the hushed words in the middle of quiet nights—this was where they broke. And this time, there would be no reconciliation, no reunion.

There was a harsh sting that came with the finality of goodbye.

Alex squeezed her fingers, refusing to let go of her hand.

"It's time." Duchess Moreau's voice was soft.

To many, she seemed the only person who wasn't losing someone to these wards. She wasn't being separated from people she loved.

But those people only had to look her in the eye to see how wrong they were. The duchess had dedicated her life to protecting magic folk. She'd hidden them from the blood-thirsty soldiers during the purge. She'd given them good lives on her land. Allowed them to live freely without risk of persecution. She'd fought the old king every step of the way and worked to show Alex that they too deserved freedom.

In erecting the wards, they were admitting defeat. They'd lost. Gaule couldn't protect magic folk from their own. The kingdom only moved in reverse.

Tyson was the first to step across the border after tearful hugs with his mother and Amalie. Ara was next.

Edmund gripped Alex's shoulder. "Don't try to die again," he said. "Next time, we won't be able to come save you."

The words sounded light, as if Edmund had no cares, but Etta knew better.

Alex brought her hand to his lips and lingered there. "I love you," he whispered.

She reached up to run her fingers along his jaw. "Stay safe, your Majesty."

He smiled sadly. "You as well, your Majesty."

He pressed a light kiss to her temple and then her lips before finally releasing her.

The deadline had passed and Belaens who had not yet left Gaule would have to fend for themselves. The Gaulean people would have their kingdom back as they'd always wanted.

Etta nodded stiffly and stepped across the border. Her power twisted and churned as if straining to be free.

She tested it, gathering every ounce of control she had. As planned, the group still in Gaule moved back away from the border. She hadn't explained everything to them, but if her magic was too powerful for her, she didn't want to hurt them. She reined in her emotions and sucked in a breath before letting the power leak from her fingertips. It hit the cold air and expanded as she shaped and molded it, invisible to all but her. She saw gold and light and everything good as it encompassed her before darkness started to creep in.

As she closed her eyes, she called forth an image of her father, separating the magic he'd possessed from any other. She saw them so clearly, the wards, a shimmering barrier only her mind knew. She didn't know how much time had passed as the power trapped her in her own mind. It took every ounce of energy not to let it burst forth as she hesitated, unsure if she could protect Gaule as her father had, if she could accomplish this feat.

*You're strong enough for this, Persinette.* Her father's voice echoed in her head. *Let the power free.*

The magic was like tiny lightning strikes along her skin as it obeyed her, taking slightly more control than she ceded willingly.

Her body sagged to the ground, utterly spent, as she opened her eyes.

Nothing looked different. Alex stood in the distance, his hands clasped behind his back as he watched her.

Her lungs expanded painfully, and she exhaled.

"I hear it," Tyson whispered.

The air itself buzzed. The magic swirled around them, inching along her skin.

"Yeah," Edmund answered. "I do too."

Ara whispered a few words that weren't for their ears. When Alex nodded, Etta sat up on her heels.

"Magic works across the wards," Ara confirmed.

"It doesn't matter," Etta said. "We can't bring them into a fight."

Edmund pulled her to her feet, and she walked to where their horses were grazing. Vérité lifted his head.

"Come on, boy." She strained to pull her tired body into the saddle. "No time to look back at a different life. It's time to go home."

Time to remind herself that Bela was her home, not Gaule.

They had a long few days ahead of them, but then they'd be back among their people. She forced herself to push Alex into a box in her mind, not wanting to cry over what she couldn't have.

Before winter was over, they had to get the new arrivals from Gaule situated, and then, they'd prepare for war.

Alex stayed until they were no longer visible across the border. Etta didn't glance back as she rode away. Tyson's eyes met his one final time and Alex wanted to run after them.

He understood why Tyson went. He needed to be part of the fight. But that didn't make it any easier.

His mother appeared beside him and hooked his arm with hers. "Goodbye is never easy."

"Tyson is still a kid, mother."

She leaned her head against his arm. "Tyson has never been a normal kid. From the moment I had Viktor Basile's child, his destiny did not run alongside ours."

"Alexandre?" Camille said tentatively from behind them.

He turned to find his sister leaning on her cane, her normally cold expression flooded with sorrow. She flicked her eyes back to where Tyson had disappeared and for the first time, he remembered he wasn't the only one who'd had to say goodbye to a brother. Camille hated Etta, but in her own way, she had loved Tyson.

He wrapped an arm around her. She might be defiant and harsh, but they had so little family left. Despite her feelings toward magic, she'd stuck by his side.

"I hate this," she whispered.

"Me too." Kissing the top of her head, he released her. "But now we have a peace to restore." He considered her for a moment. "Will you join me in meeting with Anders?"

Her watery eyes widened. "You actually want my help? Not my husband or the duchess?"

Her surprise ate away at him. Had he really shoved her aside? She was a part of the royal family and knew more about ruling than he ever would.

He glanced at his mother who was watching them carefully before grabbing his sister's arm to help her walk over the uneven ground. "Come on. We have a lot to do."

# CHAPTER 16

Etta's people greeted her warmly as if she'd been gone for more than a few mere weeks. There was no hesitancy in their loyalty. They'd been so desperate to have someone to follow they had latched on and hadn't let go.

Etta slid from Vérité's back, her feet slamming into the ground. Her ground. Home. They were in the middle of the expanded part of the village. She could see the progress right away. They'd been working hard in her absence.

Matteo appeared, shaking the shaggy hair out of his eyes. He ran in a very un-Matteo like way toward them and she braced herself to be swept along in his relief, but he passed by her with barely a glance and stopped right in front of Edmund.

"You're back," he breathed. "We've been so worried."

Edmund's face danced with amusement. "You were worried about me?"

A blush crept up Matteo's face.

"Who is that?" Ara asked, dismounting next to Etta.

"That would be Matteo," Tyson said with a laugh. "Looks like I missed the good stuff while I was in Gaule." He shot Etta a grin. "You didn't know, did you?"

"By the looks of it, Edmund didn't know either." Ara laughed.

Embarrassment froze Matteo to the spot and his eyes shifted. Before he could back away, Edmund leaned forward and pressed his lips to a shocked Matteo's.

Matteo responded after a moment, and before long, Edmund pulled back. "Thought so." He winked.

Etta groaned. She wasn't in the mood for declarations of love. Ever since leaving the border days before, her power had grown even stronger. It had taken a lot of magic to create the wards and she couldn't stop herself from drawing in more.

But the power pulled her further from the light. For a little while, Alex had been able to hold her there, but without him...

She ducked inside as she gestured for an idle boy to take care of Verite. Everything was as she left it. Her throne rested against one wall, seeming smaller than before.

With a sigh, she dropped her bag in the corner.

Matteo rushed into the room behind her, a flush still in his face.

"Welcome home, cousin." He offered her a relieved smile.

"Home." She rubbed her temples to soothe the pounding in her skull. The next words that left her mouth felt wrong, but she didn't have the energy to stop them. "I have no home."

As soon as they were out, she sighed. "I didn't mean that. Sometimes I can't–"

"Look." He wrapped his hands around her biceps. "I get it. You forget, I lived with La Dame most of my life. I've seen what too much magic can do to a person." He bent to meet her eyes. "If it's too much, promise me you'll come to me."

She didn't get a chance to agree because Esme rushed in. The Draconian woman rushed forward, looking Etta over as she did. "Are you injured? Do you need me to heal anything?"

Etta stepped away from their worried stares. How was she going to tell her cousin they had Draconian blood in their veins? That she had the healing magic?

One thing she knew for sure was that she couldn't tell Esme. The woman had helped her immensely, but there was very little trust between them.

Etta wanted nothing more than to go to sleep for the next week, but as queen, she didn't have that option. She sighed. "We have matters to discuss."

"So, we're cut off from Gaule, for good?" Matteo asked.

They'd explained the events of the past weeks, only leaving out certain things like Alex's miraculous healing.

Tyson leaned forward. "Non-magic folk can cross the border, but they are now protected against magic folk just as they once were."

"They would stand no chance against La Dame even if they did agree to help," Ara said. It pleased Etta she referred to Gauleans as "them." She was a Belaen now.

Matteo scrubbed a hand across his face. "Yeah, well we don't exactly have a chance either."

"Etta does," Edmund said confidently.

Matteo scrunched his brow. "La Dame is too powerful."

Edmund crossed his arms over his chest. "Yeah, well you didn't see Etta blow the gate at the palace of Gaule to pieces."

Matteo paused. "Wait, really?"

Etta shrugged but Ara jumped in. "I saw the aftermath. We have a chance. I wouldn't have left my family if I thought we were just going to die against the walls of Dracon."

Matteo's mouth twisted to the side as he thought for a moment. "They're just like the Gaulean soldiers with no chance, but we do have an ally."

Etta looked at him in question.

"A contingent of Madran soldiers arrived last week."

That made no sense. "Why?"

"Because La Dame has an entire army of Madran mercenaries and the king wanted to even the scales. King Rhodipus of Madra may fear Bela and our power, but he also knows La Dame is the greater threat."

"Bring me their general."

Matteo bowed his head. "Of course."

While they waited, Etta got updates on the hunting parties and food stores they had accumulated for the winter. All building had ceased in her absence as salting meat and gathering edible plants became the highest priorities. She was thankful Matteo had been able to keep Bela moving forward.

Matteo returned a few minutes later with a stocky man. Muscles bulged in his arms as he swung them with each step.

"Your Majesty," Matteo began. "This is General Landon."

The general bowed. "It is a great pleasure, Queen Persinette."

"General." Etta smiled tiredly. "Thank you for coming. Your aid will be much appreciated. I only just now returned from Gaule. Tomorrow we will begin planning an attack on La Dame and I would appreciate your presence in those discussions."

"Of course," he responded, surprise coating the words. His eyes flicked to Matteo in question. "I was under the impression we'd be waiting for her to come to us."

"No more waiting, General. As soon as the snow clears in the mountains, we bring the fight to her."

She dismissed everyone, but Matteo hung back. Once they were alone, he pulled her into a hug.

She let out a yelp of surprise before hugging him back.

"I'm glad you've returned, cousin." He released her. "We need you here."

She nodded. "We managed to stall much of the persecution of our people in Gaule. Tomorrow, I'd like a count of those who've arrived. They will need to be provided for."

"Of course." He hesitated. "Etta... do you think it's wise to launch an attack on La Dame?"

"No. But we cannot continue to sit here and wait for her to destroy us."

"I have something that may help."

"Not tonight, Matteo. I'm exhausted."

"This isn't something I can speak of at the meeting tomorrow." He met her eyes seriously.

"Out with it." She waved him on.

"We intercepted a Draconian messenger." He paused. "We have a traitor in our midst."

Distrust was a funny thing. Once it entered your mind, it stuck there, tainting every thought. Etta sat atop her throne scanning the faces of those who'd come to see their returned queen. The traitor could be any of them.

They had suspicions, but it didn't stop her from imagining each of her people at La Dame's side.

Speeches done, she stood. They gave her a wide path through the room and Edmund met her at the end of it.

"I've been following her all morning," he said. "Nothing out of the ordinary."

Etta thought for a moment. "Make sure she knows of the battle plans once they're set."

The look he gave her was meant for a crazy person.

"Trust me, I have a plan. I think we can use this."

"I always trust you."

The familiar face showed up in the distance as she weaved through residences. Etta's magic rose and she let the anger color her features.

"Etta," Edmund snapped. "If you stare any harder, you're going to burn holes into Esme. Do you want her aware we suspect?"

Etta shrugged and removed the crown from her head, resisting the urge to throw it from the highest cliff. Wearing the false crown shrouded her in ire, but wear it she would until the day she wrestled the true Basile crown from La Dame's cold hands.

Had it been planned? Had Esme intentionally told her of her family's crown's whereabouts? Probably. But why? What was she orchestrating?

The Draconian healer disappeared into one of the residences and Etta walked toward the woods with Edmund not far behind.

The meeting was to take place among the trees, away from prying eyes and curious ears. That was the reason Etta gave her trusted people for the location she chose. In truth, if she was going to plan the end of everything, she'd need the strength the forest always gave her. It wasn't the Black Forest where she'd learned to be who she was, but if she closed her eyes, she could imagine it was. She could imagine her father stood by her side. That Alex was nearby in his palace.

And that her life was still on the linear path set by the curse.

Now it diverged, and she had to choose which way to go.

Matteo spotted them first, his face going red at the sight of Edmund.

"You two still haven't talked?" Etta whispered to Edmund.

He shook his head and cast his eyes to the ground.

"Coward." She turned to her cousin and raised her voice. "Good morning, cousin."

His smile was strained, which was very unlike him. Matteo normally wore a cool emotionless mask, but it had cracked and she enjoyed seeing the man behind it.

Tyson bounded up. Even leaving behind his mother and Amalie hadn't left him bereft of energy. He smiled and slipped his arm around her. "Are you rested, Etta?"

She nodded, hoping he didn't notice the bags under her eyes. Sleep had been elusive the night before as her magic buzzed under her skin. She'd lain in the dark putting every ounce of her effort into holding it back.

After the journey into Gaule, she needed rest, but they were out of time for that.

Landon stood and issued a low bow. There was a circle of logs in the clearing. A single stream of sunlight broke through the leaves right in the very center of the seating area.

Ara stayed seated but nodded her head in respect. Etta scanned each face, making sure everyone was present. A few of Bela's best warriors had been chosen by Matteo to sit in. These would be the generals of their untrained army.

In Etta's absence, Matteo had many of the Belaens begin practicing using their magic for the fight. Each fighter would be needed–except the children. They'd remain with a few guardians, ready to run if the battle went Dracon's way.

If Etta fell, her surviving people would sail to Madra.

Matteo explained all of this in a calm voice as if he'd been practicing his speech. When he fell quiet, Etta stepped in. "You've been planning in my absence. That's good. What do you have for battle plans?"

"Did you know," Matteo began, "There is one thing La Dame wants more than anything else?"

"Hmmm..." Etta sat down, a grin spreading across her face as she leaned forward. "Tell me more."

# CHAPTER 17

Heavy footsteps provided a persistent beat against cobblestone streets. Torches lit the frigid night air. The low drone of chanting voices echoed through Gaule.

Demands.

Protests.

From high up on the hill, Alex saw a growing gathering of villagers in the center of the village. Their cries rang in the air.

No longer were they only persecuting a single person or family. All known magic folk had left the kingdom. There'd been no reported instances of magic in weeks. But still, the people rebelled.

"Should we ride?" Anders asked, waiting for the command to overtake the village to restore order, peace. But was it peace when the army had to be stationed in the streets?

"No," Alex scanned the torch-wielding mob once more and turned his horse. "If they hurt anyone, stop it. Otherwise, let them have their protests."

He kicked his horse and cantered back to where the rest of his men were camped. His guards followed, forming up tighter around him than normal. They too were nervous.

It was the sixth village they'd been called to in the weeks since the wards were put in place and that didn't include the ones the army had already taken control of.

Gaule was quickly spinning out of control.

Back at camp, his mother was waiting. She'd insisted on accompanying them, saying she cared about their kingdom as much if not more than anyone else.

She sighed when she took in his haggard appearance.

"You look like you're about to fall off that horse of yours."

He offered her a tight smile. "He wouldn't let me fall."

She pursed her lips. "Who do you think he is..." She stopped herself.

Verite. His mother was going to say Verite. That damn horse would never let Etta fall. Alex absently rubbed the arm Vérité had bitten and slid from his horse. It was good Etta had a beast that took care of her like that.

But who was he kidding? Vérité would be no help against La Dame.

He brushed by his mother on his way to his tent but she followed him. "What's happening in the village?"

"The same thing that happened in the last one." He ducked into his tent. "And the one before that."

One of the guards outside spoke quietly to his mother. "They're calling for the king's head, your Majesty."

She entered the tent and her shoulders sank as she released a sigh. "They aren't aware of what you've done for them."

"Of course not," he snapped. "They don't know La Dame could have come at any moment and our army wouldn't stand a chance. I discarded everything... everything I believed in. Why? To keep them safe!" He put his hands on his head and breathed slowly. "Magic folk had every right to be in Gaule and I practically kicked them out to restore peace. And it didn't even work. I fed them to that wretched woman in Dracon."

"Maybe Etta will put wards between Bela and Dracon to keep them safe."

He shook his head. "She thinks it's a fight that needs to happen. If she... died, the wards would disappear. The only way to protect her kingdom is to fight."

A crease formed on his mother's forehead. "So, if she loses, we'll be without the wards once again."

"If she loses..." He sat down and hunched forward to put his head in his hands. "She won't."

"We don't know that. We must prepare."

"She won't lose," he yelled. "She can't. She's Etta. No one is better equipped to face La Dame than her."

"Oh, my boy." She brushed a hand down his back. "So much faith in someone else and so little in yourself."

"Your Majesty," Simon's worried voice sounded outside the tent.

Catrine and Alex both looked up at the same time and said, "What is it?" Alex met his mother's eyes, a wry grin forming on his lips. His mother was still a queen, and she was more queenly than he'd ever be kingly.

It was as if she was the one who was meant for this life, not him.

Alex stepped outside the tent to find Simon waiting. The big man glanced towards the dowager queen and then back to the king. "They're burning the village."

"Enough," Catrine snapped. "Dammit, get me my horse."

Simon and Alex just stared at her, but one of the guards brought her white speckled mare to the tent. She climbed into the saddle unaided with all the grace she was known for and sat tall atop the horse looking down on them.

"Are you coming?" she asked.

Both men scrambled to their own mounts and then took off toward the hill where Anders still waited for orders. Their guards slowed, but Catrine dug in her heels and flew past them. Alex had no choice but to follow. As they neared the village, he rested his hand against the hilt of his sword.

Catrine didn't slow as people scrambled to get out of their way. The village square was awash in light as the flames inched up the surrounding buildings. Alex made a move toward the torchbearers, but his mother shot him a look that stopped him in his tracks.

She nudged her horse forward, making an effortless jump onto a raised platform that was just big enough for the beast to turn around.

The crowd stopped, staring up at her.

She narrowed her eyes. "People of Gaule, why do you burn your own village?"

They began shouting out reasons and Alex shrank back into the shadows as his name was yelled. The guards stayed close to Catrine as she continued to speak.

"I see." She scratched her chin. "You're angry."

They yelled in agreement.

"Well, I am too. I'm angry because my people have broken a promise to me and to my son."

A disgruntled roar wound through the mob.

"You don't agree. Hmmmm. Is Alexandre Durand not your king?"

"He chose magic over his own," someone yelled.

"Ah, I understand. Your king believes in a life free of persecution. I see the problem. That's really a horrible thing, isn't it? To have freedom?" When the yells quieted, she continued. "We've all heard the stories of La Dame and the danger she poses. Did you know that it is now magic that keeps you safe from her? Yes, magic folk protected us just as we shoved them out of their homes to go face a danger greater than we can imagine." She raised her hand, palm up and curled it into a fist.

"I love Gaule. I love my people. And so does your king."

Her horse leaped down from the platform and the people parted for her to walk through the crowd.

Alex watched her in wonder. When his father was alive, his mother's job was to plan banquets and have tea with noblewomen of the realm. To raise the royal children.

Had he ever seen what she could be?

No. Alex knew with sudden certainty that he hadn't. If he had, he would have kept her locked away for fear of the people loving her.

The guards stayed until the mob formed a bucket chain to put out the fires. It was over for now.

Back at camp, Alex dismounted and approached his mother. "You played them."

"Guilt is a motivator, Alexandre. I only had to make sure they were aware we belonged to them. We are Gauleans just as they are."

He took her hand and bowed his head over it.

Soon after, Catrine returned to the palace, but Alex moved on to the next village where rebellion brewed. He attempted a speech, trying to emulate his mother. At least the food they threw was soft. It clung to his hair but didn't hurt.

He didn't attempt a peaceful resolution in the next village. Exhausted and frustrated, he sent in the army. The villagers tried to fight back, but they were quickly disarmed and rounded up.

He was done playing nice.

Carts were found and loaded with their prisoners. If the people weren't going to listen to reason, maybe they'd listen to force.

It took two days to reach the palace once more. Repairs on the gates were going well, but a large hole still opened into the castle. Camille greeted him at the inner gates, hands on hips as she glared at the carts behind him.

"Really, Alexandre? How do you expect to feed this many prisoners when three-quarters of the farms in Gaule are refusing to send the palace any food?"

"We'll manage."

She huffed. "And you think this'll improve your relations with the people?"

"I no longer care about their love." He shouldered past her. "Only their obedience."

"Spoken just like Father," she said at his back.

"The people didn't rebel against father."

Camille chased after him, her cane slamming against the ground with each step. "That's what you want? To be just like him? You hated father. Everything he did..."

Alex turned, almost colliding with his sister. "I don't know what else to do. My kingdom is falling apart out there. It's not a long leap from rebellion to civil war."

Her mouth rounded, and she stepped back.

He met the captain of the palace guard and gestured back toward the gate. "Have your men get those people to the dungeon."

Reproof burned in the captain's eyes, but he did as he was told.

Alex shrugged off his cloak and draped it over his arm as he marched inside in search of a hot bath and a cold ale.

He stopped a servant who was rushing down the hall. "Get someone to bring hot water to my rooms." The servant bowed and scurried away.

Weeks of travel dust coated his skin. They'd bathed in streams, but only for as long as they could stand the cold. He wasn't bred to be a soldier, spending nights on the hard ground.

He passed by a room with music drifting out the door. Three women in overly embellished dresses practiced their court dances. They were beautiful, he supposed. Flawless skin. Tiny waists. All the grace of women at court.

But he didn't want grace. He wanted someone with fire. Someone who would push him with fingers roughened from time spent with a sword. Someone whose hair was not brushed to perfection but twisted back so as not to get in the way.

It was practical after all.

Even through the fog of exhaustion, his lips turned up at the image of Etta dancing with these women. She'd danced with him once before and seemed entirely out of place.

A woman with fiery red hair and painted lips caught his eye and smiled coyly as she spun. When she turned toward him once again, she crooked one long finger, beckoning him forward.

There was a time when he would have gone willingly.

He'd been the prince who loved a good party and women most of all.

He turned away with a shake of his head. Now he was a king with his own people in the dungeons and no desire to sit on his throne.

That was the biggest problem, wasn't it?

The people called for his crown and he wanted to give it to them.

He rubbed the back of his neck and walked toward his rooms without further interruption. Four servant boys arrived carrying barrels of steaming water. They poured them into the tub and left. A maid entered with a tray of food but he only had eyes for the pitcher that sat in the center. Once she was gone, he poured a mug of ale and took a long drink before setting it down.

Unbuttoning the collar of his shirt, he reached behind him and pulled it over his head, his muscles crying out in protest. As his hands moved to the waist of his pants, the door crashed open behind him.

He turned around.

"Mother," he said. "What..." He stopped himself when he noticed her knuckles turning white as she gripped the doorway. Her entire body shook.

"Alexandre Durand," she growled. "You're a stupid boy."

He drew himself up, placing a palm on his bare chest. "I am the king."

"And my son." She stepped forward and pushed the door shut. "I can call you whatever the hell I want when you arrest Gauleans and throw them into our dungeons. I thought I bred the cruel out of you by keeping you from spending too much time with your father, but I was wrong."

"Mother–"

"No, you listen to me, boy. You messed up. Fix it."

"How?" he asked, stepping back to sit on the edge of his bed. "How am I supposed to heal this kingdom?"

She opened her mouth to speak and then shut it again.

"I. Can't. Mother. Maybe Gaule will never be at peace while they have a king they despise."

"They despised your father."

Alex grunted. "No, they feared him, but they never hated him. He kept them safe from magic. They think I betrayed them for it."

She sighed. "Alexandre, I don't know what to tell you. But you can start by not making it worse. Let those people go back to their families."

He blew out a breath and nodded.

"Good." She stepped forward and patted his cheek. "I'll inform the guard for you. You stay here and bathe. You reek." She scrunched up her nose and turned to leave.

"Mother." He paused. "I'm sorry."

"Never be sorry for the actions you take to protect your people, Alexandre. They may not always be right, but your heart always will be."

When she was gone, he removed the rest of his clothes and sank beneath the warm water. But like everything in life, it too eventually turned cold, and he had to leave it behind.

# CHAPTER 18

The guards released the people from the dungeons and escorted them back to their village. Alex did not accompany them. Instead, he rode into the village near the castle gates.

The streets were deserted. Faces appeared at windows and promptly disappeared. Word of the army's intrusion into other villages had stretched across the kingdom.

When his father was king, he'd send the army into a village to force people from their homes in advance of the king's arrival. They'd have to wave and cheer as if they had not a care in the world.

Eventually, the people would come out willingly–after the purge. They were grateful for the king's removal of magic folk.

Alex had done the same thing, and yet they now cursed his name.

As he rode through the empty streets to the place where he was attacked the year before, he felt the hair rise on the back of his neck. Someone was watching them. His eyes darted around but the only other people present were his own guards.

Alex stopped and dismounted. This spot was where he'd fought with Etta and Edmund. He lifted his eyes to the healer's shop. A new sign hung over the door. The destruction of parts of the village had been cleared away and shops rebuilt on his orders.

As a boy, he'd spent a lot of time running through the streets with Etta.

But now the place seemed foreign to him.

"Alex." The voice was faint. He twisted around, looking for the source even as his mind recognized the soft quality sliding over him.

"Ara," he breathed.

"What, your Majesty?" Simon asked.

Alex held up a finger, listening.

"We need you," Ara said. "Etta will kill me for contacting you, but in two weeks' time, we march on Dracon. Etta isn't herself. Something is inside of her. Her plans... Alex, they're crazy. I hope you can hear me right now. I'm not sure if my magic is working at this distance, but I think she's losing herself. If she's going to survive this..." The words paused. "You're the one person who can keep her from letting her recklessness get her killed."

Ara continued, but Alex didn't hear it as his guards started shouting. "Get down, your Majesty." He was thrown to the ground as one of his guards tackled him and went still.

Simon took off running as the rest of the guards positioned themselves around their king. Alex couldn't see what was happening but the crash of swords rang out. The fight didn't take long and then Simon was running back toward them.

Alex pushed the man off him, but his guard didn't get up. He turned him over and sucked in a breath when he found the knife embedded in the man's back. His face was frozen in shock. Alex bowed his head and slid the dead man's eyes closed.

"We need to get you out of here, your Majesty," Simon said, sliding his sword back into the sheath.

Alex pushed to his feet. "That knife was meant for me."

"We'll make sure Riley's family is taken care of."

Riley. He hadn't even known the man's name. His body hummed with nervous energy as the shock wore off and adrenaline took over.

"Your Majesty," Simon urged. "I took care of the attacker, but there could be more."

There weren't. The attacker seemed to be working alone, so they cantered away from the village and the bodies they left behind.

Alex practically fell from his horse and stumbled back. Bile rose in his throat and he put a hand on the stable wall as the contents of his stomach emptied onto the ground below him.

"Your Majesty." A delicate hand offered him a handkerchief to wipe his mouth, and he looked up into the face of Duchess Moreau.

He took her pity, wiped his face, and stood. "I was almost..."

Simon appeared. "Your Majesty, you should go inside and rest. You're in shock." He turned his gaze on the duchess. "I'll alert the palace guards. The king was attacked. We'll increase his guard tonight."

"Thank you, Simon."

He bowed his head and hurried away.

"Alexandre." She gripped his elbow. "Come with me. You've been in battle before. An attack on your life is not the only thing on your mind."

He'd almost forgotten about Ara's message and how shaken he'd been even before the attack began.

Etta needed him, but his kingdom was on the brink of civil war because of the aid he offered magic folk. He couldn't go to her, could he?

He followed the duchess silently. She'd existed in her own world in the weeks since the wards were put into place. He'd expected her to return home as he'd ordered. The villages on the Moreau land were suffering in the wake of the exodus of the magic folk. They'd been a large part of the population on her lands and now there was a shortage of workers. The Moreau forces that marched with him to retake the palace lost many men and women to Bela as well.

But she hadn't left, claiming a duty to the crown. She sat at the head of his council and he was grateful for her steady presence.

She led him into her suite of rooms and pointed toward the couch. He ran a hand through his dark hair and sat. She walked over to a table and a minute later was pressing a cup into his hands.

He sighed and tilted it against his lips, expecting wine or even ale. When something completely different touched his tongue, he sputtered.

Duchess Moreau's face creased as a fond smile flitted across it.

"Water?" He asked skeptically. "I almost have my life taken from me. One of my men is dead. And you give me water?"

One brow arched. "You don't need a drink, your Majesty. I think you've had enough of those lately." When he started to protest, she went on. "Why else would you arrest wagons full of people in one of your own villages. The king I know would only do something so completely idiotic with a strong influencer in his system."

"I..." He sat forward to argue, but the air deflated from his lungs. "I deserved that."

"That and more, but it is not for me to chastise you."

"Actually." He rubbed his chin. "It kind of is. You're the head of the king's council. When I was ill, many of the crown's powers were transferred to you and those who sit on the council with you." He leaned back. "Essentially, I am not ruling this kingdom alone anymore because we never formally returned those powers. The proclamation has been drawn up for a reversal, but the time hasn't been right."

She narrowed her eyes, watching him. Duchess Moreau was a shrewd woman. It hadn't escaped her that the council still held more power than they had at any time since Alexandre's grandfather was king.

Their eyes met in silent standoff, each only imagining what the other was thinking.

"Your Majesty," she said.

"Duchess," he replied.

"What do you want?"

"A king's power should never be absolute," he said finally.

"No, it should not."

"My father's was, and that is how the purge happened. Never again."

"We can prevent such an occurrence."

He nodded.

"Are you sure you know what these powers mean?" she asked. "The capabilities the council will have?"

There was something lying beneath her words, but he couldn't decipher the meaning so he only nodded and sipped his water.

Her shoulders relaxed, and she poured a cup from a second pitcher. Reaching out, she took his water and passed him the new drink. He tasted it and laughed. Wine.

"Now," she said as she took a seat. "Tell me what happened today."

He didn't hold anything back as he described the empty streets. When he got to the message from Ara, he scrutinized her face. She gave nothing away, and he moved on to the attack.

When he was finished, she crossed her ankles and busied herself fanning out the skirt of her dress.

"Why does Ara think Etta needs you?"

"I'm not..." Before finishing his words, he realized they weren't true. It hadn't hit him before, why Ara was worried, but Etta had already given him all the answers he needed. "Her magic." He swallowed another gulp of wine and set the cup aside. "Before she left, she told me it was trying to control her. I saw it with my own eyes. Anger. Hatred." His brow furrowed, and he shook his head as he remembered the first time he'd seen it after she got the powers.

She'd fought La Dame, and he'd almost died. She'd told him to leave and never return. He hadn't pieced that together until this very moment. Everything. All of it. Each time she'd pushed him away since the curse was broken, it had been the magic pushing him away. And he'd let it.

He closed his eyes. "They're losing her." It was the only explanation for Ara disobeying Etta and contacting him. "She's losing herself."

"What are you going to do about it?"

The next words killed him to say. "Nothing." He brushed his hands down his embroidered jacket. "I am a king and my first responsibility must be to my people."

Duchess Moreau's lips drew down into a frown. "If Etta is lost, everything else could be as well. Even for Gaule."

###

The guards refused to let Alex out of the castle. They were on orders from the council. Alex caught Duke Caron's eye. They were already exercising some of their newfound power. Now that they knew the king was not planning a reversal of the powers, there was so much they could accomplish together.

Caron's sons had already returned to the Caron estate and would take control of it with the Duke and Camille moving full time to the palace. Alex would never admit it to her, but he was glad his sister wasn't leaving. It made him feel like Ty was close as well, like their family wasn't so distant from each other.

The council consisted of six members, each from noble families. They stood as Alex rushed into the council chambers.

"Good morning," he said, trying to keep them from noticing just how tired their leader was. It had been another night of worrying for Etta and everyone in Bela.

"Good morning, your Majesty," Duchess Moreau said. "Are you ready to begin?"

He nodded. "We have much to discuss today. General Anders reports more protests and the burning of another village. We're running out of options here. It may be time for army intervention."

Duchess Moreau's piercing eyes latched on to him. "And what are they rebelling against this time?" She crossed her arms, waiting for an answer.

Alex sighed. "Everything."

The duchess stood and moved to the front of the room to face her fellow council members. "No, your Majesty. They were protesting their king."

He scratched the side of his face. "Does this have a purpose? What do you want me to say?"

"We want you to take responsibility for destroying Gaule."

It was as if the air in the room had been sucked out. Every eye turned to the duchess. Jaws fell open.

"Rae," Catrine warned. "That's enough."

Alex followed the locked gazes of his mother and the duchess as they held a silent conversation. Was this what happened when the council actually had power? Was this why his father had disbanded them?

"I assure you, Duchess," he began. "I am doing everything possible to heal our kingdom."

Duchess Moreau tore her eyes from the dowager queen and rounded on him. "Does that include arresting those who've done nothing but voice their discontent? You got us into this mess with your rushed policy changes on magic folk. A king cannot just follow his every desire..." Her eyes met his. "Simply because he fell in love."

"I–"

"What about receiving magical messages without informing your council?" she asked.

His hands shook at his sides. How dare she use what he told her in confidence against him now? Duke Caron leaned forward.

"Ara?" he asked hopefully.

"It doesn't matter who it was," the duchess snapped as she pointed one long finger at Alex. "This man is not fit to be king. Even if he were, Gaule will not be at peace while the crown sits on his head."

Alex had no words.

Betrayal burned through him. "You can't take my throne. I am the rightful heir."

Her icy gaze flew over the rest of the council, her face set in grim determination. "Actually, your Majesty, we can."

She gestured to a guard who stood by the wall. He opened the door, and a servant walked in, handed a rolled parchment to the duchess, and left.

She unrolled it slowly.

"I hold in my hand a declaration of transfer, signed by all members of this council save one." Her eyes flicked to Catrine who had a disturbed grimace on her face.

The moment rushed by, happening too quickly for Alex to fully grasp it. They were taking his throne.

And he knew, this was the reason his father stripped them of power. They could have destroyed him.

One of the few allies he thought he'd had was destroying the only thing he'd ever wanted in life.

But even that was a glorious lie. He'd never wanted it; he'd just had no other choice.

It didn't change the facts though. Gaule was his.

"You've been planning this," he rasped. "Since the day I was attacked. You convinced each member of my council..."

"I am sorry, your Majesty, but we do what we must for the good of the people." She turned to Catrine once more. "We need one final signature."

Her sad eyes found her son, glassing over as she considered her decision. Without taking her pained gaze from his, she picked up the pen to sign the transfer and Alex could only watch as even his mother stole his kingdom out from under him.

"It is done," the duchess said, rolling the proclamation and tying it with a ribbon. "Alexandre." No title, just his name. "You are no longer part of this council. I'm afraid I must ask you to leave."

A guard appeared at his side as if he'd protest, but he couldn't think clearly enough for that. He stood frozen for a moment.

"You can't to this." His words sounded hollow as if they had no meaning. "I am the king. Gaule is my birthright."

The duchess' expression softened. "Gaule will always be yours, Alexandre, to love and to protect. But it is now ours to rule. There is a grander purpose for you, I'm afraid." She nodded to the guard.

A firm hand gripped his arm, leading him into the hall as the door shut with a definitive slam. It was gone. His purpose. His duty. Everything.

He started toward the courtyard, disbelief clouding his mind. None of it felt real. One meeting and everything he'd worked his life for was finished.

If only Father could see him now. He'd know he'd been right. Alex had failed. No guards followed him. Why would they? He was no longer king. Instead, he was simply a prince. He sucked in a breath as his slow steps brought him to the north tower. Amalie and Camille were sitting atop the wall and they spotted him before he could back away.

"Are you coming up or what?" Camille asked.

He sighed and climbed the steps before dropping down beside them.

"Alex, what's wrong?" Amalie touched his arm lightly.

He closed his eyes, a single tear escaping. He'd done such a good job holding it together, but now as they looked to him for answers, all the emotion broke free.

"They took it," he said softly.

"Took what?" Camille asked.

"My crown." The words pierced his heart. How could this happen? How could he lose the one thing he'd been born for? "Duchess Moreau convinced them. They removed me from the throne."

"They can't do that!"

"They can, sister. And your husband was part of it."

"I'll talk to him. Alex, you're the king. No one else. It can only be you. Who is going to rule if not the first-born Durand? It has to be a Durand and I refuse."

He lifted his shoulders in a shrug. "It's over. There's nothing you can do."

"There's–" Amalie cut her off.

"I'm sorry."

Alex grunted.

Silence fell over the three of them like a blanket.

"You're going to leave me too, aren't you?" Camille asked in resignation. "Wait, don't even answer that because I know what you're going to say and it'll be wrong."

"Camille, I–"

Camille started to laugh and Alex couldn't remember the last time he'd heard that sound coming from her. Confusion mixed with amusement in his eyes as she clutched her stomach.

"I think she's finally lost it," Amalie whispered.

When Camille calmed enough to speak, her eyes were swimming. "You never did want to be king. All those years, I resented you for being father's heir when you didn't even want it." She breathed out slowly, one hand still gripping her side. "But then I saw what it did to you."

"What it did to me?"

"Yes, Alexandre. This role that was thrust upon you. Gone was the easy smile I'd always been envious of and the obvious joy. The crown weighed on your head like chains around your neck." She shook her head. "My jealousy turned into pity... and a bit of respect."

"Just a bit?"

She held up two fingers close together. "This much." A smile softened her harsh face. "I didn't want it anymore after that. How did Gaule end up with two heirs who don't want the title and a third who was no heir at all?"

Amalie chewed on her lip at the mention of Tyson. They should have seen it all along. Ty was the best of them, too good to have been fathered by the man who led Gaule into the purge.

"But, Alexandre." She leaned across Amalie to look him directly in the eye. "You're free." The sun reflected off her irises, making them glow as they held steady with his own. "The only question left is what are you going to do with this freedom?"

Amalie didn't wait for him to respond to his sister before she jumped in. "I'm coming with you."

"What?" he asked.

"To Bela. I assume that's where you're going."

"Um..."

"She's right, brother," Camille said. "We've all heard about Ara's message."

"What?" He sighed. It shouldn't surprise him that the news had wound through the palace. If Duchess Moreau was planning to denounce him, she'd have wanted to put rumors into play. Only, this time they weren't rumors.

"I don't like Etta," Camille stated bluntly.

Amalie rolled her eyes. "Here we go."

"No, hear me out. I don't like her. I think magic is dangerous still. BUT, there are things far more dangerous than Persinette Basile. Gaule cannot help Bela in this fight. We'd stand no chance." She scanned her brother's face. "You, Alexandre, no longer represent all of Gaule. Perhaps it's time you go fight for something greater than a throne you never wanted. You and Etta are connected. You're probably the one person who can help her in this."

"As long as I get to come." Amalie crossed her arms over her chest. "If you get to fight for Etta, I can fight for Ty. Plus, I'm probably better with a sword than you, anyway."

Camille grinned over the top of Amalie's head. "She's got you there, brother. You're shit with a sword."

He smiled. "Thank you, Camille."

"For the insult?"

"No, for everything."

He stood and pulled his sister to her feet, slipping her cane back into her hand. Looking over his shoulder, he caught the determination in Amalie's eyes.

"Fine," he said to her. "We leave at first light."

She nodded once, trying to conceal the satisfied smile on her lips as she broke off from them to head for her rooms.

Alex and Camille walked in silence toward the royal family wing and found Simon outside Alex's rooms.

Alex knew what that meant. He pushed inside to find his mother waiting. She paced the length of the room nervously, stopping in her tracks when she noticed her son and daughter. Tears streamed down her face.

The door shut and Duchess Moreau appeared behind them.

Alex held back the growl that tried to work its way up his throat for the woman who had just usurped his throne.

Instead, he cleared his throat, not giving any of them time to speak. "I am going to inform you of a decision that you now have no say over. Without a crown on my head, the council does not decide my movements inside Gaule... or across the border." His voice was cold as he tried to keep the emotion from it.

"This palace has always been my home, but it is no longer where my path lies. Tomorrow, I will leave for Dracon. Any who will join me are welcome." He nodded toward the duchess. "You may go. We have no need of each other any longer."

She didn't move. "Alexandre." There was no sadness or regret in her voice, only... hope? "We have named a replacement and will hold the coronation in three weeks' time once the villages and estates across the realm have been informed as to what has occurred this day."

"How could you possibly have named a new heir? Gaulean law states it must be of the royal family. Tyson is gone. Camille would refuse you. You have already betrayed me."

A moment of silence stretched into two and it was his mother who spoke next. "There is yet one person who wants to heal Gaule."

Why hadn't he seen it? It was so simple. She'd been able to quiet the mob with a single speech. The people loved her in a way they'd never loved him. If he hadn't been so determined to hold on to his crown, he'd have given it to her himself.

"Queen Catrine," he whispered, raising his eyes to meet his mother's. "Was that the plan all along?"

"No," she gasped. "Of course not."

Camille's hand slid into his and she squeezed.

"Alexandre." Duchess Moreau clasped her hands in front of her. "I am sorry it had to happen this way, but there would never be peace with you as a king. You said it yourself." She walked toward him, her dark hair swinging down her back. "You must go. If Ara says you are needed, I believe her. For all of us, you have to leave. Your place is there."

Realization crashed into him and he stepped back. "You did all of this just so I would join the battle against La Dame?"

"These are dark times, Alexandre." She pursed her lips. "There is a village near my estate where you will find some who will join you in your journey into Dracon to join the fight. I wish you well. Tell Persinette that she holds all of our lives in her hands."

With those words, she left. Catrine rushed to her children and pulled them both against her. The betrayal Alex felt before now extinguished slightly, leaving only a few lingering doubts. They'd done what was best for both Gaule and Bela. At least, he hoped they did.

"I'm sorry," his mother whispered.

He leaned back so he could look into her face and brushed aside her tears. "You're going to give this kingdom a peace they've never known, mother."

She smiled. "Thank you for saying that."

Camille sniffled and Alex laughed. "Are you crying, Camille?"

"Shut up," she groaned.

"I just don't think I've seen you cry since we were kids."

"I have something in my eye."

"Yeah, those are called tears."

Catrine swatted the back of his head. "Alexandre, stop teasing your sister. She's just worried about you."

Camille groaned again. "Mother."

"What? When someone in your family is about to leave the kingdom to go fight against a woman who is more powerful than pretty much the rest of the world put together, I think you're allowed to worry."

"You're my mother," Alex said. "Aren't you supposed to give me more confidence?"

"No." She snorted and slapped a hand over her mouth in embarrassment. "I'm supposed to let you know that we love you."

He hugged her again and this time, when he released her, he knew he was doing the right thing. It no longer felt like something had been taken from him. Instead, he'd gained it all. Everything. A different future than he'd ever expected. A chance to fight for what he believed in.

Etta.

She needed him.

*I'm coming.* He sent the thought into the atmosphere as he prepared for a new kind of journey, a new kind of battle.

*Don't give up. I'll be there.*

# CHAPTER 19

Ice encased Dracon. Or, it would be more accurate to say ice encased the walls surrounding the dark kingdom. The black gates rose before the Belaen army, spanning the length of the pass between two mountains. Fog swirled through the valley as Etta nudged Vérité forward. The cobbled-together army of Bela waited behind her.

They'd never been in battle. For most of their lives, they hadn't even been able to use their magic. Now, she was asking them to wield it like a weapon.

Etta let her hand drift to the sword hanging at her waist, getting more comfort from that than the power in her blood. She'd spent more of her life practicing with sword or pole than with magic. It would always center her. The weight of the blade. The memories of it slicing through her enemies.

"How are we supposed to get past those?" Tyson asked, gesturing to the gates.

Edmund met Etta's eyes. "We're not."

"Oh."

Etta jerked Vérité around and faced her people without a word. A crown sat atop her head, but it didn't belong to her, and it was time the true crown returned to Bela.

"Make camp," she ordered brusquely before sliding down from Vérité's back.

Landon approached tentatively.

"General," Etta acknowledged with barely a nod.

"Your Majesty." He lowered his head.

"Have your men prepare a watch."

"I'm a little unsure of this battle plan. In Madra, we believe in striking first. He who catches the others unawares will win the day."

Etta studied the older man. He'd seen many battles from what she'd been told. The Madran forces told her people tales of their kingdom's constant wars. But he'd never faced magic.

"Tell me, general, do you truly think La Dame doesn't already know we're here? That she hasn't known we've been coming since the day we left Bela?"

His brow furrowed, deepening the lines on his face.

"I didn't think so." Her eyes drifted back toward the gates. "No. We will wait. She will let us enter through this very gate."

His jaw clenched. "And it will surely be a trap."

"Well, I am the queen. I will decide which traps we fall into."

"You're insane."

"Probably, but I also understand what she wants and I plan to give it to her."

"What does she want?"

"Me."

Someone tried to take Vérité away to feed him. "I'll take care of him," Etta snapped.

"But, your Majesty, that's what I'm here for," a young boy stammered.

"I said I'd handle him."

The boy ran off. She didn't like to be away from Vérité on a night such as this. It might very well be her final night.

She didn't need to take Vérité's reins. He followed her through the mess of people setting up tents and stoking fires. There was no point in trying to hide their presence.

Once Vérité finished grazing, she left him near her tent. Edmund fell into step beside her and she wondered how long he'd been following her.

"I don't like the silence coming from the wall," he said. "There should be lines of archers atop them. I still don't like your plan. She may not do as we anticipated?"

"No, Edmund, La Dame has a fatal flaw."

Behind those walls should be an army of Madran mercenaries, every Draconian with magic, and the most powerful sorcerer in the world.

Etta didn't expect they'd beat a full army, but they didn't need to. Everything had been orchestrated to get her close to La Dame to end this once and for all.

La Dame's fatal flaw? She would sacrifice every person in Dracon for a chance at her revenge. Killing Etta would mean ending the direct line of the Belaen king, the very source of the Basile power. If she took Tyson and Matteo out as well, the entire Basile line would be no more.

Her single-mindedness in her desires made her predictable. Or, at least Etta hoped it did.

The other possibility was as Esme said—that La Dame wanted Etta and her power to stand beside her.

She wasn't sure which was more worrisome.

She entered the command tent to find Ara, Tyson, and Landon in a heated debate.

"The Madrans are the most skilled fighters here," Landon claimed. "We will not be pushed aside."

"But you don't have magic," Tyson argued. "That makes you vulnerable."

Ara's mind had gone in a different direction. "I'll challenge your best fighter and then we'll see who the most skilled is."

"Enough," Matteo snapped, his eyes finding Etta. "We will stick to the original battle plan."

"I don't like it," Landon grumbled.

Etta sat in an empty chair and leaned toward him. "No one said you have to like it. Look, my goal is to get to La Dame, but I will not sacrifice everyone else to do it. We stick with the original formation. Landon, you will position your men among mine. My most powerful magic wielders will take up their positions in an outside ring. I'm sorry, but if we face the Draconians right away, and without magic, we will be rendered useless."

Landon crossed his arms over his chest but leaned back and nodded. He'd been trained to take orders. Ara and Tyson had not.

"Ara," Etta began, preparing herself for an imminent argument. "I need you to remain with the small force I'm leaving outside the gates."

"You can't be serious." Ara scowled. "You need me."

"I do," Etta agreed. "But think with your magic right now, not your sword. We don't know what La Dame has in store for us and I need you to find somewhere where you can watch for any surprises to warn us."

Ara sagged back in defeat. "That's..." She sighed. "A good idea."

"I know." Etta turned to the rest of her most trusted people. "I..." She stopped, fiddling with the end of her braid. Her fingers inched up and she removed the false crown. She wouldn't enter Dracon wearing it.

"You don't have to give us the speech, Etta," Tyson said. "We all understand the stakes."

"She probably wouldn't be good at the death speech, anyway." Edmund laughed, and it sounded wrong in the tense atmosphere.

"Death speech?" Matteo raised an eyebrow, but the fond look he gave Edmund spoke of hidden depths.

"Yeah. She'd say something awkward like 'we probably won't all make it out of this'. Then there'd be silence because she never knows any comforting words to say and we'd all leave with the singular thought that we were probably going to die because the speech had never moved past that point."

"You would speak to your queen this way?" Landon asked. Etta almost laughed at him. His defense of her was admirable, but he didn't understand Edmund.

So instead, she fixed Edmund with an unblinking stare. He met her eyes.

"You're an ass," she said finally. "I'm not that bad at speeches."

He draped an arm over her shoulder. "Trust me, I just saved us all. When you speak to the army in the morning, make sure you leave out the doom and gloom we love you for."

She scowled, and he laughed. How did he take everything so lightly? She envied that about him.

"You have a bit of an emotional streak," he went on.

Etta pushed him away. She'd never told anyone other than Alex how the Basile power tore her up on the inside, infusing anger into every thought and action. If she did, they wouldn't fear her, but they'd fear for her. They'd try to prevent her from everything she'd planned.

She'd spent so much effort learning to gain control over the magic, but that wasn't how she'd beat La Dame. She'd win by ceding her will. By giving in. By letting it overpower her and unleashing its wrath.

But none of them knew that. They might be going into battle against the Draconian forces, but when the real war began, she'd be utterly alone.

She left them in search of her own tent. A bedroll sat inside and not much else. Bela didn't have a lot of the luxuries of Gaule so even the queen must make do. She didn't mind though.

She left behind the emptiness of her tent and found Vérité outside. As she closed her eyes, she ran a hand along his soft mane. "Remember when it was just you and me, boy?"

He snorted as if he too recalled the wide-open forests and their time riding among the flowers. The only power she'd had then was magic that made plants grow.

"Would you go back?" she asked, leaning into him. "Me either. They've always needed a queen, needed a kingdom." Back then, Bela had been an empty land, the idea of a thriving kingdom that only existed in the minds of magic folk hiding in Gaule. "We may not make it out of there. Dammit! Stupid Edmund." His words ran through her mind. A death speech. She would not give a death speech.

Vérité nudged her as if agreeing with her assessment of Edmund. For the first time all night, Etta grinned. "You've always known he was an idiot, haven't you?"

She sat down and Vérité lowered himself beside her. "I'm going to need a miracle, Vérité. Are you ready to be a hero?" She wouldn't be there without the horse. He'd gotten her out of more than a few situations.

"Can I tell you a secret?" she asked. "I told Alex we wouldn't need them, but I wish I had him by my side."

He bared his teeth, and she laughed.

"You have no reason not to like him, you stubborn beast."

Another voice broke through Etta's one-sided conversation. "I used to think that was really weird."

Tyson sat on the other side of Vérité and stroked his back.

"Used to?" Etta asked.

"Yeah, now I understand you two."

"What do you mean?"

"I've never seen anyone with a relationship like yours. Vérité is your soul mate."

He said it so simply, but it wasn't simple at all. From the time she'd found the wild horse in the woods, there'd been a connection between them. He'd started following her and soon she'd attempted to ride him. Nothing had ever been so right as that first time she sat high on his back.

"Alex—"

"Is special to you," Tyson cut her off. "But that doesn't mean he has to be your soul mate. Most people fall in love, but few ever really find the one being who is so attuned to them it's like they're one person."

"How did you learn about this stuff?"

Tyson shrugged. "Amalie." His eyes pinched in sadness.

Etta reached across Vérité–her soul mate–and gripped her brother's hand. "I'm glad you're my brother."

She'd hated her father when she found out. Hated that it tarnished the memory of her mother. But she'd come to accept that some things couldn't be held on to.

Tyson grinned, flashing his teeth. "I love you, Etta. And Vérité. I love him too."

Before she responded, the massive gates shuddered and began to drift apart, turning outward as they did.

Etta jumped to her feet and started running toward the gates with Tyson following her. She stopped at the edge of camp to watch them open fully.

La Dame had set her trap.

Etta raised her eyes to the full moon hanging overhead and shook her head. "We aren't going in while it's still dark." She turned to Edmund. "I want a watch on guard until the sun rises. If anything comes out of those gates–even the tiniest bit of magic, I hear about it." To Landon, she said, "We need to rouse the camp. No eye closes while we sit at the mouth of Dracon."

He issued a sharp nod and left to wake his men. Ara went to prepare the Belaens.

Etta returned to her tent to don the armor that had been put there. She'd left her mail shirt behind, opting for the lighter leather armor she'd always worn when practicing with her father in the woods.

She didn't expect to need protection against swords as much as magic so the agility the leather gave her would prove a better defense.

Her armor firmly in place, she hooked the sword belt around her waist. After strapping a sheath to her leg, she slid a thin knife into it.

Edmund pushed the tent flap aside and stepped in. "The watch is set."

She nodded, her eyes sliding over his shining armor.

He stepped toward her, reaching around to pull the tight braid over her shoulder. "In Bela, we learned of your likeness to Queen Aurora, but we've both heard the stories of Rapunzel. Now that we know there is Draconian blood in your veins as well as Belaen blood, we have answers to all the questions we've been asking. It's funny, your father gave you all the answers you needed when he named you Persinette."

"The Draconian word for Rapunzel," she said softly. "How long have you known?"

"Esme told me about the translation and then I saw you heal Alex. That's how Draconian blood entered the Basile line. King Philip didn't kidnap her. She went willingly. She must have fallen in love with Phillip and Aurora's son—the first man to fall under the curse."

She ran a hand down her braid, stopping at the ribbon tying it together. She pulled it free, and it fluttered to the ground as Etta—Persinette untwisted her hair and let the waves fall down her back.

Edmund gave her an approving nod. "Use this. Let La Dame see who's coming for her."

"Yes." Etta nodded. "She's going to regret the day she raised her magic against my kingdom."

When the dawn came, the Belaens mounted their horses and Etta rode to the front. Esme waited for her. The Draconian healer was the only person they had who knew her way around La Dame's fortress under the mountain and Etta had a crown to find. Esme would lead her straight to La Dame. Etta had never been more sure of anything.

Edmund sat on her other side. "No death speech," he muttered.

This time, she grinned and raised her voice. "We are doing exactly what La Dame wants us to do. And she knows we will. It's a circle and we will go round and round guessing what the other will do. OR we end it. They are waiting for us. They are hidden, hoping to surprise us. But we are Belaens. We have spent generations being hunted and persecuted. Decades denied our rightful kingdom. La Dame destroyed Bela once, but we are stronger than our ancestors because we've had to be."

She stopped speaking and nodded to Ara who put her hand to her throat. Silken, spine-chilling words settled over them. "We're coming for you."

Etta wanted the Draconians to fear them. She nodded again.

"Are you ready?" Ara asked quietly, sending her words across the land.

Etta nudged Vérité forward, knowing her people would follow her every move. Her hawk-like eyes scanned the gates as she passed between them.

The town that lay on the other side had been carved into the very side of the mountain. Flat stone rooflines extended far into the mountains. They rode through what looked like a marketplace, but empty streets greeted them. No archers lined the roofs. No magic men appeared in the doors or windows, waiting for them to approach.

The farther in they walked, the more Etta expected attackers to descend on them.

"Where are they?" Tyson asked.

It was a miscalculation. Etta had been so sure of the trap La Dame would set. Roads stretched before them like spokes of a wheel, leading up into the mountains.

"The one on the left leads to the palace," Esme said.

Etta clenched her teeth, her magic wanting to lash out at the woman.

A crash sounded behind them as the gates shut abruptly, then silence.

Then she heard it, the rumble of hooves on stone.

"Form up," she screamed.

Landon and Edmund both started barking orders as they prepared for the onslaught. The first riders appeared. One man held his sword aloft and stood on the back of a galloping horse.

"It's the mercenaries," Landon said.

"Not the Draconians." Edmund shot her a sharp look.

"They're sacrifices." The horror struck Etta. "They just don't know it. They're a distraction." Why else would she send the mercenaries against magic folk to start the battle?

"Esme," Etta yelled. "We need to get to that palace."

The mercenaries met them in a clash of swords. Landon led his force against their own countrymen while the Belaens fended them off with their magic.

Etta jerked Vérité's reins. Mercenaries continued to pour down every road, save one. La Dame was calling Etta to her.

With one swift kick, Vérité cantered away from the battle ensuing behind them with Esme and her horse beside them.

The mountain drew closer, its black face serving as the front of the palace. "No guards?"

"Does La Dame need them?" Esme asked.

"Good point."

The doors stood open in invitation and Etta slid down from Vérité's back. "She's in there." She turned to the healer. "Where would the crown be held?"

"She has a treasure room."

Setting foot into the palace was like taking a walk in the darkness of La Dame's soul. Pillars of black onyx lined a grand entryway. Etta strode across the dark marble floor, a tiny gasp escaping her when she reached the painting at the end of the entryway. It was the same woman she'd seen in the palace of Bela and thought Aurora. But now she knew for certain she was looking into the face of someone else. "Rapunzel."

Had the man in the painting in Bela not been King Philip at all? Maybe his son?

"Why didn't you tell me?" Etta asked Esme. "She looks like me. I..."

"I thought you knew."

Etta backed away from the painting, shaking her head. She couldn't tear her gaze away from the woman with her crystal eyes and golden hair. She tried to breathe as her magic slid within her, cutting off any air. She clutched at her throat and she bent over. Control. Control. She forced out a breath and sucked in harshly, pushed the power down. Her throat loosened, but the rage remained.

She was going to raze this place to the ground.

"Take me to my crown," she bit out, knowing with sudden clarity wherever that crown lay, La Dame would appear as well.

Esme yanked on her arm and pulled her away from the painting to drag her down a long hall and around the corner. A stairwell of dark stone descended into the earth. Damp air greeted them as they took the steps slowly.

Torches hung along the walls, illuminating a massive cavern under the palace. Etta barely took in her surroundings before finding what she was looking for.

Each detail—down to the row of gems at the base—was so utterly familiar.

"Why did she keep it, Esme?" Etta whispered. The cavernous room demanded hushed tones of respect.

Glass cases on silver pedestals held La Dame's most prized possessions, but only one called to Etta. She yearned to fold her fingers around it and rest it against her hair. Hair she'd thought a remnant of Aurora's part in the Basile bloodline. Now she knew better.

"Because it belonged to her daughter," a familiar voice said, the sound of her boots on stone echoing off the arched ceilings.

Esme's eyes widened and Etta knew exactly what she'd see when she turned around. Maiya walked across the far end of the room and stopped.

The shock of seeing her old friend again—the girl who'd betrayed her—made Etta struggle to recall what she'd said. When she finally did, it all made sense. She'd had the thought in the back of her mind ever since she'd learned of her Draconian healing powers.

Maiya moved forward again. "Hello, mother."

Etta looked between them as Esme shot Maiya a warning glance. "You led me here," Etta accused the older woman.

"Just as you asked me to."

Etta clenched her jaw and glanced back at the crown. "I did. Everything we've done has brought us to this moment."

Maiya continued closing the distance between them. Her eyes flicked to her mother, and she frowned. In that moment, Etta knew her suspicions had been right. It had been too easy.

Nothing in life was coincidental. Esme had betrayed La Dame just when they needed a healer.

Because La Dame hadn't wanted her to realize her new powers included the Draconian ones.

She'd been right about her.

"She's been manipulating everything." Etta spoke to herself and for a moment, she would have sworn regret flashed through Maiya's eyes.

"Why are you here?" she asked Maiya.

Esme moved behind her daughter and put a hand on each of her shoulders.

Uncertainty crossed the younger girl's face.

"Etta," Esme said. "Come here."

Etta lurched forward as Esme's magic took hold but she held herself back.

"Persinette Basile," the woman boomed. "Obey."

"No," Etta growled through her resistance.

Esme's eyes narrowed. "Rapunzel."

"I. Am. Not. Rapunzel!" Power burst out of Etta in a flash of light. It was too fast for her to control. Esme and Maiya flew into the air as if they weighed nothing at all. They didn't crash to the ground, instead they hung, suspended midair, unconscious.

A slow clap seemed to come from every direction at once. Etta whipped her head around looking for the source, finally finding La Dame bathed in shadows. Had she been there the whole time? She snapped her fingers and light pushed the darkness away.

It was a face Etta had seen in her dreams, haunting her every thought.

La Dame waved a hand and the two unconscious women dropped to the ground. A cry lodged in Etta's throat as she saw Maiya's head loll to the side.

"Interesting," La Dame said.

Magic raged through Etta, knowing its target. She breathed heavily. "Another sacrifice." Just like the mercenary forces who'd been sent against the magic folk of Bela. A distraction.

"Hmmm." La Dame tapped her chin. "Sacrifice is an interesting word. It implies the girl was valuable to me. My dear Persinette, the only person of value to me is you."

She walked forward, her long silver dress dragging behind her. Etta backed away. "I'm nothing to you."

A smirk spread across La Dame's face. "Phillip said the same thing, but he was wrong. He was everything to me. I wanted to destroy him for stealing my darling Rapunzel."

"But he didn't steal her, did he?" Etta didn't know where the courage came from but the power swirled through her chest. "She went with him to escape you."

"No," La Dame roared.

"Rapunzel healed Aurora, woke her, and then chose not to return." Etta pulled her knife free and sliced it across her own forearm before La Dame could stop her. "She married their son. That's how I got this." She raised her arm and sent a bolt of warmth along her skin, watching as the wound closed before her eyes. After wiping the blood off on her pants, she raised her eyes once more. La Dame had moved beside Maiya.

"So young. So beautiful. She's not here as my sacrifice, Persinette." Dark eyes met hers. "She's yours."

"No!" Etta forced her magic to shoot straight for La Dame's heart.

The sorceress waved the power away.

Etta pulled her sword from the scabbard at her waist. Instinct. Everything her father had taught her. Fight first. Think second. No time for hesitation. She lunged forward into a sprint and jumped toward the raven-haired sorcerer, twisting her sword arm to bring it down at an angle. La Dame pushed a hand out in front of her, sending Etta sailing backward. She rolled as she landed and popped back up.

La Dame raised one brow. "I see Viktor's influence in you."

Etta ground her teeth. "Do not speak of my father. You knew nothing of him."

"My dear, I fear it is you who are gloriously misinformed. Viktor was a dear friend."

"You lie."

"Well, we all have our opinions, don't we? It saddened me to hear of his untimely demise."

Etta lurched forward, flinging her knife with every bit of strength she possessed.

La Dame laughed as it clattered to the ground. "So very Basile of you. Viktor always thought of conventional weapons before his magic as well. Though, he didn't possess the great Basile powers." She cocked her head mockingly. "You can't control them, can you?"

A crunch snapped her attention to Esme and Maiya who were stirring. Maiya scrambled out of the way, her doe eyes huge. Etta tried not to pity the scared girl who'd been dragged into her parents scheming, and for a moment it worked. Her magic found its target, and a flame rose, spreading toward the two women Etta once counted as friends.

Maiya screamed as the fire engulfed her mother's body and Etta felt nothing at all. She no longer had to direct the magic, it took control on its own.

La Dame's laughter slammed into Etta and it was only then she realized what she was doing. The flames extinguished immediately and Esme coughed.

"Yes," La Dame said, standing still among the shadows. She smoothed her hands calmly down over her black dress before settling her blazing eyes on Etta. "Good, Persinette. Give in to the darkness."

White-hot fury raced through Etta and it took everything she had to control the power it brought with it.

"You can sense it." La Dame grinned. "I know you can. The emotion. It feels good."

Magic expelled from every part of Etta, twisting around the room. Every glass case shattered at once, the shards lifting into the air.

Etta pointed them at La Dame and flicked her hand. They sped through the room, dropping with a clatter before reaching their intended target. One made it farther, scraping against La Dame's cheek before falling. She wiped at the tiny trickle of blood in surprise.

Etta's chest expanded rapidly. La Dame was right. She felt the power, and the intensity was exhilarating.

Fire raged in Etta's eyes.

"Feed it, Persinette. Let it take you over."

"I-I can't." Etta stumbled back. "No."

"You came to me for a reason. I've been waiting for you for a long time. Your father thought he could thwart me by marrying a woman with no power. He thought that would keep the curse at bay. But I own you. I've always owned you."

La Dame threw a force at her that sucked the air from her lungs. Her knees buckled and slammed into the stone floor beneath her. Anger. Hatred. It was all she had. All that had existed since the curse no longer filled her.

Blackness clouded her vision as a scream rose up around her. It sounded like her, but she was so very far away.

"Yes!" La Dame laughed.

"Etta, no!" Maiya yelled. She was cut off abruptly as La Dame forced her back against the wall.

Etta sent wave after wave of power toward La Dame and she fought each of them off easily. With every moment, the magic took more control. Etta faded into the background and Persinette was relentless.

Her golden hair glowed and whipped around her shoulders. When her blazing eyes met La Dame's, she sensed approval, respect even.

"This is what you've wanted," La Dame said. "Ever since the day these powers invaded your heart. They are who you are, who you're supposed to be. My Rapunzel."

"Rapunzel," Etta whispered, the name sounded wrong. She wasn't Rapunzel. Rapunzel had been courageous. She'd given up everything to escape this life. She'd never ceded control. No, Etta wasn't her. She was weak. The darkness crumbled everything beneath her until her feet no longer stood on solid ground.

She thrust her fist against the floor. Tiny shards of glass embedded themselves in her skin. She hit it again. The blood trickled between her fingers. On the third time, the ground rumbled as if she called her magic from the depths of the earth. The mountain that housed the palace shook. Pillars of stone fell around them.

"More," La Dame yelled. "Release it all."

Maiya screamed as she dodged falling stone, her dark curls coated in raining debris. "Etta, you're going to bury us."

She didn't care. All that mattered was tearing it down. Holes punched into her soul and she screamed as if it was ripping her apart. Her body couldn't hold it. The magic must be released. She raised up on her hands and knees as someone else ran into the room. "Etta!" Tyson yelled.

"No." She shook her head, unable to see anything but darkness. "No!"

"Etta stop," Maiya pleaded. "She's trying to drain your magic. To make the Basile power leave you! If you use too much of it, you won't get it back."

Tyson acted quickly, sending a tunnel of water straight for her, but La Dame blocked it. The force of his halted magic threw Tyson into Maiya and they crumpled to the ground.

La Dame laughed as Etta's power built. The dark queen jumped away from falling stone. "Come to me, Rapunzel. Together, we can hold the world."

She held out a hand.

Etta stood slowly and stepped forward. "I am not Rapunzel," she gritted out, forcing breath into her lungs. Her feet moved as if stuck in quicksand as it pulled her down, trying to take the words before she could say them. "I am not yours. My father was Viktor Basile. I am the rightful Belaen queen. You will not control me." La Dame brought up her hands to ward off Etta's magic with her own, but it was no use. The burst of light broke through her shield, striking La Dame in the center of her chest.

She stumbled back but remained upright. Etta advanced, her power begging to test itself against La Dame's again.

The Basile magic and La Dame's existed to balance each other. To make sure each always had an equal, an opponent. It was never meant to be on the same side.

The hatred that burned through Etta was strongest when staring into the eyes of her greatest enemy—the woman who'd destroyed her kingdom, her family.

"No more," Etta said, mostly to herself. Power twisted in the palms of her hands as she raised them in the air. It writhed and fought for supremacy, matching the darkness in her eyes.

She didn't notice Tyson and Maiya dragging Esme out of the way as her eyes were solely focused on her opponent who was now finding it hard to breathe. La Dame clutched at her throat, trying to break the magic.

But she couldn't. She knew it the moment Etta lifted her into the air. She'd pushed her too far, past the point of conversation, past the road that led to redemption.

The ancient Basile power that had seen kingdoms rise and fall and lain dormant for generations gathered within Etta's heart, pulling in all its strength.

She threw La Dame back against the wall with so much force, the mountain shook once more. Her lip curled up, and she hardened her eyes as the magic detonated like a bomb inside of her, ripping her soul to shreds before slamming into La Dame. It curled with her own power before light burst from her every orifice.

La Dame dropped to the ground, her face twisted in pain, and her body charred almost beyond recognition.

Power blasted from La Dame, latching onto Etta's. She wouldn't let it go.

Etta stared at her, the rage continuing to burn. She wanted to hurt them all. The ones who betrayed her. The ones who fought for La Dame. They would pay.

"Etta," Tyson called.

She turned. Her brother stood next to Maiya and a now upright Esme. Their ending would come with one flick of her hand. The desire to see their pain pierced what was left of her heart and she ran towards them. They didn't deserve her magic. She picked up her sword on the way and lunged, expecting blade to meet flesh.

Steel flashed in front of her face as Tyson blocked her thrust.

"Etta," he said. "Stop."

"You don't give me orders," she growled as she lunged for Maiya again. Maiya jumped away and metal clanged against metal as Tyson blocked her once again.

"This isn't you," he yelled. "Fight it. Fight the magic."

"The magic is me." Her voice shook with crazed intensity. "I am the Basile heir."

"Please." His eyes flicked between her and what remained of La Dame. "We need you, Etta. We're losing out there."

"Etta," a voice sounded around her. Ara. "There's another force moving in from the South. We can't hold our position here. Get us inside those walls."

Some sense of purpose returned to her. Maiya's fate had to wait. Sword in hand, she took off running. Along the palace halls, tables lay on end, chairs were strewn about, paintings had fallen from walls.

Everything was a blur as she tried to find her way. The past melted away until all that existed was the power. Where was she? Who was she? The magic took hold of the beat of her heart, her every breath. Pain sliced through her chest, the power tearing her up from the inside.

She couldn't stop.

It wanted to ravage.

Blackness swam before her eyes but she pushed on.

Outside those walls were people who deserved its wrath. They'd followed the woman who tried to keep the power from its rightful owner.

She paused at the entrance to the palace. The onyx pillars that had been so ominous before, now leaned, doing their best to hold up a falling roof. The earth shook again with the tremors of what her magic had done.

Wood cracked and her eyes snapped to the source. The portrait of Rapunzel had fallen from its place of honor, its cherry red frame broken. The woman in the painting stared at Etta through her own eyes.

"Rapunzel," Etta breathed, only slightly aware of Tyson's approach. Her father thought he was so clever, using a different language to name her for the first woman who defied La Dame—her own daughter.

Persinette was the last. The final. La Dame was no more. At that thought, Etta's power leaped inside of her and she turned her back on the girl they all wanted her to be.

She might have had the golden hair and the defiant eyes, but she was no Rapunzel.

Outside the palace, chaos reigned. The battle had closed in on them. Madrans faced off against mercenaries from their own kingdom. Belaen sorcerers fought those from Dracon. None of them knew La Dame was gone. She'd disappeared from this land without everything breaking apart and Etta had never felt more powerful because of it.

Before, her power had only been part of a whole, but the magic she'd taken from La Dame made it complete.

"Etta," Tyson said. "We need to get to the gatehouse." He pointed down the road that would lead to the structure containing the mechanism that opened the large gate. Etta shook her head. How did he expect her to follow him when there were so many enemies to be dealt with here?

She balled up her fist, letting the magic pool together before throwing it forward. Draconians, Belaens, and Madrans alike flew through the sky, blasted apart, leaving behind a gaping hole in the earth.

One side of Etta's mouth curled up, and she held her sword aloft as she charged toward a group of Draconians. They gave her everything they had, sending their magic her way, but she brushed each bit of power away. Nothing could stop her.

Pulling back her own power, she dove into the fight, only releasing it in pieces as she sliced through her enemies. Warm blood splattered onto her face and she laughed. A tall Draconian man with thick tattoos snaking down both arms charged at her. She held up one palm, and he stopped, clutching at his throat as she sucked every bit of air from his lungs.

His face contorted, and he fell to his knees. Other Draconians tried to help him and she fought them off while maintaining her hold.

The magic seeped deep into her mind, stealing everything from her except for her need to fight.

When his body stopped twitching, she raised her eyes to the horror-filled face of a battle-weary Balean soldier. Edmund. His name was Edmund. She tried to recall anything else about him but shook her head when she couldn't and tried to bull by him.

He blocked her path, putting a hand on her arm to hold her back.

"Etta," he said.

She flicked her eyes from his face to the hand on her arm, the magic goading her into doing something about it. One last shred of sanity reminded her Belaens weren't the enemy, but that was as far as it went. If they weren't her enemies, what were they? She didn't know. The confusion locked with the darkness swirling inside of her. Nothing. They were nothing.

A blast sounded behind them and Etta turned, ready to meet whoever sent rock raining down on them. She froze when her eyes met those of the woman she'd come to destroy.

La Dame's charred body healed itself, pink skin slowly smoothing over the burned surface. Soon, only her eyes spoke of fire.

Fear tried to intrude on Etta's mind but she pushed it away. There was no time to be afraid.

Edmund stepped up to her side as if he would be any help against the sorceress. The battle swirled around them. Grunts of pain. Clashes of steel. Bodies dropping to the ground. But none of it would make any difference. It didn't matter how many Draconians were killed if their sorcerer lived; how much blood was spilled if Etta lost.

"You have something that belongs to me," La Dame said, not a hint of emotion in her voice. She narrowed her eyes.

Etta breathed heavily, control unraveling in her chest.

"You feel it." La Dame cocked her head. "My magic fights with yours."

Pain sliced through Etta's chest and she doubled over.

"Etta," Edmund yelled.

La Dame took a step forward. "It's going to destroy you. That much power. You must release it all."

Etta sucked air through her teeth and shook her head. "I can't let it return to you."

"Shame. We could have done great things together."

Etta's ribs cracked as if being broken apart from the inside. She screamed and fell to her knees.

La Dame advanced with the eyes of a predator. She circled Etta but Edmund drew his sword, blocking her way. Etta's cry ripped through the air as the magic pulsed through her limbs, hitting every nerve along her bones. A soldier fell beside her, hitting the ground with a thud and going still.

La Dame flicked her eyes from Edmund's sword to Etta who struggled to rise. "You can't protect her, boy. Not when the thing she needs protection from is herself." She advanced.

Etta lifted her eyes as her stomach cramped and sweat beaded across her brow. A growl ripped from her throat. "No!"

Sympathy entered La Dame's gaze but Etta thought she imagined it. Why would the woman feel sorry for her? She wanted to destroy her. To recover the power squeezing around Etta's heart.

"You feel it." La Dame's lip curled. "The darkness. You want to give in to it. Your magic pulled mine in like two of the same kind, but they aren't the same at all, are they? Soon, what you took from me will overcome everything inside of you. Every light will be extinguished and you will finally understand."

A tear tracked down Etta's soot-covered face as she gave in to the agony breaking her. "Understand what?"

La Dame leaned down, her black eyes dangerous. "What it truly means to be me. I am not the villain in your story, Persinette, dear. You are."

The words sank into Etta, ringing truer than any before them. Was La Dame right? Etta shook her head, trying to let the buzzing of her magic drown out the battle cries around them. Soldiers died because of her. She'd brought them here. She'd been determined to break the curse and to destroy the woman who'd taken everything from her. But at what cost? She'd been right. La Dame knew they'd come. She knew Etta would surrender herself to the power, to the darkness.

She'd planned for it.

A smile tilted La Dame's lips. Whichever army defeated the other this day, the ancient sorceress thought she'd won.

But she was just a woman now. Only a Draconian with an ability to heal. Unless Etta released it, she no longer had the power to do as she wished; to finally take the last curse-bearer under her power.

Etta gritted her teeth, pushing a stab of pain away from her mind. "You," she breathed, her voice growing louder with each word. "Will. Not. Destroy." She rose to her feet, her magic curling in her palms. "Me."

She did as La Dame wished. She released it, but it wasn't La Dame's own power that struck the space between them. Basile magic, once trapped by La Dame's curse, struck her in the chest, burning through her. Light exploded from every orifice and a scream fractured everything the world knew to be true.

La Dame had been the most powerful woman there was. She'd terrorized people for centuries, trapping three entire kingdoms in the palm of her hand.

No longer.

Now there was Persinette.

Beside her, Edmund gasped as La Dame's body withered until only a cloud of ash remained. No more healing. No more magic.

Etta's magic snapped back into her chest, sending her stumbling back in shock. Was La Dame really gone.

"Etta, watch out!"

Seconds after Edmund's warning, the sun glinted off an oncoming blade. Etta ducked, rolling to the ground and retrieved a knife laying abandoned nearby. Her attacker swung his sword down and she lunged for his legs, slicing the blade across the armor gaps behind each knee.

The large man dropped his sword, pitching forward with a roar leaving his mouth. Etta scrambled out of the way as he fell where she'd been only moments before.

He wasn't dead, but Etta no longer cared. Her eyes returned to the place La Dame had disappeared from as her lungs struggled for breath. Her magic and La Dame's continued to battle within her, making her head feel as if it had cracked open.

"Get us through that gate!" The cry surrounded them, spreading through the air, blanketing them in the desperation of the small force they'd left outside Dracon. Ara's voice grew frantic, but Etta felt the girl's magic weakening.

Bela was being overwhelmed.

A horn blared from a distance.

Landon ran toward them, blood and grit dripping down his face. "That's a Madran horn," he panted, putting his hands on his knees and shaking his head.

"She kept a part of her mercenary army from the fight and now..." Edmund's mouth dropped open in horror.

Tyson joined them and finished the thought. "They're outside the gates." He covered his mouth with his hand. "Ara."

A low hum rumbled through Etta's chest and she gave one short shake of her head. "We aren't losing this fight."

They tried to follow her as she walked directly through the center of the battle, but she threw a magical barrier behind her to make them stay. In this, she must be alone.

The Belaen's were outmatched. These people barely had any training and had spent most of their lives trying to hide the fact their magic existed inside of them.

Hers no longer only existed. It lived. It grew. It pushed her to new limits.

It became her.

No one could touch her when she left the Belaen defenses to move directly among the Draconians. Every slash of a sword or blast of magic was met with bone-crushing resistance. She barely had to make a move. The magic flowed out of her effortlessly.

"Enough," she said to no one but herself.

A battle is loud. It's dirty and chaotic and everything Etta never wanted to see in her life. But once she'd seen it, it called to her.

Etta blocked out the call. She pushed away every crash of a weapon and the screams of the injured. The only thing that existed to her was the song of the magic in her veins; the pain of the war within her. She funneled the power down her arms and into her hands, her golden hair once again picking up the ethereal glow.

Her lips tilted up, but the concentration in her face was unmistakable. Closing her eyes, she let the darkness consume her. Inhaling deeply, she pushed the magic out of her, tunneling it down directly into the earth.

Her body vibrated with the energy and it felt good. When the earth began to shake and crack open, she didn't move. A deafening sound came from deep in the ground as her magic tore it apart.

She didn't open her eyes until something hard slammed into her from the side and she fell. Her eyes snapped open to find Edmund on top of her.

"Get off," she yelled.

He rolled sideways, a flash of pain crossing his weary face. It was only then that she saw the gash in his stomach.

"You're hurt," she accused. Was she supposed to care? She remembered time spent with the man, but the magic blocked her from feeling anything at all, yet something told her to pause and make sure he wasn't going to die.

"You trying to get yourself killed?" He pressed a hand to the open wound to stop the bleeding.

He stared behind her and she turned to find a rip in the earth separating the two armies. Some tried to cross it, but it was too wide. The fighting inside Dracon was paused for now.

As she decided on her next move, something didn't let her leave him. "Dammit," she growled, lunging for the blond man's arm. Jerking him to her roughly, she put a hand against his wound and it began to close.

"You are still in there." His stare hurt as if he tried to see something that was no longer there. She turned away.

"Etta," Ara's voice sounded again. Another horn blasted through the confusion, different from the one before.

"That's not a Madran horn." Edmund's eyes widened. "It's..."

Etta took off running, needing to get to the gates. Her feet picked up speed, and she launched herself across the gully, barely coming up short of the other side. She slammed into the edge and grappled for something to hold on to, using her magic to call forth vines. As she climbed to the surface, Draconian eyes followed her. No one made a move against her as she pulled herself to her feet, not bothering to draw her sword. Her magic was all she needed.

There was a rumble from the direction of the palace as the earth groaned and shifted. Still, no one struck. She walked through the gaggle of enemy soldiers to reach the wall. The gatehouse was still a fair distance away, and she knew what she had to do.

She found a set of steps to the top of the wall. It had been abandoned even before the battle. She pounded up the steps, ascending to the top of Dracon.

*Tear it all down,* her magic begged. *Unleash the Basile wrath.*

She reached the top of the wall. On one side were Belaens and Draconians still trying to figure out how to cross the divide to resume the fight. On the other side, two armies faced off with a tiny force in the middle. That would be Ara.

From the direction of the mountains, the larger part of the Madran Mercenary army came into view.

And then there was the other force.

*He came.* A small part of her still held on to the Gaulean king, but any love for him or joy or worry was hidden beneath the rage of her magic.

She crouched down, laying her hands upon the rough stones protecting Dracon.

She clenched her jaw and sweat poured down her face as she battled for control. Her throat constricted before an explosion in her chest pushed heat down her limbs. Magic pulsed out of her. For a moment, nothing happened. Then the wall shook. She steadied herself and poured every ounce of power she had remaining to bring this kingdom to its knees. This was her final vengeance. This was what the power wanted.

Destroy.

Crush.

Bring the barrier down.

The wall undulated, the stones rising and falling with each pulse of magic. Yet she kept going. It would have all of her. When the wall started to break, the section she stood on tilted forward, the ground beneath it moving in sync with the beat of her magic, preparing to swallow it whole.

Her feet left the ground as the rocks sailed through the air and the wall of Dracon crumbled to the ground.

# CHAPTER 20

"They're moving into position," someone called. At this point, Alex wasn't sure who the voice belonged to. He and his entirely too small force of Gauleans had been riding hard for days with very little time for rest and still, they may have arrived too late.

The ground shook beneath his feet. Etta. Or La Dame. Only they would have that kind of power.

He sent out a prayer that Etta was okay.

"Alexandre." Amalie pushed her horse up beside him. When he didn't answer, she tried again. "Your Highness."

Yes, that was right. He wasn't a king any longer. He glanced behind him. Yet these people continued to follow him.

"Alex," Ara's voice rang in his ears. "Please tell me that's you." His eyes jerked to the small group of soldiers standing between the two forces. As if sensing his questions, Ara kept going. "Etta is inside the walls. I've reached out to her but have received no response."

"We have to get to Ara." Alex turned to Amalie. "Are you prepared for this?"

"I've never been more ready for anything in my life." Her eyes drifted to the walls of Dracon. "If Etta is in there, it means Tyson is as well. We have to help them."

Alex lingered for a moment, watching the girl who'd once been his betrothed. She was no longer the shy flower of the Leroy family. They were all hardened now, and he wondered if any of them would be able to find their way back to who they'd been before.

"Let's move." He kicked his horse, leading his troops from the relative safety of their position. "Horn."

The horn of Gaule pierced the air. Who was the other force? They could be non-magic mercenaries or Draconians who would defeat them easily. But now they'd know the once-king of Gaule was coming for them.

A volley of arrows arced toward them but fell short of their thundering horses as they neared Ara's position.

Alex jumped from his horse and ran to greet her.

"I am beyond glad to see you, your Majesty," she said, a relieved smile tilting her lips.

He wouldn't correct her just now. There'd be time for that later.

"We've moved out of range," she said. "But they're preparing to press forward. The queen needed me out here to watch for surprises and alert them. I've been telling them to get those damn gates open, but her Majesty might not be able to receive my messages. She might be—"

"Don't," Alex grunted. "There's no time to think like that. Not when La Dame lies beyond those walls and we don't know who we face here."

"It's Madran mercenaries. If they were Draconians, they'd be able to reach us with their magic. Plus, La Dame is probably surrounding herself with the more powerful fighters."

Alex scratched the back of his neck. That was good news then.

Ara continued. "I don't have many magic folk. Etta couldn't spare them. She left me with a contingent of Madran soldiers."

He tried to push all worries of Etta, Edmund, and Tyson from his mind but as he lifted his eyes to the wall, he saw her.

Etta was unmistakable with her blazing golden hair.

"What is she doing?" Amalie asked.

Alex didn't answer, too relieved to see her there and alive. There was something different about her, he could tell even at this distance. It was almost as if an aura of magic surrounded her, distorting the air.

Ara grinned. "She heard me." She met Alex's gaze. "She's bringing down the wall."

A boom burst through the air and Etta rose up with the wall beneath her before it slammed back to the ground. It cracked and broke apart at the base, happening in slow motion. All they could do was watch as Etta was thrown forward.

Alex waited for her to use her power to stop her descent, to save herself. That moment never came. She rushed to meet the ground, stones large and small raining down around her, burying her in the rubble.

Alex didn't think before jumping back into his saddle and jerking the reins around while digging his heels into the horse's flanks. They took off with the speed of an arrow, loosed expertly toward its target.

Draconians rushed through the fallen wall and Alex yanked his bow free from where it was hooked behind him. Drawing an arrow was as easy to him as drawing a breath. He fired in rapid succession as he neared the place where she'd fallen.

He didn't hear his force thundering after him or the Madran mercenaries joining in the rush toward the center of Dracon. All he heard was the twang of his bowstring and the steady drumming of his horse's hooves.

When he loosed his last arrow, he pulled his sword free and jumped from the horse without bothering to pull him to a stop.

He'd never claimed to be skilled with a sword, but no one could stop him from getting to her.

His soldiers' arrival turned the tide of the battle as they bolstered the Belaen spirits. By the time they were embroiled in the fight, magic had been drained from Belaens and Draconians alike.

He caught sight of the familiar form of his brother, cutting his way through entire hordes of men to get to the wall. Matteo and Edmund held each other up as they fought one handed.

Tyson reached Alex, his eyes flicking to the piles of stones. None of them could see Etta.

"La Dame is dead," Tyson confirmed breathlessly. "Etta killed her."

Alex barely heard his words. "Where is she? I saw her fall." His eyes drifted to the canyon that now stretched far into Dracon. He shook his head. "No."

Tears shone in Tyson's tired eyes and Amalie moved closer to him. As they stood still, their worlds falling apart, the battle continued to rage around them.

"La Dame is dead." Ara's voice fell around each soldier—Belaen, Draconian, Madran. "The queen of Dracon is dead. Throw down your weapons. There is no more reason for our fight."

Alex turned from the dead-strewn battlefield as weapons were thrown down.

"They're doing it," Tyson said in surprise, his voice choked.

"Of course they are." A man Alex didn't recognize said. "Without La Dame, there is no one to pay the Madran mercenaries. And with her gone, the Draconians are free."

Dazed men and women drifted across the broken city. Buildings lay in ruins, roads were cracked, and right at the center was a dark pit that had stolen everything.

Everything. That's what Etta was. She was the reason Alex hadn't fought for his crown.

She was the queen who'd made her people believe again.

"We can't tell them," Ara said quietly, her eyes drifting to the exhausted Belaen warriors who were now checking their dead. "Some will have seen, but we can't... not yet."

Alex walked away without another word, back through the rubble of the fallen wall and away from everything he'd thought he could save.

Persinette Basile wasn't someone you could hold on to. She wasn't someone who could be saved.

He'd known it and yet...

His foot slipped on a pile of tiny rocks and he fell, his butt slamming into the ground. He knew he should still be on guard. He wasn't an idiot. The Draconians were still the enemy—maybe... hell, no one knew what they were without La Dame.

But he didn't care.

He bent his knees and rested his elbows on them, letting his chin dip to his chest as people streamed by. The chaos of battle hadn't ended, only shifted to something else, and he got lost in it.

When Etta thought she was losing him, she'd found magic within herself to prevent that fate. But he had no magic. He couldn't change this.

She'd accomplished everything she'd set out to do. La Dame would no longer terrorize the world. Dracon was defeated.

But so were they.

They'd lost because she was lost.

Persinette wasn't only the Belaen queen, she was his. He would have followed her anywhere.

A warm nose nudged the side of his face and he lifted his eyes to familiar brown ones. "We lost her, boy."

Vérité snorted and stomped his foot.

"I'm sorry," Alex whispered before narrowing his eyes in accusation. "Where were you? You're supposed to protect her."

It didn't escape his notice that for once, Vérité wasn't trying to bite him. In this sorrow, they were together.

Vérité kicked again.

"I'm sorry." He buried his face in his hands. "It wasn't your fault."

He'd always thought it was weird that Etta talked to a horse and now he found himself doing the same thing. If only he could figure out what those intense eyes were trying to tell him.

Vérité bared his teeth and lowered his head to catch the edge of Alex's chain mail between them and tugged.

Alex snapped his head up. "What?"

Vérité tugged again.

It was a foolish hope, but hope was a foolish emotion and he wanted nothing more than to give into it, so he jumped to his feet. Vérité snorted and started walking back into Dracon.

Edmund and Tyson called out to Alex, but he ignored them and kept going.

Vérité stopped at the side of the canyon and stomped his foot. When Alex didn't move, he stomped it again.

Alex couldn't see over the edge so he got to his knees and leaned out farther, trying not to lose his balance. The first thing he saw was the golden hair. It no longer glowed, but it still called to him. Etta was pressed to the side of the canyon with thick vines crossing her back, keeping her from falling.

Etta's eyelids slid open against their will. The blackness pulled her toward its peaceful nothingness.

No.

She wouldn't give in.

When she came back to herself, she was suspended over a wide-open hole. A hole she'd created. She didn't know what was happening above but the last few moments came back to her. She'd taken down the wall and given all the magic she had left. It had rushed out of her and then she was falling, unable to call it back.

With the last bit of power she could summon, she'd brought forth the vines. It was the most basic of her magic, not a part of the Basile power. Making things grow was only her, just Etta. It had seemed right for that to be the last thing she ever did.

She hadn't expected to wake. Not when she'd drained herself so completely.

Someone called to her, but the voice seemed far away.

"Etta."

It was like waking from a dream. She remembered it all. Every person she'd slain. The charred, broken body of La Dame. The harsh words she'd spoken. But they didn't feel like her memories. The rage and the hate weren't her emotions.

For the first time since the Basile magic coursed through her, her mind was truly clear. She knew who she was. She was the queen of Bela. She was Persinette Basile. But most of all, she was still Etta.

Reaching up, she grabbed onto the vines holding her and pulled. Her magic released.

The vines pulled her up to the lip of the ravine and she prepared to rejoin the battle, with her sword, not her magic, pulling it free of its scabbard.

Her vision cleared and two faces looked down on her. Chocolate eyes scanned her face. Her best friend. Vérité shook his head, his mane flopping to the side.

The second was a face she never thought she'd see again, and it felt as if she was seeing him for the first time. There was no curse holding them together and no magic keeping them apart. She reached the top, and he held out his hand. She took it without hesitation and allowed him to pull her the rest of the way up. He fell back on his knees clutching her to him. She let herself sink into his embrace as she tentatively ran her fingers over his jaw and down to his chest.

A throat cleared behind them and for the first time, she saw something other than Alex. The battle no longer roared with its ugly song. People wept alongside fallen friends. Others tried to gather themselves and get far from this tainted place.

Tyson rushed forward and dropped down next to Etta, wrapping his arms around both her and Alex.

"We thought you were gone." His voice clogged with tears.

As the memories assaulted her, she knew he didn't just mean after the wall fell.

"I was," she whispered. "I—" She sucked in a breath and buried her face in Alex's shoulder. "It took control of me."

Tyson nodded in his too-damn-understanding way. "But you did it. La Dame is gone. You beat her."

Etta shook her head. She could picture the woman's final moment, but she wouldn't truly believe it until she saw her palace empty. She pushed away from Alex and tried to stand. Her legs were too weak, but he jumped up to steady her.

"I need to see it," she pleaded.

He led her to Vérité. The horse took a moment to nuzzle her before Alex lifted her into the saddle. He climbed up behind her and she directed him toward the palace.

The grand home of La Dame built into the side of the mountain now lay as broken as the rest of the kingdom. The doorway was all but collapsed, with only a small opening. They left Vérité outside and climbed over fallen pillars and past the image of Rapunzel.

Etta hoped she'd done her ancestor proud. Rapunzel was the first to defy La Dame when she let Phillip spirit her away. Persinette was the last to defy her. Maybe that was why her father had given her such a powerful name. It didn't mean much to Etta, but it would to the Draconians. Maybe it would allow for peace.

Etta had never been trained to break the curse. Her father told her it couldn't be done. She'd thought that meant he didn't believe in her. Maybe giving her the name Persinette was his way of showing her what he'd feared she'd been meant for. Maybe he'd had faith in her after all.

Etta's legs strengthened with each step she took, her energy returning to her. It wasn't the same as the Basile magic, but if all she had left was the Basile determination, she'd take it.

The doorway to the treasure room was still intact but the room itself was in disarray. Shattered glass, scattered prizes, and a single body.

When Etta peered into the home of her family's greatest enemy, she only felt sorrow. La Dame's curse destroyed Bela and imprisoned generations of Basiles, but in the end, Etta saw her for what she was. A lonely woman who'd been twisted by magic.

Etta had a taste of it. The Basile magic had been too much. That much power wasn't meant to be held by one person. It only created anger and hatred. When she'd taken La Dame's power into her as well, it destroyed everything she was. The dark Draconian magic warred with the Basile until they crushed each other, almost taking Etta with it.

Never again.

That power was gone, released into the atmosphere. Drained from Etta. In the throes of her rage, she'd used too much magic at once and it had saved her life.

Tearing her eyes from the spot she'd taken the only thing La Dame truly cared about—her magic, Etta caught sight of a flash of dark curls.

"Maiya," she said. "I'm not going to hurt you."

The young girl appeared, her hands clasped behind her back and her lip between her teeth.

Alex narrowed his eyes, but Etta put a hand on his arm. She was tired of animosity.

"Come here." It wasn't a demand, but Maiya took it as such. "Is your mother..."

"Dead," Maiya confirmed, no remorse in her voice.

"I see."

Maiya dropped to her knees as tears spilled from her eyes. "I'm sorry, Etta, I didn't have a choice."

"You will call her by her title," Alex barked.

"Alex." Etta sighed. "Please. No more anger. Let her speak."

"Thank you, y-your Majesty," she stuttered. "I didn't know my mother. That was true. And my father didn't have a choice. La Dame was threatening me."

La Dame's words ran through Etta's mind. *She is a sacrifice. She's not my sacrifice, she's yours.*

She'd tried to get Etta to kill an innocent, hoping it would push her further into the dark corners of her power.

La Dame knew Maiya to be an innocent.

"What do you have behind your back, Maiya," Etta asked calmly.

Maiya lifted her eyes to meet Etta's and pulled her hands around, holding up the Basile crown for Etta to take. "For you, your Majesty."

Etta' s hands shook as she folded them around the golden circlet, its jewels shining. Alex took it from her and she met his gaze in question.

He lifted the corners of his mouth. "Allow me, my queen." He set the crown atop her golden hair.

A commotion sounded from the door and Edmund was all but carrying Matteo through. "Etta," he began. "Now that you aren't super angry or super dead, do you think you can heal Matteo so I can stop carrying his ass around? I didn't trust any of the Draconians to do it."

Etta laughed despite herself. "Super dead as opposed to just dead? I'm glad to know you're happy I'm still breathing."

"Just heal Matteo and then I can celebrate properly the fact you're alive, La Dame is dead, and Alex showed up at the last moment to act like he had a hand in winning the battle when all he really did was steal some of our glory."

Matteo snorted. "Real funny, but kind of in pain here."

Etta's brows drew together. "I can't," she admitted quietly.

"Etta," Edmund chastised. "We all know Matteo can be kind of an ass, but that's no reason to withhold some of your magic goodness."

"I think I should be offended," Matteo said with a wince. "But I just want to close my eyes." His body started to slump and Edmund caught him.

"Etta," Edmund yelled. "Stop playing around." He lowered him to the ground, his voice growing frantic. "Do it now!"

Etta slid to her knees beside her cousin. "I can't." She looked down at her hands as if they'd betrayed her. Her next words were barely above a whisper but every person present heard her. "My magic is gone. La Dame's power and the Basile power… they destroyed each other. When I took down the wall, every bit of both magics left me."

The room went so silent, they could have heard a snowflake hit the ground.

Matteo groaned.

"I can do it," Maiya's small voice echoed behind them.

Etta glanced from Maiya to Alex. Could they trust her?

"We don't have a choice," she said finally. "Do it, Maiya."

Maiya knelt beside Etta, laying her hands on Matteo's chest. Before long, his breathing became more regular and his eyes opened once again. He coughed weakly and the entire room exhaled.

Alex pulled Etta up beside him. "Is your magic really gone?"

"The Basile power is. I still have the magic I was born with. It's all I feel."

He pressed his nose to the side of her face. "Are you okay?"

She nodded, realizing the truth. She was glad it was gone.

"Etta," Tyson said, hesitating. "You scared me... before... when we were down here."

She thought back on the fight. Tyson had been there. She closed her eyes, wishing he hadn't seen that. When she opened them again, she walked toward him and wrapped her arms around him.

"It's over," she said.

After a few moments, his arms circled her waist and tightened. "It's over," he mimicked, his voice breaking on the words.

She repeated the phrase in her head, trying to believe it. Everything was done, finished. The curse. The vengeful power she'd had within her for so long. La Dame. All of it. Squeezing her brother tighter, she released a breath and felt the emptiness she'd had since the breaking of the curse begin to fill.

# CHAPTER 21

"As the world ended, all we could do was watch," Alex said, leaning back on his arms. He sat far from the walls of Dracon in a camp of their own making. None of them wanted to sleep amongst the ghosts of that fallen kingdom for one single night.

"Um." Edmund shot him a strange look from where he rested against a sleeping Matteo. "The world didn't end, dumbass."

"It sort of did. At least the world we knew." Alex had never seen Edmund openly affectionate with another man. He'd always known Edmund's preferences but through the lens of his friend's feelings toward him.

The odd thing was that it didn't feel odd to him. When his father lived, Edmund would have been imprisoned and perhaps even executed for it in Gaule, but as he'd said, that world no longer existed and his friend seemed happy.

Etta sat a safe distance from Alex. She'd been different toward him since the shock of the day's events wore off, but as she watched him, he knew something had changed. She'd once told him the magic was trying to control her. Now that it was gone, she'd become the girl who'd won the tournament in Gaule again. The one who'd created a meadow of flowers in the Black Forest and who'd given everything she had to save him from the tower.

Alex met her intense gaze as he went on to explain himself. "For hundreds of years, La Dame has controlled this world. She destroyed kingdoms and struck such fear in others that they went to great lengths to avoid crossing her. Her own people served as nothing more than slaves to her whims. Now we're all free. The Madrans and Belaens can once again control the seas with trade. The Gauleans can break free of the fear that rules their lives. The Draconians can live their lives as they wish." He looked at them each in turn, finally landing on Etta. "Both La Dame's magic and the Basile magic are no more."

"We're free," Etta breathed. "All of us."

"I still have a problem with your original statement," Edmund cut in. "Some of us did a lot more than watch."

"You're right." Tyson smirked. "Etta broke the chains."

Edmund opened his mouth to protest again, but Etta shrugged, a beautiful grin appearing on her face. She touched the crown that sat on the table beside her. "I don't know what you guys are talking about. I only came today to retrieve my crown." Her grin widened. "La Dame died of old age."

Tyson nodded seriously. "Plausible. She was very old."

"The oldest," Alex agreed.

Edmund crossed his arms over his chest. "You aren't going to take any of the glory, are you?"

"What glory?" Etta asked. "I tripped on my way to the palace and knocked myself out." She shrugged. "I only woke when I was dangling above a ravine. Missed the entire battle."

Alex laughed and Tyson joined him. Soon, a smile broke out on Edmund's face as well.

Tyson held a finger to his lips as he glanced toward the sleeping Amalie.

Ara pushed into the tent and stopped abruptly when she saw the four of them awake. Camp had been hastily constructed and Etta invited all of them to share her tent. It would be tight, but she needed them surrounding her that night.

"Your Majesties." Ara dipped her head.

"Ara," Etta said. "It's about damn time you call me Etta. Although the next time you go behind my back and fetch us some assistance..." She paused, shaking her head. "Thank you for disobeying me."

"Uh—you're welcome, your—Etta."

"I'm going to need a council," Etta said. "Ara, I'd like you to be on it." She looked to Alex. "I will need a council, won't I?"

The words slipped out before he could stop them. "I don't know. You should probably ask a king."

Etta snapped her jaw shut, her eyes never leaving him. "Alex," she warned.

"Come outside with me," he said. "Please."

Alex led her to the edge of camp where a fire still lingered. Other than the posted guards, most people had gone to bed. It was too dark to see the ruins of the Draconian walls in the distance, but their presence still loomed.

Etta breathed in deeply and raised her eyes to the cloudless sky above. The clear night revealed thousands of tiny winking stars only partially obscured with the waning light of the fire. "Have you ever seen anything so beautiful?" she asked. Since the Basile magic left her, she'd felt like everything was new, fresh, like she was finally alive.

"Never," Alex breathed.

She lowered her gaze to him, feeling the intensity of his words in every part of her. She touched her golden hair self-consciously, knowing she'd never again experience the brilliant glow. Her hair fell loose and wild down her back, still unkempt from battle.

Alex stepped closer and pushed her hand away from her hair.

"What did you mean before?" she asked quietly. "When you told me to ask a king."

His throat worked to swallow, and he pressed his lips together as he brought his hand up to touch his thumb to her bottom lip.

"Alex." She sighed.

"I'm no longer the king of Gaule." His voice strained as if the words physically hurt to say.

His words took a while to sink into her mind and her eyes rounded. "Y-you..."

"Gaule would never have peace with a king they rebelled against. I love my kingdom, but I had to leave." He continued to stroke her lip. "I shouldn't be King of Gaule when that throne is not where my loyalty lies." He dropped to his knees, his eyes never leaving hers. "Persinette Basile, I pledge loyalty to the throne of Bela. I will fight for the queen until my dying breath. A life spent in service to her will be a life worth living. The Belaen people will be my people, the land my land. If the queen will have me as a loyal subject."

Tears built in Etta's eyes as she saw a future she'd never thought could be hers, but there was one problem. "Get up," she said. When he did, she smacked his arm. "What are you thinking? You can't give up your throne. Your entire life, you've been meant to be king. You're such an idiot, Alex. I can't believe you left Gaule. You will go back tomorrow and tell them that you're king and no one else deserves to sit their ass on that throne and—"

He kissed her, cutting off her rant. She didn't respond at first and felt him begin to pull back, but then she made a sound in the back of her throat and pulled him closer, wrapping her arms around his neck and parting her lips to deepen the kiss.

He pressed her to him, lifting her off her feet.

"Etta," he whispered, dropping kisses down her face to her neck. "My Etta. My protector, my charge, my love."

"You're still an idiot," she said, shivering under his touch.

He chuckled against her skin. "The thing you don't understand about me, Etta, is that I was never meant to be king. I was simply meant to love a queen."

"Then yes," she said. "This queen accepts you into her kingdom for as long as you'll stay." She kissed him again. "I love you, Alex. Even when the magic was twisting me up on the inside, I loved you."

"I will always love you."

"I think you're wrong though." She grinned, her eyes twinkling.

"You always think I'm wrong."

She laughed. "What I mean is that you were meant to be king, you were just in the wrong kingdom."

"Don't you dare..." he said.

"Why not?"

"We just finished basically saving the world."

She raised an eyebrow in response.

"Okay, you just finished saving the world. Everyone is exhausted. We're sleeping within sight of the Draconian ruins. La Dame has been gone for less than a day. Right now is not the time for big decisions."

She put her hands on her hips. "I think it's the perfect time. Don't you contradict your queen, Alexandre Durand."

"Wow, you've been my queen for not even ten minutes and already exercising your power."

She winked. "Basically. Alex, I love you. That's never going to change. For the first time I'm finally seeing everything clearly. Today has been the most insane day in all the histories of our kingdoms. Please just let me have this right now."

When he didn't respond, she smirked. "Do I have to make some big declaration?" She ran back toward her tent. "Edmund, Tyson get out here."

They scrambled out. "Is someone attacking?" Edmund asked. For months, she'd been locked inside herself unable to break free. Now, there were no curses, no chains, only a crown, but the crown didn't mean anything to her without the people she loved. Etta had never expected to fall in love. She hadn't imagined having friends or family other than her father. The world she'd grown up in was so small, only existing among the trees of the Black Forest. It hadn't allowed her to think of any kind of happiness for herself.

Exhaustion tugged at her, but she wouldn't wait a moment longer for the future to begin.

"Etta," Tyson said carefully. "Are you okay? You look flushed. You've been through so much today. You should lie down."

She shook her head. "I'm not closing my eyes this time. Not when it's all right in front of me."

Matteo stumbled out of the tent rubbing his eyes. "What are you all doing out here?"

The fire shrank down to glowing embers. A targeted burst of air brushed past Etta and she grinned as the flames kicked up once again. The Basile magic might be gone, but she loved knowing she was surrounded by other magic every day.

Edmund flashed his teeth.

Ara joined them and for a moment, no one spoke as they soaked in the peace none of them had been sure they'd ever see again.

Etta faced the people she trusted most in this world. The ones who'd put their faith in her. Who'd believed in what she could do even when she doubted.

"Kneel," she commanded.

They didn't hesitate.

"Matteo, Tyson, Edmund, Ara... I name you to the queen's council. Some of you earned this right by blood." Tyson and Matteo glanced up. "All of you have earned it by sacrifice and courage. Rise."

Edmund was the first to break the silence that followed. "I think we're going to need some more experienced council members."

"I agree. That's why your first task is to decide if there is a problem with me taking a non-Belaen as my husband."

Alex started choking beside her and Edmund laughed.

Matteo, ever the serious one, was the person who answered. "Phillip allowed his son to wed a Draconian when he took Rapunzel to wife, did he not? And now we don't have to worry about diluting the Basile magic."

Etta closed her eyes. She hadn't thought of that. Just another reminder that her ancestral right had vanished. If the Basile magic were still within her, she'd need to worry about the effects of taking someone without magic as her husband.

She opened her eyes and sucked in a breath. Alex's eyes were fixed on her face, the fire reflecting off his irises, making the flames dance in his gaze.

The Basile power was gone, but perhaps this was a kind of magic as well.

Matteo continued to speak about Belaen history, but his voice faded into the background. Etta had gone into the day thinking she wouldn't make it out alive, but she had. Now the question stood, what was she going to do with her second chance?

"Marry me," she said, her words cutting Matteo off mid-sentence.

Alex's lip twitched.

"Marry me," she said again. "This world has worked so damn hard to keep us apart and I won't let it anymore." She took a step toward him. "Marry me because this is the only kind of magic I need. Marry me because—"

"I love you," he finished for her, pulling her to him once again. "Marry me."

"I already asked you that."

He grinned. "Forever." He kissed her again.

She smiled against his lips, knowing that forever was something she could finally have. Their lives were theirs now and there was no more time to waste.

# EPILOGUE

The queen of Bela sat alone on the edge of the white cliffs. She let her legs drop over the side as she peered down into the calm waters below. It was a rare day that didn't see the churning ocean thrashing against the rocky face.

There hadn't been a day of such importance since the time of Aurora and Phillip.

She held her hand at her side, palm down, pulling the grasses from the earth with her magic. It was all she could do now. She created flowers and helped with the clearing of land for new building projects.

When she wasn't ruling her people.

Two years had passed since the day her people were freed from the threat of La Dame. They'd been an uneventful two years, and that was okay with Etta.

Bela made progress. They'd lost a lot in the battle. Many of her people didn't make it home, but she was glad for what they had left.

Behind her stood the royal residence, built right next to the ruins of the old Belaen seat of power. It wasn't some grand palace like the one before it. Instead, it consisted only of a small throne room and living space the size of a large cottage. It wasn't opulent, but it was home.

A presence appeared behind her and she knew who it was before he even spoke.

"You know I don't like when you get so close to the cliffs." Alex sighed indulgently.

The traitor who called himself Edmund had been filling Alex's ears with stories of Etta on these same cliffs.

"I told you before," she said, her eyes continuing to sweep the horizon. "I was only testing my magic."

"And Edmund had to save you."

She shrugged. "Payback for all the times I've saved his ass."

He laughed. "Well, your Majesty, I've come to tell you our first wave of guests have arrived."

She scooted away from the edge and stood. "Thank you, your Majesty." She grinned up at him and stole a quick kiss.

They'd combined a wedding with a coronation for Alex. He hadn't enjoyed ruling Gaule alone, and she didn't like the idea of doing the same with Bela. Plus, Alexandre Durand was meant to have a crown on his head.

He held out her crown. "You need it to greet them."

She took it and set the golden circlet on top of her short blonde hair. She'd been pleased to find it easy to cut once the power had left her. She'd wanted a fresh start, separated from the deeds of her ancestors.

She hooked her arm through Alex's and allowed him to lead her toward their home.

Horses had been left outside and stable lads hurried to lead them to the stables.

Inside were faces so familiar they made her heart stop. She ran forward to greet the delegation from Gaule.

Catrine's wide smile greeted her. "Etta." When Etta reached her, she pulled her into her arms. "It's wonderful to see you, your Majesty."

"And you, your Majesty," Etta said, pulling back.

Alex greeted his mother and those who'd accompanied her. Simon was with her as well as Duchess Moreau, Duke Caron, Camille, and a few others.

When Tyson and Amalie appeared to greet Catrine, pandemonium ensued.

The wards surrounding Gaule had disappeared the moment her Basile power was gone. Tyson traveled back and forth frequently as Etta's emissary to Gaule, but the rest of them were busy running their kingdoms.

In the following days, representatives from Madra and others across the sea would arrive. Even Dracon sent someone to represent their interests. With their queen dead, they'd chosen a new ruler, and he had been reaching out to help Dracon rejoin the rest of the world.

Trade between the kingdoms thrived, the world once again at peace. For now.

They were entering a new era.

Having everyone join her in Bela reminded Etta what she'd fought for. It was this, these people, this life. Her family.

She still had moments when anger or hatred would overtake her, remnants of the magic that had controlled her so completely. But they never lasted. How could they?

###

Days after the rulers and representatives of their allied kingdoms left, Etta found herself sitting with Vérité.

Her father's warnings rang in her head and she laughed. He'd said Vérité was dangerous, wild. But then, she had been as well. Viktor Basile had been a great many things, but he hadn't been everything and she only now realized that was okay. He'd made mistakes, just as she had.

She'd once thought he didn't believe in her because he told her not to attempt to break the curse, but that wasn't true at all. It was because he'd known La Dame. It was an impossible task.

Not everyone is meant to attempt the impossible.

She looked up at Vérité. And not everyone was meant to attempt it alone.

"What are you two up to?" Alex asked, walking around the side of the house with a knowing smirk.

"Trouble," she answered. "Lots and lots of trouble."

He laughed and bent down to kiss the top of her head. He tried to pull away, but she pulled him back and breathed him in.

Vérité nipped at him and he jumped back. "Hey," he protested. "I thought we were moving past that."

Etta shrugged, trying to hide her grin. "Can't chain a wild beast."

"Yeah, yeah," he said, leaning in to kiss her again. "We all saw what happened when they tried to chain you."

Vérité snorted and Etta pushed Alex away before the jealous horse bit. "Go," she said with a laugh. "Isn't Edmund waiting for you?"

"I'm going. I have to get some time in with him before he leaves for his new position as ambassador to Madra." He shook his head sadly. "Be nice to her, Vérité."

Etta raised an eyebrow. They all knew Vérité would never harm her. Once Alex was out of sight, Etta climbed to her feet.

"How about a ride?"

Vérité stomped his foot.

She didn't bother with a saddle as she hauled herself onto his back and braided her hands through his mane. With a gentle squeeze of her calves, he took off.

All of Bela stretched out before her. Most of it was still untamed. Thick forests. Wildflowers. Running streams.

They crested the hill that led down into the village. Etta turned Vérité to the other side of it instead. His hooves thundered down an unused path and into the trees. She breathed in the fresh air as it whipped around her face.

They were right. Alex may have been her heart's mate, but Vérité owned her soul. With them, she was complete. With them, she was whole.

For she was Persinette Basile. Daughter of a great man. Breaker of curses. Queen of Bela. No chains could hold her for she was finally free, and the free had no more battles to wage.

# ACKNOWLEDGMENTS

I've written enough books now where writing the acknowledgments seems to say the same thing again and again. But "thank you" is always something worth repeating because the people who help me and are there for me don't only do it once. They continue to hold me up when I'm falling down. They fix my mistakes when my brain doesn't want to operate any longer.

First and foremost is my family. I work a lot of long hours sometimes, demanding solitude and getting antsy with interruptions. Thank you for understanding and for doing what you can to help me reach my dream.

My friends who make me leave the house and see something other than the four walls of my workspace. But who also understand when I need to be a hermit.

Melissa, my close friend and editor. Your honesty and sometimes harshness is needed and so very appreciated. This series wouldn't be what it is without you.

Patrick, who always comes through.

My beta team. I'd never have the courage to send my books to editing without you.

Daqri Bernardo. Just no words on this cover and every other cover you've done for me.

And of course, my readers. I love you guys. Thank you.

www.ingramcontent.com/pod-product-compliance
Lightning Source LLC
Chambersburg PA
CBHW030527310726
48979CB00010B/1824/J
*9781970052688*